1

ISBN: 1979275122

Original text: The War Workers, Edmée Elizabeth Monica Dashwood. 1917

The War Workers

Edmée Elizabeth Monica Dashwood

CHAPTER I

AT the Hostel for Voluntary Workers, in Questerham, Miss Vivian, Director of the Midland Supply Depot, was under discussion that evening.

Half a dozen people, all of whom had been working for Miss Vivian ever since ten o'clock that morning, as they had worked the day before and would work again the next day, sat in the Hostel sitting-room and talked about their work and about Miss Vivian.

No one ever talked anything but "shop," either in the office or at the

Hostel. "Didn't you think Miss Vivian looked awfully tired to-day?"

"No wonder, after Monday night. You know the train wasn't in till past ten o'clock. I think those troop-trains tire her more than anything."

"She doesn't have to cut cake and bread-and-butter and sandwiches for two hours before the train gets in, though. I've got the usual blister to-day," said an anaemic-looking girl of twenty, examining her forefinger.

There was a low scoffing laugh from her neighbour.

"Miss Vivian cutting bread-and-butter! She does quite enough without that, Henderson. She had the D.G.V.O. in there yesterday afternoon for ages. I thought he was never going. I stood outside her door for half an hour, I should think, absolutely hung up over the whole of my work, and I knew she was fearfully busy herself."

"It's all very well for you, Miss Delmege you're her secretary and work in her room, but we can't get at her unless we're sent for. I simply didn't know what to do about those surgical supplies for the Town Hospital this morning, and Miss Vivian never sent for me till past eleven o'clock. It simply wasted half my morning."

"She didn't have a minute; the telephone was going the whole time," said Miss Delmege quickly. "But yesterday, you know, when the D.G.V.O. wouldn't go, I thought she was going to be late at the station for that troop-train, and things were fairly desperate, so what d'you suppose I did?"

"Dashed into her room and got your head snapped off?" someone suggested languidly. "I shall never forget one day last week when *I* didn't know which way to turn, we were so busy, and I went in without being sent for, and Miss Vivian--"

"Oh yes, I remember," said Miss Delmege rapidly. She was a tall girl with eyeglasses and a superior manner. She did not remember Miss Marsh's irruption into her chief's sanctum with any particular clearness, but she was anxious to finish her own anecdote. "But as *I* was telling you," she hurried on, affecting to be unaware that Miss Marsh and her neighbour were exchanging glances, "when I saw that it was getting later every minute, and the D.G.V.O. seemed rooted to the spot, I simply went straight downstairs and rang up Miss Vivian on the telephone. Miss Cox was on telephone duty, and she was absolutely horrified. She said, 'You don't mean to say you're going to ring up Miss Vivian,' she said;

and I said, 'Yes, I am. Yes, I am,' I said, and I did it. Miss Cox simply couldn't get over it."

Miss Delmege paused to laugh in solitary enjoyment of her story.

"'Who's there?' Miss Vivian said you know what she's like when she's in a hurry. 'It's Miss Delmege,' I said. 'I thought you might want to know that the train will be in at eight o'clock, Miss Vivian, and it's half-past seven now.' She just said ' Thank you,' and rang off; but she must have told the D.G.V.O., because he came downstairs two minutes later. And she simply flung on her hat and dashed down into the car and to the station."

"And, after all, the train wasn't in till past ten, so she might just as well have stayed to put her hat on straight," said Miss Henderson boldly. She had a reputation for being "downright" of which she was aware, and which she strenuously sought to maintain by occasionally making small oblique sallies at Miss Vivian's expense.

"I must say it was most awfully crooked. I noticed it myself," said a pretty little giggling girl whom the others always called Tony, because her surname was Anthony. "How killing, I thought; there's Miss Vivian with her hat on quite crooked."

"Yes, wasn't it killing?"

"Simply killing. I thought the minute I saw her: How killing to see Miss Vivian with her hat on like that!"

"She looked perfectly lolling hurrying down the platform," remarked Miss Marsh, with an air of originality. "She was carrying cigarettes for the men, and her hat got crookeder every minute. I was pining to tell her."

"Go on, Marshy! She'd have had your head off. Fancy Marsh stopping Miss Vivian in the middle of a troop-train to say her hat was on crooked!"

Everyone laughed.

"I should think she'd be shot at dawn," suggested Tony. "That's the official penalty for making personal remarks to your C.O., I believe."

"You know," said Miss Delmege, in the tones whose refinement was always calculated to show up the unmodulated accents of her neighbours, "one day I absolutely did tell Miss Vivian when her hat was crooked. I said right out: 'Do excuse me, Miss Vivian, but your hat isn't quite straight.' She didn't mind a bit."

"I suppose she knows she always looks nice anyway," said Tony easily.

"I mean she didn't mind me telling her," explained Miss Delmege. "She's most awfully human, you know, really. That's what I like about Miss Vivian. She's so frightfully human."

"Yes, she is human," Miss Marsh agreed. "Awfully human." Miss Delmege raised her eyebrows.

"Of course," she said, with quiet emphasis, "working in her room, as I do, I suppose I see quite another side of her the human side, you know."

There was a silence. Nobody felt disposed to encourage Miss Vivian's secretary in her all-too-frequent recapitulations of the privileges which she enjoyed.

Presently another worker came in, looking inky and harassed. "You're late to-night, Mrs. Potter, aren't you?" Tony asked her.

"Oh yes. It's those awful Belgians, you know. Wherever I put them, they're miserable, and write and ask to be taken away. There's a family now that I settled simply beautifully at Little Quester village only a month ago, and this afternoon the mother came in to say the air doesn't suit them at all she has a consumptive son or something and could they be moved to the seaside at once. So I told Miss Vivian, and she said I was to get them moved directly. At once to-day, you know. Of course, it was perfectly absurd they couldn't even get packed up and I told her so; but she said, 'Oh, settle it all by telephone 'you know her way. 'But, Miss Vivian,' I said, 'really I don't see how it can be managed. I've got a most fearful amount of work,' I said. 'Well,' she said, 'if you can't get through it, Mrs. Potter, I must simply put someone else at the head of the department who can.' It's too bad, you know."

Mrs. Potter sank into the only unoccupied wicker arm-chair in the room, looking very much jaded indeed.

Tony said sympathetically:

"What a shame! Miss Vivian doesn't realize what an awful lot you do, I'm perfectly certain."

"Well, considering that every letter and every bit of work in the whole office passes through Miss Vivian's hands, that's absurd," said Miss Delmege sharply. "She knows exactly what each department has to do, but, of course, she's such a quick worker herself that she can't understand anyone not being able to get through the same amount."

Mrs. Potter looked far from enchanted with the proffered explanation.

"It isn't that I can't get through the work," she said resentfully. "Of course I can get through the regular work all right. But I must say, I do think she's inconsiderate over these lightning touches of hers. What on earth was the sense of making those people move to-night, I should like to know?"

"Miss Vivian never will let the work get behindhand if she can help it," exclaimed Miss Marsh; and Miss Henderson at the same instant said, rather defiantly:

"Well, of course, Miss Vivian always puts the work before everything. She never spares herself, so I don't quite see why she should spare any of us."

"The fact is," said the small, cool voice of Miss Delmege, as usual contriving to filter through every other less refined sound, "she is extraordinarily tender-hearted. She can't bear to think anyone is suffering when she could possibly help them; she'll simply go miles out of her way to do something for a wounded soldier or a Belgian refugee. I see that in her correspondence so much. You know the letters she writes about quite little things, because someone or other wants her to. She'll take endless trouble."

"I know she's wonderful," said Mrs. Potter, looking remorseful.

She was a middle-aged woman with light wispy hair, always untidy, and wearing a permanent expression of fluster. She had only been at the Hostel a few weeks.

"Isn't it nearly supper-time?" yawned Tony. "I want to go to bed." "Tired, Tony?"

"Yes, awfully. I was on telephone duty last night, stamping the letters, and I didn't get off till nearly eleven."

"There must have been a lot of letters," said Miss Delmege, with the hint of scepticism which she always managed to infuse into her tones when speaking of other people's work.

"About a hundred and thirty odd, but they didn't come down till very late. Miss Vivian was still signing the last lot at ten o'clock."

"She must have been very late getting out to Plessing. It's all very well for us," remarked Miss Marsh instructively; "we finish work at about six or seven o'clock, and then just come across the road, and here we are. But poor Miss Vivian has about an hour's drive before she gets home at all."

"She's always at the office by ten every morning, too."

"She ought to have someone to help her," sighed Miss Delmege. "Of course, I'd do anything to take some of the work off her hands, and I think she knows it. I think she knows I'd do simply anything for her; but she really wants someone who could take her place when she has to be away, and sign the letters for her, and see people. That's what she really needs."

"Thank goodness, there's the supper bell," said

Tony. They trooped downstairs.

The house was the ordinary high, narrow building of a provincial town, and held an insufficiency of rooms for the number of people domiciled there. The girls slept three or four in a room; the Superintendent had a tiny bedroom, and a slightly larger sitting-room adjoining the large room on the ground floor where they congregated in the evenings and on Sundays, and the dining-room was in the basement.

Gas flared on to the white shining American-cloth covering the long table and on the wooden kitchen chairs. The windows were set high up in the walls, and gave a view of area railings and, at certain angles, of a piece of pavement..

One or two coloured lithographs hung on the walls.

There was a hideous sound of scraping as chairs were drawn back or pulled forwards over the uncarpeted boards.

"Sit next me, duck."

"All right. Come on, Tony; get the other side of Sprouts."

Miss Delmege, aloof and superior, received no invitation to place herself beside anyone, and settled herself with genteel swishings of her skirt at the foot of the table.

The Superintendent sat at the head.

She was a small, delicate-looking Irish woman with an enthusiastic manner, who had married late in life, and been left a widow within two years of her marriage. She worked very hard, and it was her constant endeavour to maintain an atmosphere of perpetual brightness in the Hostel.

It was with this end in view that she invariably changed her blouse for a slightly cleaner one at suppertime, although all the girls were in uniform, and many of them still wearing a hat. But little Mrs. Bullivant always appeared in a rather pallid example of the dyer or cleaner's art, and said hopefully: "One of these days I must make a rule that all you girls dress for dinner. We shall find ourselves growing dreadfully uncivilized, I'm afraid, if we go on like this."

The Hostel liked Mrs. Bullivant, although she was a bad manager and could never keep a servant for long. She made no secret of the fact that she could not afford to be a voluntary worker.

Every Hostel in the district, and they were numerous owing to the recently-opened Munitions Factory near Questerham, had rapidly become, as it were, fish for Miss Vivian's net. Each and all were under her control, and the rivalry between the Questerham Hostel "for Miss Vivian's own workers" and those reserved for the munition-makers was an embittered one.

"What has everyone been doing to-day?" Mrs. Bullivant asked cheerfully. The inquiry was readily responded to. The angle of Miss Vivian's hat, when she had gone down to meet the troop-train, was again the subject of comment, and Miss Delmege was again reminded of the story, which she told with quiet and undiminished enjoyment, of her erstwhile daring in approaching Miss Vivian upon the subject.

"Did you really?" said Mrs. Bullivant admiringly. "Of course, it's different for you, Miss Delmege, working in her room all day. You see so much more of her than anyone else does."

Everyone except the complacent Miss Delmege looked reproachfully at the little Superintendent. She was incapable of snubbing anyone, but the Hostel thought her encouragement of Miss Delmege unnecessary in the extreme.

Mrs. Bullivant changed the conversation rather hurriedly.

"Who is on telephone duty to-night?" she inquired. "I am, worse

luck." "Miss Plumtree? And your head is bad again, isn't it, dear?"

"Yes," said Miss Plumtree wearily. She was a fair, round-faced girl of five or six and twenty who suffered from frequent sick headaches. She worked for longer hours than anyone else, and had a reputation for "making muddles." It was popularly supposed that Miss Vivian "had a down on her," but the Hostel liked Miss Plumtree, and affectionately called her Greengage and Gooseberrybush.

"Greengage got another headache?" Miss Marsh asked concernedly. "I can take your duty to-night, dear, quite well."

"Thank's awfully, Marsh; it's sweet of you, but I haven't got leave to change. You know last time, when Tony took duty for me, Miss Vivian asked why I wasn't there."

"I can say you're sick."

"Oh, I'm sure she wouldn't like it," said Miss Plumtree, looking nervous and undecided.

"I think you ought to be in bed, I must say," said Mrs. Bullivant uncertainly.

"She certainly doesn't look fit to sit at that awful telephone for two and a half hours; and there are heaps of letters to-night. I can answer for the Hospital Department, anyway," sighed Miss Henderson. "Marshy, you look pretty tired yourself. I can quite well take the telephone if you like. I'm not doing anything."

"I thought you were going to the cinema."

"I don't care. I can do that another night. I'm not a bit keen on pictures, really, and it's raining hard."

"Thanks most awfully, both of you," repeated Miss Plumtree, "but I really think I'd better go myself. You know what Miss Vivian is, if she thinks one's shirking, and I'm not at all in her good books at the moment, either. There was the most ghastly muddle about those returns last month, and I sent in the averages as wrong as they could be."

"That's nothing to do with your being unfit for telephone duty to-night," said Miss Delmege, with acid sweetness. "I think I can answer for it that Miss Vivian would be the first person to say you ought to let someone else take duty for you. I'd do it myself, only I really must get some letters written to-night. One never has a minute here. But I think I can answer for Miss Vivian."

In spite of the number of times that Miss Delmege expressed herself as ready to answer for Miss Vivian, no one had ever yet failed to be moved to exasperation by her pretensions.

"On the whole, Plumtree, you may be right not to risk it," said Miss Henderson freezingly, as she rose from the table.

"I'll manage all right," declared Miss Plumtree; but her round apple-blossom face was drawn with pain, and she stumbled up the dark stairs.

In the hall there was a hurried consultation between Miss Marsh and Miss Anthony.

"I say, Tony, old Gooseberry-bush isn't fit to stir. She ought to be tucked up in her bye-byes this minute. Shall I risk it, and go instead of her, leave or no leave?"

"I should think so, yes. What have things been like to-day?"

"Oh, fairly serene. I didn't see Miss Vivian this morning, myself, but nobody seems to have had their heads snapped off. There wasn't a fearful lot of work for her, either, because Miss Delmege came in quite early."

"Delmege makes me sick, the way she goes on! As though nobody else knew anything about Miss Vivian, and she was a sort of connecting-link between her and us. Didn't you hear her to-night? 'I think I can answer for Miss Vivian,'" mimicked Tony in an exaggerated falsetto. "I should jolly well like Miss Vivian to hear her one of these days. She'd appreciate being answered for like that by her secretary I don't think!"

"I say, Marshy, can you keep a secret?"

"Rather!"

"Well, swear not to tell, and, mind, I'm speaking absolutely unofficially. I've no business to know it officially at all, because I only saw it on a telegram I sent for the Billeting Department. Miss Delmege is going to get her nose put out of joint with Miss V. Another secretary is coming."

"She's not! D'you mean Delmege has got the sack?"

"Oh, Lord, no! It's only somebody coming to help her, because there is so much work for one secretary. She's coming from Wales, and her name is Jones."

"I seem to have heard that name before."

They both giggled explosively; then made a simultaneous dash at the hall-door as Miss Plurntree, in hat and coat, came slowly out of the sitting-room.

"No, you don't, Plumtree! You're going straight up to bed, and I'll tell Miss Vivian you were ill. It'll be all right."

"You are a brick, Marsh."

"Nonsense! You'll do as much for me some day. Good-night, dear."

Miss Marsh hurried out, and Miss Plumtree thankfully took the felt uniform hat off her aching head.

"Get into bed," directed Tony, "and take an aspirin." "Haven't got one left, worse

luck."

"I'll see if anyone else has any. I believe Mrs. Potter has."

Tony hurried into the sitting-room. Mrs. Potter had no aspirin, but she hoisted herself out of her arm-chair and said she would go round to the chemist and get some. She went out into the rain.

Tony borrowed a rubber hot-water bottle from Miss Henderson, and a kettle from somebody else, and went upstairs to boil some water, forgetting that she was tired and had meant to go to bed after supper.

Presently little Mrs. Bullivant came upstairs with a cup of tea and the aspirin, both of which she administered to the patient.

"You'll go to sleep after that, I expect," she said consolingly. "I'll tell the girls to

get into bed quietly," Tony whispered.

Miss Plumtree shared a room with Miss Delmege and Miss Henderson.

"I never do make any noise in the room that I am aware of," said Miss Delmege coldly; but she and her room-mate both crept upstairs soon after nine o'clock, lest their entrance later should awaken the sufferer, and they undressed with the gas turned as low as it would go, and in silence.

Padding softly in dressing-slippers to the bathroom later on, for the lukewarm water which was all that they could hope to get until the solitary gas-ring should have served the turn of numerous waiting kettles, they heard Miss Marsh returning from telephone duty, bolting the hall-door, and putting up the chain.

"You're back early," whispered Miss Henderson. coining halfway downstairs in her pink flannelette dressing-gown, her scanty fair hair screwed back into a tight plait.

"Wasn't much doing. Miss Vivian got off at half-past nine. Jolly good thing, too; she's been late every night this week."

"Was it all right about your taking duty?"

"Ab-solutely. Said she was glad Miss Plumtree had gone to bed, and asked if she had anything to take for her head."

"How awfully decent of her!"

"Wasn't it? It'll buck old Greengage up, too. She always thinks Miss Vivian has a down on her."

Miss Delmege leant over the banisters and said in a subdued but very complacent undertone:

"I thought Miss Vivian would be all right. I thought I could safely answer for her."

CHAPTER II

PLESSING was also speaking of Miss Vivian that evening.

"Where is this to end, Miss Bruce? I ask you, where is it to end?" demanded Miss Vivian's mother.

Miss Bruce knew quite well that Lady Vivian was not asking her at all, in the sense of expecting to receive from her any suggestion of a term to that which in fact appeared to be interminable, so she only made a clicking sound of sympathy with her tongue and went on rapidly stamping postcards.

"I am not unpatriotic, though I do dislike Flagdays, and I was the first person to say that Char must go and do work somewhere nurse in a hospital if she liked, or do censor's work at the War Office. Sir Piers said ' No ' at first you know he's old-fashioned in many ways and then he said Char wasn't strong enough, and to a certain extent I agreed with him. But I put aside all that and absolutely encouraged her, as you know, to organize this Supply Depot. But I must say, Miss Bruce, that I never expected the thing to grow to these dimensions. Of course, it may be a very splendid work in fact, I'm sure it is, and everyone says how proud I must be of such a wonderful daughter but is it all absolutely necessary?"

"Oh, Lady Vivian," said the secretary reproachfully. "Why, the very War Office itself knows the value of dear Charmian's work. They are always asking her to take on fresh branches."

"That's just what I am complaining of. Why should the Midland Supply Depot do all these odd jobs? Hospital supplies are all very well, but when it comes to meeting all the troop-trains and supplying all the bandages, and being central Depot for sphagnum moss, and all the rest of it all I can say is, that it's beyond a joke."

Miss Bruce took instant advantage of her employer's infelicitous final cliche to remark austerely:

"Certainly one would never dream of looking upon it as a joke, Lady Vivian. I quite feel with you about her working so fearfully hard, and keeping these strange, irregular hours, but I'm convinced that it's perfectly unavoidable perfectly unavoidable. Charmian owns herself that no one can possibly take her place at the Depot, even for a day."

This striking testimony to the irreplacableness of her daughter appeared to leave Lady Vivian cold.

"I dare say," she said curtly. "Of course, she's got a gift for organization, and all she's done is perfectly marvellous, but I must say I wish she'd taken up nursing or something reasonable, like anybody else, when she could have had proper holidays and kept regular hours."

Miss Bruce gave the secretarial equivalent for laughing the suggestion to scorn.

"As though nursing wasn't something that anyone could do! Why, any ordinary girl can work in a hospital. But I should like to know what other woman could do Charmian's work. Why, if she left, the whole organization would break down in a week."

"Well," said the goaded Lady Vivian, "the war wouldn't go on any the longer if it did, I don't suppose any more than it's going to end twenty-four hours sooner because Char has dinner at eleven o'clock every night and spends five pounds a day on postage stamps."

Miss Bruce looked hurt, as she went on applying halfpenny stamps to the postcards that formed an increasing mountain on the writing-table in front of her.

"I suppose you're working for her now?"

"I only wish I could do more," said the secretary fervently. "She gives me these odd jobs because I'm always imploring her to let me do some of the mechanical work that anyone can manage, and spare her for other things. But, of course, no one can really do anything much to help her."

"I'm sorry to hear it, since she has a staff of thirty or forty people there. Pray, are they all being paid out of Red Cross funds for doing nothing at all?" inquired Lady Vivian satirically.

"Oh, of course they all do their bit. Routine work, as Charmian calls it. But she has to superintend everything hold the whole thing together. She looks through every letter that leaves that office, and knows the workings of every single department, and they come and ask her about every little thing."

"Yes, they do. She enjoys that."

Lady Vivian's tone held nothing more than reflectiveness, but the little secretary reddened unbecomingly, and said in a strongly protesting voice:

"Of course, it's a very big responsibility, and she knows that it all rests on her."

"Well, well," said Lady Vivian soothingly. "No one is ever a prophet in his own country, and I suppose Char is no exception. Anyhow, she has a most devoted champion in you, Miss Bruce."

"It has nothing to do with any--any personal liking, Lady Vivian, I assure you," said the secretary, her voice trembling and her colour rising yet more. "I don't say it because it's her, but quite dispassionately. I hope that even if I knew nothing of Charmian's own persona] attractiveness and and kindness, I should still be able to see how wonderful her devotion and self-sacrifice are, and admire her extraordinary capacity for work. Speaking quite impersonally, you know."

Anything less impersonal than her secretary's impassioned utterances, it seemed to Lady Vivian. would have been hard to find, and she shrugged her shoulders very slightly.

"Well, Char certainly needs a champion, for she's making herself very unpopular in the county. All these people who ran their small organizations and war charities quite comfortably for the first six or eight months of the war naturally don't like the way everything has been snatched away and affiliated to this Central Depot--"

"Official co-ordination is absolutely-"

"Yes, yes, I know; that's Char's *cri de bataille*. But there are ways and ways of doing things, and I must say that some of the things she's said and written, to perfectly well-meaning people who've been doing their best and giving endless time and trouble to the work, seem to me tactless to a degree."

"She says herself that anyone in her position is bound to give offence sometimes."

"Position fiddlesticks!" said Miss Vivian's parent briskly. "Why can't she behave like anybody else? She might be the War Office and the Admiralty rolled into one, to hear her talk sometimes. Of course, people who've known her ever since she was a little scrap in short petticoats aren't going to stand it. Why, she won't even be thirty till next month! though, I must say, she might be sixty from the way she talks. But then she always was like that, from the time she was five years old. It worried poor Sir Piers dreadfully when he wanted to show her how to manage her hoop, and she insisted on arguing with him about the law of gravitation instead. I suppose I ought to have smacked her then."

Miss Bruce choked, but any protest at the thought of the obviously-regretted opportunity lost by Lady Vivian for the perpetration of the suggested outrage remained unuttered.

The sharp sound of the telephone-bell cut across the air.

Miss Bruce attempted to rise, but was hampered by the paraphernalia of her clerical work, and Lady Vivian said:

"Sir Piers will answer it. He is in the hall, and you know he likes telephoning, because then he can think he isn't really getting as deaf as he sometimes thinks he is."

Miss Bruce, respecting this rather complicated reason, sat down again, and Lady Vivian remarked dispassionately:

"Of course it's Char, probably to say she can't come back to dinner. You know, I specially asked her to get back early to-night because John Trevellyan is dining with us. There! what did I tell you?"

They listened to the one-sided conversation.

"Sir Piers Vivian speaking. What's that? Oh, you'll put me through to Miss Vivian. Very well; I'll hold on. That you, my dear? Your mother and I are most anxious you should be back for dinner Trevellyan is coming.... We'll put off dinner for half an hour if that would help you.... But, my dear, he'll be very much disappointed not to see you, and it really seems a pity, when the poor chap is just back... he'll be so disappointed.... Yes, yes, I see. I'm sure it's very good of you, but couldn't they manage without you just for once?... Very well, my dear, I'll tell him.... It's really very good of you, my poor dear child...."

Lady Vivian stamped her foot noiselessly as her husband's voice reached her; but when Sir Piers had put back the receiver and come slowly into the room, she greeted him with a smile.

"Was that Char? To say she couldn't be back in time for dinner to-night, I suppose?"

Quick-tempered, sharp-tongued woman as she was, Joanna Vivian's voice was always gentle in speaking to her white-haired husband, twenty years her senior. "The poor child seems to think she can't be spared. Very good of her, but isn't she overdoing it just a little eh, Joanna? Aren't they working her rather too hard?"

"It's mostly her own doing, Piers. She's head of this show, you know. I suppose that's why she thinks she can't leave it."

"The whole thing would go to pieces without her," thrust in the secretary, in the sudden falsetto with which she always impressed upon Sir Piers her recollection of his increasing deafness. "She supervises the whole organization, and if she's away there isn't anyone to take her place."

16

"But they don't want to work after six o'clock," said the old man, looking puzzled. "Ten to six that's office hours. She oughtn't to want to be there after the place is shut up."

"Oh, there's no ' close time ' for the Midland Supply Depot," said Miss Bruce, looking superior. "They may have orders to meet a train at any hour of the day or night, and the telephone often goes on ringing till eleven or twelve o'clock, I believe. And Charmian never leaves till everyone else has finished work."

Sir Piers looked bewildered, and his wife said quietly:

"I'm thinking of suggesting to Char that she should sleep at the Hostel they opened last year, instead of coming back here at impossible hours every night. It really is very hard on the servants, and, besides, I don't think we shall have enough petrol this winter for it to be possible. She could always come home for week-ends, and on the whole it would be tiring foi her to be altogether in Questerham during the week."

"But is it necessary?" inquired Sir Piers piteously.

His wife shrugged her shoulders.

"If she'd been a boy she would be in the trenches now. I suppose we must let her do what she can, even though she's a girl. Other parents have to make greater sacrifices than ours, Piers."

"Yes, yes, to be sure," he assented. "And it's very good of the dear child to give up all her time as she does. But I'm sorry she can't be back for dinner to-night, Joanna very sorry. Poor Trevellyan will be disappointed."

"Yes," said Lady Vivian, and refrained from adding, "I hope he will be."

She had once hoped that Char and John Trevellyan might marry; but Char's easy contempt for her cousin's Philistinism was only equalled by his unconcealed regret that so much prettiness should be allied to such alarming quick-wittedness.

"Miss Bruce," she said, turning to her secretary, "I hope you will dine with us to-night. Captain Trevellyan is bringing over a brother-officer and his wife, and we shall be an odd number, since there is no hope of Char."

"What's that, my dear?" said Sir Piers. "I hadn't heard that. Who is Trevellyan bringing with him?"

"Major Willoughby and his wife. She used to be Lesbia Carroll, and I knew her years ago before she married. I shall be rather curious to see her again."

"Are they motoring?"

"Yes, in Johnnie's new car."

The dressing-gong reverberated through the hall.

"They will very likely be late," remarked Lady Vivian, "but I must go and dress at once."

She went across the long room, a tall, upright woman with a beautiful figure, obviously betterlooking at fifty-two than she could ever have been as a girl. Her hair was thick and dark, with more than a sprinkling of white, and two deep vertical lines ran from the corners of her nostrils to her rather square chin. But her blue eyes were brilliant, and deeply set under a forehead that was singularly unlined.

As Joanna Trevellyan, ungainly and devoid of beauty, she had been far too outspoken to conceal her native cleverness, and had never known popularity. As the wife of Sir Piers Vivian, the only man who had ever wished to marry her, and mistress of Plessing, her wit and shrewdness became her, and as the years went on she was even accounted good-looking.

Miss Bruce, returning to her postcards after a hurried toilet, thought that Lady Vivian looked very handsome as she came down in her black-lace eveningdress with a high amethyst comb in her hair.

"Have the evening papers come?" was her first inquiry.I think Sir Piers had them

taken upstairs."

Lady Vivian frowned quickly.

"How I wish he wouldn't do that! The casualty lists depress him so dreadfully. We must try and keep off the subject of the war at dinner, Miss Bruce, or he won't sleep all night."

Miss Bruce said nothing, but she pursed up her lips in a manner which meant that a possibly wakeful night for Sir Piers Vivian ought not to be weighed in the balance against the universal tendency to discuss the war. That the subject was never willingly embarked upon at Plessing, except by Char Vivian, seemed to her a confession of weakness.

Lady Vivian was perfectly aware of her secretary's point of view, and profoundly indifferent to it. She even took a rather malicious pleasure in saying lightly and yet very decidedly:

"John is safe enough, but I don't know what Lesbia Willoughby may choose to talk about. As a girl she had the voice of a pea-hen, and never stopped chattering. So, if you can, please head her off war-talk at dinner."

Her employer's trenchant simile as to Mrs. Willoughby's vocal powers could not but recur to Miss Bruce with a sense of its extreme appositeness when the guests entered.

Mrs. Willoughby billowed into the room. There was really no other word to describe that rapid, undulating, and yet buoyant advance. Tall as Lady Vivian was, and by no means slightly built, she seemed to Miss Bruce to be at once physically overpowered and almost eclipsed in the strident and voluminous greeting of her old acquaintance.

"My dear Joanna! After all these years... how too, too delightful to see you so absolutely and utterly unchanged! Dear old days! And now we meet in the midst of all these horrors!"

The exaggeration of the look she cast round her seemed to include the drawing-room and its occupants alike in the pleasing category.

"I'm sorry you don't like my Louis XV.," said Lady Vivian flippantly, and turned to greet the rest of the party.

Her cousin John, who looked, even in khaki, a great deal less than his thirty years, smiled at her with steady blue eyes that bore a great resemblance to her own, and wrung her hand, saying, "This is very jolly, Cousin Joanna," in a pleasant, rather serious voice.

""And here," said Lesbia Willoughby piercingly "here is my Lewis."

Her Lewis advanced, looking not unnaturally sheepish, and Trevellyan said conscientiously:

"May I introduce Major Willoughby to you? My Lady Vivian,"

"You never told me, Joanna, that this dear thing was a cousin of yours," shrieked Lesbia reproachfully, "I think it quite disgustingly mean of you, considering that we were girls together."

"In the days when we were girls together," said Lady Vivian ruthlessly, "he wasn't born or thought of. Have they announced dinner, Miss Bruce?"

"This moment."

"Then, do let's go in at once. You must all be very hungry after such a drive."

"I never eat nowadays simply never," proclaimed Mrs. Willoughby as she crossed the hall on Sir Piers's arm. "I think it most unpatriotic. We're all going to be starving quite soon, and the poor are living on simply nothing a day as it is. And one can't bear to touch food while our poor dear boys in the trenches and in Germany are literally starving."

Mrs. Willoughby's voice was of a very piercing quality, and she emphasized her words by rolling round a pair of enormous and over-prominent light grey eyes as she spoke. Seated at the dinner-table, she contrived to present an appearance that almost amounted to impropriety, by merely putting a large bare elbow on the table and flinging back an elaborately dressed head set on a short neck and opulent shoulders, thickly dredged with heavily scented powder. Miss Bruce, on the opposite side of the table, eyed her with distrustful disapproval. It did not appear to her likely that she would be able to carry out Lady Vivian's injunction that war-talk was to be avoided.

"Isn't Char at home?" Trevellyan inquired of his hostess.

"She's at Questerham, and the car has gone in for her, but she telephoned to say that she couldn't get back till late. It's this Supply Depot of hers; she's giving every minute of the day and night to it," said Lady Vivian, characteristically allowing no tinge of disapproval or disappointment to colour her voice.

"Is that your delightful girl?" inquired Lesbia across the table, and pronouncing the word as though it rhymed with "curl." "Isn't it too wonderful to see all these young things devoting themselves? As for me, I'm literally run off my feet in town. I'm having a holiday here just to see something of Lewis, who's stationed in these parts indefinitely, poor dear lamb because my doctor said I was killing myself literally killing myself."

"Really?" said Lady Vivian placidly. "I hope you're going to be here for some time. Are you staying--"

"Only till I'm fit to move. That moment," said Lesbia impressively, "that very moment, I must simply dash back to London. My dear, I can't tell you what it's like. I never have an instant to call my own have I, Lewis?"

"Rather not," said Lewis hastily.

He was a small, brown-faced man, who had won his D.S.O. in South Africa, and whom no doctor could now be induced to pass for service abroad.

"Perhaps some charitable organization takes up your time," suggested Sir Piers to Mrs. Willoughby. His deafness seldom permitted him to follow more than the drift of general conversation. "Now, Charmian, our daughter, has taken up a most creditable piece of work, most creditable--although, perhaps, she is a little inclined to overdo things just at present."

"No one can possibly overdo war-work," Mrs. Willoughby told him trenchantly. "Nothing that we women of England can do could ever be enough for the brave fathers, and husbands, and brothers, and sweethearts, who are risking their lives for us out there. Think of what the trenches are 'just hell, as a boy said to me the other day hell let loose!"

Sir Piers looked very much distressed, and his white head began to shake. He had only heard part of Lesbia's discourse. Trevellyan's boyishly fair face flushed scarlet. He had fought in Belgium, and in Flanders, until a bullet lodged in his knee, and now his next Medical Board might send him to France to rejoin his regiment. But it would have occurred to no one to suppose that the poignant description quoted by Mrs. Willoughby had ever emanated from Trevellyan.

From the head of the table Joanna Vivian said smoothly:

"You've made us all very curious as to your work, Lesbia. Do tell us what you do."

Mrs. Willoughby gave her high, strident laugh.

"Everything," was her modest claim. "Absolutely everything, my dear. Packing for prisoners three mornings a week, canteen work twice, and every Flag-day going. I can't tell you the hours I've stood outside Claridge's carrying a tray and seeing insolent wretches walk past me without buying. I've been so exhausted by the end of the day I've had to have an hour's massage before I could drag myself out to patronize some Red Cross entertainment. But, of course, my real work is the Colonial officers. Dear, sweet things! I take them all over London!"

"By Jove, though, do you really!" said Trevellyan admiringly.

Only a certain naive quality of sincerity in his simplicities, Joanna reflected, saved Johnnie from appearing absolutely stupid. But, her husband excepted, she was secretly fonder and more proud of Johnnie than of any one, in the world, and she did not make the mistake of supposing that his easy chivalry denoted any admiration for the screeching monologue of which Lesbia was delivering herself.

"I make a speciality of South Africans," she proclaimed to the table. "They're so delightfully rural even more so than the dear Australians, though I have a pasgion for Anzacs. But I take some of them somewhere every day just show them London, you know. Not one of them knows a soul in England, and of course London is a perfect marvel to them. I simply live in taxis, rushing the dear things round."

"Ah, we had a couple of Canadians here last week very fine fellows," said Sir Piers. "Been in hospital in Questerham, both of them, and Char thought they'd enjoy a day out in the country. She manages everything, you know even the hospitals. The doctors all come to her for everything, I believe. She tells me that all the hospitals round about are affiliated to her office."

"Ranks as a sort of Universal Provider what?" said Trevellyan.

"Yes; isn't it wonderful?" said Miss Bruce eagerly; and availed herself of the full of the double opportunity for obeying, even at the eleventh hour, Lady Vivian's injunctions as to the trend of the conversation, and at the same time making the utmost of her favourite topic, Char Vivian's work at the Midland Supply Depot.

For the rest of dinner, in spite of several strenuous efforts from Lesbia Willoughby, nothing else was discussed.

CHAPTER III

TEN o'clock in the morning, and little Miss Anthony flew up Questerham High Street on her bicycle, conscious that her hurried choice of a winter hat had not only been highly unsatisfactory, owing to the extreme haste with which she had conducted it, but was also about to make her late in arriving at the office. She threw an anxious glance at the Post-Office clock, and redoubled her speed at the sight of it, though no amount of haste would get her to the Midland Supply Depot Headquarters under another seven minutes.

But she sped gallantly across the tram-lines and in and out of the slow-moving stream of market-carts, and arrived breathless at the offices in Pollard Street just as Miss Vivian's small open car drew up at the door.

"Damn!" automatically muttered Tony under her breath, and seeing nothing for it but to put her bicycle into a corner and efface herself respectfully to let Miss Vivian pass.

But Miss Vivian, generally so unaware of any member of her staff as not even to exchange a "Goodmorning," elected suddenly to reverse this policy.

"Good-morning," she said graciously. "We're both late to-day, I'm afraid."

The clerk in the hall, who drew an ominous line in her book under the last signature as the clock struck ten, laughed in a rather awestruck way and said, "Oh, Miss Vivian!"

"I think you must let Miss Anthony off to-day," said Char Vivian, smiling. "As I am late myself, you know."

She went slowly upstairs, just hearing an ecstatic gasp from the two girls in the hall.

She was vaguely aware that those few gracious words and tone of easy kindness had secured for her little Miss Anthony's unswerving loyalty and admiration. Girls of that age and class were like that, she told herself with a slight smile.

The smile died away into an expression of weary concentration as she entered her private office.

"Good-morning, Miss Delmege. Is there much in, to-day?"

"Good-morning, Miss Vivian," said Miss Delmege, elegantly rising from her knees, in which lowly position she had been trying to coax the small, indifferent fire to burn. I am afraid there are a lot of letters."

Miss Vivian sighed and moved to the looking-glass to take off her hat. She also was in uniform, and wore several curly stripes of gold braid on her coat collar and cuffs to denote her exalted position.

Even when she had taken off her ugly and unbecoming felt hat and run her fingers through the thick, straight masses of reddish hair that hung over her forehead, Char Vivian contrived to look at least ten years older than her actual twenty-nine years.

She was very good-looking, with delicate aquiline features, a pale, fair skin powdered all over with tiny freckles, and beautiful deep-set brown eyes surrounded by unexpectedly dark lashes.

It was something quite indefinable in the lines round her pretty, decided mouth, and under her eyes that gave the odd impression of maturity. Her manner had always, from the age of five, been one of extreme self-security.

"Now, then, for the letters," she said, as she sat down before the great roll-top desk. Char Vivian's voice was deep and rather drawling in character, and she used it with great effect.

"Miss Delmege, did you put these heavenly liliesof-the-valley here? You really mustn't but they're too lovely. Thank you so much. They do make such a difference!"

She sniffed delicately, and Miss Delmege smiled with gratification. The lilies-of-the-valley had really cost more than she could afford, but those few words of appreciation sent her to her small table in the corner with a sense of great satisfaction.

Char tore open one envelope after another with murmured comments. She frequently affected an absence of mind denoted by fragmentary monologue.

"Transport wanted for fifty men going from the King Street Hospital to-day--and they want more sphagnum moss. There ought to be five hundred bags ready to go out this morning.... I wonder if they've seen to it. Inquiries 'inquiries inquiries! When are people ever going to stop asking me questions? Hospital accounts 'that can go to the Finance Department.... The Stores bill to the Commissariat. What's all this transport for that man in Hospital? I shall have to see to that myself. Look me up the War Office letters as to Petrol regulations, Miss Delmege, will you? Belgians again; they're very difficult to satisfy, poor people. Madame Van Damm I don't remember them I must send for the files. Here are some more of those tiresome muddles of Mrs. Potter's. I told her all about those people on Monday. Why on earth hasn't it been arranged? Nothing is ever done unless one sees to it oneself.
The Medical Officer of Health wants to see me. What are my appointments for to-day, Miss Delmege?"

"The man from the building contractors is coming at twelve, and the Matron from the Overseas Hospital at three, and then there's that Miss Jones who's coming to work here. And it's the day you generally go to the Convalescent Homes."

"I see. Ring up the Medical Officer and say I can give him a quarter of an hour at two o'clock. I can't really spare that," sighed Miss Vivian, "but I suppose I shall have to see him."

Miss Delmege knew that, whatever else her chief might depute to her, she never relinquished to anyone a business interview, so she merely looked concerned and said: "I'm afraid it will be a great rush for you."

Miss Vivian gave her subtle, infrequent smile, and began the customary series of morning interviews which were supposed to settle the perplexities of each department for the day. That this supposition was not invariably correct was made manifest on this occasion by the demeanour of the unhappy Miss Plumtree, when her chief had made short work of a series of difficulties haltingly and stammeringly put before her in sentences made involved and awkward through sheer nervousness.

"Let me have those Requisition Averages by twelve o'clock, please and I think that completes you, Miss Plumtree?" concluded Miss Vivian rapidly.

"Thank you, Miss Vivian. Is are do these averages include the first day of the month as well as the last?"

"Yes, of course. And remember to give the gross weight of the supplies as well as the nett weight."

"And I I divide by the number of days in each month. Yes, I see," faltered Miss Plumtree, seeing nothing at all except the brisk tapping of Miss Vivian's long, slight fingers on the blotting-paper in front of her, denoting with sufficient clearness that in her opinion the interview had reached it's conclusion some moments since.

"It's for August, September, and October, isn't it?"

"Yes."

Miss Vivian's tone implied that the question was unnecessary in the extreme, as indeed it was, since Miss Plumtree had been engaged in conducting the quarterly Requisition Averages to an unsuccessful issue for the past eighteen months.

"Thank you."

Miss Plumtree faltered from the room, with the consciousness of past failures heavy upon her.

Char did not like an attitude of sycophantic dejection, and Miss Plumtree may therefore have been responsible for the very modified enthusiasm with which the next applicant's request for an afternoon off duty was received.

"It rather depends, Miss Cox," said Char, her drawl slightly emphasized. "I thought the work in that department was behindhand?"

"Not now, Miss Vivian," said the grey-haired spinster anxiously. "Mrs. Tweedale and I cleared it all up last night; I'm quite up to date."

"Well, I'm afraid there's a good deal for you here," said Char rather cruelly, handing her a bundle of papers. "However, please take your afternoon off if you want to, and if you feel that the work can be left.--"

"Thank you, Miss Vivian."

Miss Cox, who was meek and deferential, left the room, the pleasurable anticipation of a holiday quite gone from her tired face.

Char looked at the neatly coiled twist of Miss Delmege's sand-coloured hair.

"Was I a wet-blanket?" she inquired whimsically. "Really, the way these people are always asking for leave! I wonder what would happen if *I* took an afternoon off. How long is it since I had a holiday, Miss Delmege?"

"You've not had one since I've been here," declared her secretary, "and that's nearly a year."

"Exactly. But then I can't understand putting anything before the work, personally."

Char returned to her pile of letters and Miss Delmege went on with her writing in a glow of admiration, and resolved that, after all, she would come and work on Sunday morning, although nominally no one came to the office on Sundays except the clerks who took turns for telephone duty, and Miss Vivian herself in the afternoon.

The morning was a busy one. Telephone calls seemed incessant, and the operator downstairs was unintelligent and twice cut Miss Vivian off in the midst of an important trunk call.

"Hallo! hallo! are you there? Miss Henderson, what the dickens are you doing? You've cut me off again."

Char banged the receiver down impatiently with one hand, while the other continued to make rapid calculations on a large sheet of foolscap. She possessed and exercised to the full the faculty of following two or more trains of thought at the same moment.

Presently she rang her bell sharply, the customary signal that she was ready to dictate her letters.

Each department was supposed to possess its own typewriter and to make use of it, and the services of the shorthand-typist, who was amongst the few paid workers in the office, were exclusively reserved for Miss Vivian.

The work entailed was no sinecure, the more especially since Miss Collins was obdurate as to her time-limit of ten to five-thirty. But it was never difficult for Miss Vivian to commandeer volunteer typists from the departments when her enormous correspondence appeared to her to require it.

"Good-morning, Miss Vivian."

"Good-morning," said Char curtly, unsmiling. Miss Collins always gave her a sense of irritation. She was BO jauntily competent, so consciously independent of the office.

Horthand-typists could always find work in the big Questerham manufacturing works, and Miss Collins had only been secured for the Supply Depot with difficulty. She received two pounds ten shillings a week, never worked overtime, and had every Saturday afternoon off. Miss Vivian had once, in the early days of Miss Collins, suggested that she might like to wear uniform, and had received a smiling and unqualified negative, coupled with a candid statement of Miss Collins V views as to the undesirability of combining clerical work with the exhausting activities required in meeting and feeding the troop-trains.

"I should be sorry to think that any of my staff would shirk the little additional work which brings them into contact with the men who have risked their lives for England," had been the freezing finale with which the dialogue had been brought to a close by the disgusted Miss Vivian.

Since then her stenographer had continued to frequent her presence in transparent and decolletees blouses, with short skirts swinging above silkstockinged ankles and suede shoes. Even her red, fluffy curls were unnecessarily decked with half a dozen sparkling prongs. But she was very quick and intelligent, and Miss Vivian had perforce to accept her impudent prettiness and complete independence.

Char never, after the first week, made the mistake of supposing that Miss Collins would ever fall under that spell of personal magnetism to which the rest of the office was in more or less complete subjection, and she consequently wasted no smile upon her morning greeting.

"This is to the Director-General of Voluntary Organizations, and please do not use abbreviations. Kindly head the letter in full."

Miss Collins's small manicured hand ran easily over her notebook, leaving a trail of cabalistic signs behind it. Char leant back, half-closing her eyes in a way which served to emphasize the tired shadows beneath them, and proceeded with her fluent, unhampered dictation.

She was seldom at a loss for a word, and had a positive gift for the production of rhetorical periods which never failed to impress Miss Delmege, still writing at her corner table. In spite of frequent interruptions, Char proceeded unconcernedly enough, until at the eleventh entry of a messenger she broke into an impatient exclamation:

"Miss Delmege, please deal for me!" Miss Delmege swept forward, annihilating the unhappy bearer of the card with a look of deep reproach, as she took it from her.

"I'm afraid it's someone to see you," she faltered deprecatingly.

Char frowned and took the card impatiently, and Miss Delmege stood by looking nervous, as she invariably did when her chief appeared annoyed. Char Vivian, however, although frequently impatient, was not a passionate woman, and however much she might give rein to her tongue, seldom lost control of her temper, for the simple reason that she never lost sight of herself or of her own effect upon her surroundings.

Her face cleared as she read the card. "Please ask Captain Trevellyan to come up here." The messenger disappeared thankfully and Miss Delmege retreated relievedly to her corner.

Char leant back again in her capacious chair, a sheaf of papers, at which she only cast an occasional glance, before her.

She was not at all averse to being found in this attitude, which she judged to be most typical of herself and her work, and for an instant after Captain Trevellyan's booted tread had paused upon the threshold she affected unawareness of his presence and did not raise her eyes.

"... I am in receipt of your letter of even date, and would inform you in

reply..." "Oh, John! So you've come for an official inspection?"

"Since you're never to be seen any other way," he returned, laughing, and grasping her hand.

"I ought to send you away; we're in the midst of a heavy day's work."

"Don't you think you might call a a sort of truce of God, for the moment, and tell me something about this office of yours? I'm much impressed by all I hear."

Miss Delmege, judging from her chief's smile that this suggestion was approved of, brought forward a chair, and acknowledged Captain Trevellyan's protesting thanks with a genteel bend at the waist and a small, tight smile.

The amenities of social intercourse were always strictly held in check by the limits of officialdom by Miss Vivian's staff, with the exception of the unregenerate Miss Collins, who tucked her pencil into her belt, uncrossed her knees, and rose from her chair.

"I'm afraid I'm interrupting you," said Trevellyan politely, addressing his remark to Char, but casting a quite unnecessary look at the now smiling Miss Collins.

"I've nearly finished," said Char.

"Shall I come back later?" suggested Miss Collins gaily, swinging a turquoise heart from the end of an outrageously long gold chain.

"I will ring if I want you," said Miss Vivian in tones eminently calculated to allay any assumption of indispensability on the part of her employee.

With a freezing eye she watched Miss Collins swing jauntily from the room, her red head cocked at an angle that enabled her to throw a farewell dimple in the direction of Captain Trevellyan.

"Is that one of your helpers?" was the rather infelicitously worded inquiry which John was inspired to put as Miss Collins disappeared.

"The office stenographer," said Char curtly.

"Why don't you have poor old Miss Bruce up here? She's longing to help you couldn't talk about anything but this place last night."

"Dear old Brucey!" said Char, with more languor than enthusiasm in her voice. "But there are one or two reasons why it wouldn't quite do to have her in the office; we have to be desperately official here, you know. Besides, it's such a comfort to get back in the evenings to someone who doesn't look upon me as the Director of the Midland Supply Depot! I sometimes feel I'm turning into an organization instead of a human being."

Miss Vivian, needless to say, had never felt anything of the sort, but there was something rather gallantly pathetic in the half-laughing turn of the phrase, and it sufficed for a weighty addition to Miss Delmege's treasured collections of Glimpses into Miss Vivian's Real Self.

She received yet another such a few minutes later, when Captain Trevellyan began to urge Miss Vivian to come out with him in the new car waiting at the office door.

"Do! I'll take you anywhere you want to go, and I really do want you to see how beautifully she runs. Come and lunch somewhere?"

"I'd love it," declared Char wistfully, "but I really mustn't, Johnnie. There's so much to do."

Either the cousinly diminutive, or something unusually unofficial in Miss Vivian's regretful voice, caused the discreet Miss Delmege to rise and glide quietly from the room.

"Miss Vivian really is most awfully human," she declared to a fellow-worker whom she met upon the stairs. "What do you think I've left her doing?"

The fellow-worker leant comfortably against the wall, balancing a wire basket full of official-looking documents on her hip, and said interestedly:

"Do tell me."

"Refusing to go for a motor ride with a cousin of hers, an officer, who wants her to see his new car. And she awfully wants to go I could see that it's only the work that's keeping her."

"I must say she is splendid!" "Yes, isn't she?"

"I think I saw the cousin, waiting downstairs about a quarter of an hour ago. Is he a Staff Officer, very tall and large, and awfully fair?"

"Yes. Rather nice-looking, isn't he?"

"Quite, and I do like them to be tall. He's got a nice voice, too. You know I mean his voice is nice."

"Yes; he has got a nice voice, hasn't he? I noticed it myself. Of course, that awful Miss Collins made eyes at him like anything. She was taking letters when he came in."

"Rotten little minx! I wonder if he's engaged to Miss Vivian?"

"I couldn't say," primly returned Miss Delmege, with a sudden access of discretion, implying a reticence which in point of fact she was not in a position to exercise.

She did not go upstairs again until Captain Trevellyan and his motor-car had safely negotiated the corner of Pollard Street, unaccompanied by Miss Vivian.

This Miss Delmege ascertained from a ground-floor window, and then returned to her corner table, wearing an expression of compassionate admiration that Char was perfectly able to interpret.

"I'm afraid that was an interruption to our morning's work," she said kindly. "What time is it?"

"Nearly one o'clock, Miss Vivian."

"Oh, good heavens! Just bring me the Belgian files, will you? and then you'd better go to lunch."

"I can quite well go later," said Miss Delmege eagerly. "I I thought perhaps you'd be lunching out to-day."

"No," drawled Char decisively; "in spite of the inducement of the new car, I shan't leave the office till I have to go to the Convalescent Homes. I'll send for some lunch when I want it."

Miss Delmege went to her own lunch with a vexed soul.

"I do wish one could get Miss Vivian to eat something," she murmured distractedly to her neighbour. "I know exactly what it'll be, you know. She'll sit there writing, writing, writing, and forget all about food, and then it'll be two o'clock, and she has to see the M.O. of Health and somebody else coming at three and she'll have had no lunch at all."

"Doesn't she ever go out to lunch?"

"Only on slack days, and you know how often we get them, especially now that the work is simply increasing by leaps and bounds every day."

"Couldn't you take her some sandwiches?" asked Mrs. Bullivant from the head of the table. "I could cut some in a minute."

"Oh no, thank you. She wouldn't like it. She hates a fuss," Miss Delmege declared decidedly.

The refusal, with its attendant tag of explanatory ingratitude, was received in matter-of-fact silence by everyone.

Miss Vivian's hatred of a fuss, as interpreted by her secretary, merely redounded to her credit in the eyes of the Hostel.

They ate indifferent pressed beef and tepid milkpudding, and those who could afford it for the most part accompanied by those who could not afford it-- supplemented the meal with coffee and cakes devoured in haste at the High Street confectioner's, and then hurried back to the office.

It was nearly three o'clock before Miss Delrnege ventured to address her

chief. "I'm afraid you haven't had lunch. Do let me send for something."

Miss Vivian looked up, flushed and tired. "Dear me, yes. It's much later than I thought. Send out one of the Scouts for a couple of buns and a piece of chocolate."

"Oh!" protested Miss Delmege, as she invariably did on receipt of this menu.

Char Vivian did not raise her eyes from the letter she was rapidly inditing, and her secretary retreated to give the order.

Miss Plumtree, counting on her fingers and looking acutely distressed, sat at a small table in the hall from whence the Scout was despatched.

"Is that all she's having for lunch?" she paused in her pursuit of ever-elusive averages to inquire in awestruck tones.

"Yes, and she's been simply worked to death this morning. And it's nearly three now, and she won't get back to dinner till long after ten o'clock, probably; but she never will have more for lunch, when she's very busy, than just buns and a penny piece of chocolate. That," said Miss Delmege, with a sort of desperate admiration "that is just Miss Vivian all over!"

CHAPTER IV

CHAR looked wearily at the clock.

The buns and chocolate hastily disposed of in the intervals of work during the afternoon had only served to spoil the successive cups of strong tea, which formed her only indulgence, brought to her at five o'clock. They were guiltless of sustaining qualities. It was not yet seven, and she never ordered the car until nine o'clock or later.

Her eyes dropped to the diminished, but still formidable, pile of papers on the table. She was excessively tired, and she knew that the papers before her could be dealt with in the morning.

But it was characteristic of Char Vivian that she did not make up her mind then and there to order the car round and arrive at Plessing in time for eight o'clock dinner and early bed, much as she needed both. To do so would have jarred with her own and her staff's conception of her self-sacrificing, untiring energy, her devotion to an immense and indispensable task, just as surely as would a trivial, easy interruption to the day's work in the shape of John Trevellyan and his new car, or an hour consecrated to fresh air and luncheon. Necessity compelled Char to work twelve hours a day some two evenings a week, in order that the amount undertaken by the Midland Supply Depot might be duly accomplished; but on the remaining days, when work was comparatively light, and over early in the evening, she did not choose to spoil the picture which she carried always in her mind's eye of the indefatigable and overtaxed Director of the Midland Supply Depot.

So Miss Vivian applied herself wearily, once again, to her inspection of those Army Forms which were to be sent up to the London office on the morrow.

Presently the door opened and Miss Delmege came in with her hat and coat on, prepared to go.

"I thought I'd just tell you," she said hesitatingly, "that Miss Jones has come the new clerk. Shall I take her over to the Hostel?"

Char sighed wearily.

"Oh, I suppose I'd better see her. If it isn't to-night, it will have to be to-morrow. I'd rather get it over. Send her up."

"Oh, Miss Vivian!"

"Never mind. I shan't be long."

Miss Vivian smiled resignedly.

As a matter of fact, she was rather relieved at the prospect of an interview to break the monotony of the evening. The Army Forms in question had failed to repay inspection, in the sense of presenting any glaring errors for which the Medical Officer in charge of the Hospital could have been brought sharply to book.

She unconsciously strewed the papers on the desk into a rather more elaborate confusion in front of her, and began to open the inkpot, although she had no further writing to do. The pen was poised between her fingers when Miss Delmege noiselessly opened the door, and shut it again on the entry of Miss Jones.

Char put down her pen, raised her heavy-lidded eyes, and said in her deep, effective voice:

"Good-evening, Miss--er--Jones."

She almost always hesitated and drawled for an instant before pronouncing the name of any member of her staff. The trick was purely instinctive, and indicated both her own overcharged memory and the insignificance of the unit, among many, whom she was addressing.

"How do you do?" said Miss Jones.

Her voice possessed the indefinable and quite unmistakable intonation of good-breeding, and Char instantly observed that she did not wind up her brief greeting with Miss Vivian's name.

She looked at her with an instant's surprise. Miss Jones was short and squarely built, looked about twenty-seven, and was not pretty. But she had a fine pair of grey eyes in her little colourless face, and her slim, ungloved hands, which Char immediately noticed, were unusually beautiful.

"You are from Wales, I believe?" said Char, unexpectedly even to herself. She made a point of avoiding personalities with the staff. But there appeared to be something which required explanation in Miss Jones.

"Yes. My father is the Dean of Penally. I have had some secretarial experience with him during the last five years."

Evidently Miss Jones wished to keep to the matter in hand. Char was rather amused, reflecting on the fluttered gratification which Miss Delmege or Miss Henderson would have displayed at any directing of the conversation into more personal channels.

"I see," she said, smiling a little. "Now, I wonder what you call secretarial experience?"

"My father naturally has a great deal of correspondence," returned Miss Jones, without any answering smile on her smaJl, serious face. "I have been his only secretary for four years. Since the war he has employed someone else for most of his letters, so as to set me free for other work."

"Yes; I understood from your letter that you had been working in a hospital." "As

clerk."

"Excellent. That will be most useful experience here. You know this office controls the hospitals in Questerham and round about. I want you to work in this room with my secretary, and learn her work, so that she can use you as her second."

"I will do my best."

"I'm sure of that," said Miss Vivian, redoubling her charm of manner, and eyeing the impassive Miss Jones narrowly. "I hope you'll be happy here and like the work. You must always let me know if there's anything you don't like. I think you're billeted just across the road, at our Questerham Hostel?"

"Yes."

"I'll send someone to show you the way."

"Thank you; I know where it is. I left my luggage there before coming here."

"The new workers generally come to report to me before doing anything else," said Char, indefinably vexed at having failed to obtain the expected smile of gratitude.

"However, if you know the way I must let you go now, so as to be in time for supper. Good-night, Miss Jones."

"Good-night," responded Miss Jones placidly, and closed the door noiselessly behind her. Her movements were very quiet in spite of her solid build, and she moved lightly enough, but the Hostel perceived a certain irony, nevertheless, in the fact that Miss Jones's parents had bestowed upon her the baptismal name of Grace.

The appeal thus made to a rather elementary sense of humour resulted in Miss Jones holding the solitary privilege of being the only person in the Hostel who was almost invariably called by her Christian name. She enjoyed from the first a strange sort of popularity, nominally due to the fact that "you never knew what she was going to say next "; in reality owing to a curious quality of absolute sincerity which was best translated by her surroundings as "originality." Another manifestation of it, less easily denned, was the complete good faith which she placed in all those with whom she came into contact. Only a decided tincture of Welsh shrewdness preserved her from the absolute credulity of the simpleton.

Almost the first question put to Miss Jones was that favourite test one of the enthusiastic Tony, "And what do you think of Miss Vivian?"

"I think," said Miss Jones thoughtfully, "that she is a reincarnation of Queen Elizabeth."

There was a rather stunned silence in the Hostel sitting-room.

Reincarnation was not a word which had ever sounded there before, and it carried with it a subtle suggestion of impropriety to several listeners. Nor was anyone at the moment sufficiently au courant with the Virgin Queen's leading characteristics to feel certain whether the comparison instituted was meant to be complimentary or insulting in the extreme.

Miss Delmege for once voiced the popular feeling by ejaculating

coldly: "That's rather a strange thing to say, surely!"

"Why? Hasn't it ever struck anybody before? I should have thought it so obvious. Why, even to look at, you know that sandy colouring, and the way she holds her head: just as though there ought to be a ruff behind it."

"Oh, you mean to look at," said Miss Marsh, the general tension considerably relaxed as the trend of the conversation shifted from that dreaded line of abstract discussion whither the indiscreet Miss Jones had appeared, for one horrid moment, to conduct it.

"Had Queen Elizabeth got freckles? I really don't know much about her, except that they found a thousand dresses in her wardrobe when she died," said Tony, voicing, as it happened, the solitary fact concerning the Sovereign under discussion which anyone present was able to remember, as outcome of each one's varying form of a solid English education.

"Her power of administration and personal magnetism, you know," explained Miss Jones.

"Oh, of course she's perfectly wonderful," Miss Delmege exclaimed, sure of her ground. "You'll see that more and more, working in her room."

Whether such increased perception was indeed the result of Miss Jones's activities in the room of the Director might remain open to question.

Char found her very quick, exceedingly accurate, and more conscientious than the quick-witted can generally boast of being. She remained entirely selfpossessed under praise, blame, or indifference, and Miss Vivian was half-unconsciously irritated at this tacit assumption of an independence more significant and no less secure than that of Miss Collins the typist.

"Gracie, I wish you'd tell me what you really think of Miss Vivian," her room-mate demanded one night as they were undressing together.

Screens were chastely placed round each bed, and it was a matter of some surprise to Miss Marsh that her companion so frequently neglected these modest adjuncts to privacy, and often took off her stockings, or folded up even more intimate garments, under the full light, such as it was, of the gas-jet in the middle of the room.

Miss Jones was extremely orderly, and always folded her clothes with scrupulous tidiness. She rolled up a pair of black stockings with exactitude before answering.

"I think she's rather interesting."

"Good Lord, Gracie! if Delmege could only hear you! Rather interesting! The Director of the sacred Supply Depot! You really are the limit, the things you say, you know."

"Well, that's all I do think. She is very capable, and a fairly good organizer, but I don't think her as marvellous as you or Miss Delmege or Tony do. In fact, I think you're all rather detraquees about Miss Vivian."

Miss Marsh was as well aware as anybody in the Hostel that the insertion of a foreign word into a British discourse is the height of affectation and of bad form; and although she could not believe Grace to be at all an affected person, she felt it due to her own nationality to assume a very disapproving expression and to allow an interval of at least three seconds to elapse before she continued the conversation,

"Don't you like her?"

"I'm not sure."

"I suppose you don't know her well enough to say yet?" Miss Marsh suggested.

"Do you think that has anything to do with it? I often like people without knowing them a bit," said Grace cordially; "and certainly I quite often dislike them thoroughly, even if I've only heard them speak once, or perhaps not at all."

"Then you judge by appearances, which is a great mistake."

Miss Jones said in a thoughtful manner that she didn't think it was that exactly, and supposed regretfully that Miss Marsh would think she was "swanking" if she explained that she considered herself a sound and rapid judge of character.

"Oh, what a sweet camisole, dear!"

"My petticoat-bodice," said Grace matter-of-factly. "I'm glad you like it. The ribbon always takes a long time to put in, but it does look rather nice. I like mauve better than pink or blue."

There came a knock at the door.

"Come in!" called Miss Jones, bare-armed and bare-legged in the middle of the room.

"Wait a minute!" exclaimed the scandalized Miss Marsh, in the midst of a shuffling process by which her clothes were removed under the nightgown which hung round her with empty flapping sleeves.

"It's only me," said Miss Plumtree in melancholy tones, walking in. "I'm just waiting for my kettle to boil."

The gas-ring was on the landing just outside the bedroom door.

Grace looked up.

"How pretty you look with your hair down!" she said admiringly.

"Me? Rubbish!" exclaimed Miss Plumtree, colouring with astonishment and embarrassment, but with a much livelier note in her voice.

"Your hair is so nice," explained Grace, gazing at the soft brown mop of curls.

"Oh, lovely, of course."

Miss Plumtree wriggled with confusion, and had no mind to betray how much the unaffected little bit of praise had restored her spirits. But she sat down on Grace's bed in her pink cotton kimono in a distinctly more cheerful frame of mind than that in which she had entered the room.

"Are you in the blues, Gooseberry-bush?" was the sympathetic inquiry of Miss Marsh.

"Well, I am, rather. It's Miss Vivian, you know. She can be awfully down on one when she likes."

"I know; you always do seem to get on the wrong side of her. Grace will sympathize; she's just been abusing her like a pickpocket," said Miss Marsh, apparently believing herself to be speaking the truth.

Miss Jones raised her eyebrows rather protestingly, said nothing. She supposed that in an atmosphere of adulation such as that which appeared to her to surround Miss Vivian, even such negative criticism as was implied in an absence of comment might be regarded seriously enough.

"But even if one doesn't like her awfully much, she has a sort of fascination, don't you think?" said Miss Plumtree eagerly. "I always feel like a a sort of bird with a sort of snake, you know."

The modification which she wished to put into this trenchant comparison was successfully conveyed by the qualifying "sort of," an adverb distinctly in favour at the Hostel.

"I know what you mean exactly, dear," Miss Marsh assured her. "And of course she does work one fearfully hard. I sometimes think I shall have to leave."

"She works every bit as hard as we do harder. I suppose you'll admit that, Gracie?"

"Oh yes."

"Don't go on like that," protested Miss Marsh, presumably with reference to some indefinable quality detected by her in these two simple monosyllables.

"I only meant," said Grace Jones diffidently, "that it might really be better if she didn't do quite so much. If she could have her luncheon regularly, for instance."

"My dear, she simply hasn't the time." "She could make it."

"The work comes before everything with Miss Vivian. I mean, really it does," said Miss Plumtree solemnly.

Miss Jones finished off the end of a thick plait of dark hair with a neat blue bow, and said nothing.

"I suppose even you'll admit that, Gracie?"

Grace gave a sudden little laugh, and said in the midst of

it: "Really, I'm not sure."

"My dear girl, what on earth do you mean?"

"I think I mean that I don't feel certain Miss Vivian would work quite so hard or keep such very strenuous hours if she lived on a desert island, for instance."

The other two exchanged glances.

"Dotty, isn't she?"

"Mad as a hatter, I should imagine."

"Perhaps you'll explain what sort of war-work people do on desert islands?"

"That isn't what I mean, quite," Gracie explained. "My idea is that perhaps Miss Vivian does partly work so very hard because there are so many people looking on. If she was on a desert isle she might find time for luncheon."

"My dear girl, you're ab-solutely raving, in my opinion," said Miss Plumtree with simple directness. "There! That's my kettle."

She dashed out of the room, as a hissing sound betrayed that her kettle had overboiled on to the gas-ring, as it invariably did.

After the rescue had been effected she looked in again and said:

"I suppose you wouldn't let me come in for some of your tea to-morrow morning, would you, dear? Ours is absolutely finished, and that ass Henderson forgot to get any more."

"Rather," said Miss Marsh cordially. "This extraordinary girl doesn't take any, so you can have the second cup."

"Thanks most awfully. I can do without most things, but I can't do without my tea. Good-night, girls."

It was an accepted fact all through the Hostel that, although one could do without most things, one could not do without one's tea.

This requirement was of an elastic nature, and might extend from early morning to a late return from meeting a troop-train at night. Grace every morning refused the urgent offer of her room-mate to "make her a cup of nice hot tea," and watched, with a sort of interested surprise, while Miss Marsh got out of bed a quarter of an hour earlier than was necessary in order to fill and boil a small kettle and make herself three and sometimes four successive cups of very strong tea. She was always willing to share this refreshment with anyone, but every room in the Hostel had its own appliances for tea-making, and made daily and ample use of them.

Although Miss Jones did not drink tea, she often washed up the cup and saucer and the little teapot. Miss Marsh suffered from a chronic inability to arrive at the office punctually, although breakfast was at nine o'clock, and she had only to walk across the road. But she frequently said, in a very agitated way, as she rose from the breakfast-table:

"Excuse me. I simply must go and do my washing. It's Monday, and I've left it to the last moment."

This meant that the counting and despatching of Miss Marsh's weekly bundle for the laundry would occupy all her energies until the desperate moment when she would look at her wrist-watch, exclaim in a mechanical sort of way, "Oh, damn! I shall never do it!" and dash out of the house and across Pollard Street as the clock struck ten.

"I'll wash the tea-things for you."

"Oh no, dear! Why should you? I can quite well do them to-night."

But Grace knew that when her room-mate came in tired at seven o'clock that evening she might very likely want "a good hot cup of tea "then and there, and she accordingly took the little heap of crockery into the bathroom. Standing over the tiny basin jutting out of the wall, Miss Jones, with her sleeves carefully rolled up over a very solid pair of forearms. washed and dried each piece with orderly deliberation, and replaced them in the corner of Miss Marsh's cupboard.

"I'm afraid you'll be late. Can't I help you?"

"Thanks, dear, but I dare say I can just scramble through. What about your washing?"

"Oh, I did all that on Saturday night," said Grace, indicating a respectable brown-paper parcel tied up with string and with an orderly list pinned on to the outside.

"You're a marvel!" sighed Miss Marsh. "Don't wait, Gracie."

Miss Jones went downstairs and out into Pollard Street. She moved rather well, and had never been known to swing her arms as she walked. Her face was very serious. She often thought how kind it was of the others not to call her a prig, since her methodical habits and innate neatness appeared to be in such startling contrast to the standards prevailing at the Hostel. She had never been sent to school, or seen much of other girls, and the universal liking shown to her by her fellow-workers gave her almost daily a fresh sense of pleased surprise.

Arrived at the office, she signed her name at the door, and proceeded upstairs to Miss Vivian's room.

Miss Vivian came in, chilled from her motor drive and with that rather pinky tinge on her aquiline nose which generally forecasted a troubled morning. The observant Miss Jones regarded this law very matterof-factly as an example of cause and effect. She felt sure that Miss Vivian only felt at her best when conscious of looking her best, and hoped very much that the winter would not be a very cold one. It was obvious that Miss Vivian suffered from defective circulation, which her sedentary existence had not improved.

But it was Miss Delmege who solicitously suggested fetching a foot-warmer from the Supplies Department, and who placed it tenderly at the disposal of Miss Vivian.

After that the atmosphere lightened, and it was with comparative equanimity that Miss Vivian received the announcement that a lady had called and desired to see her.

"Please send up her name and her business on a slip of paper, and you can tell the clerk in the outer hall that I won't have those slipshod messages sent up," was the reception of the emissary.

"Yes, Miss Vivian."

Miss Delmege gathered up a sheaf of papers from her table and glided from the room. Grace, whose powers of mental detachment permitted her to concentrate on whatever she was doing without regard to her surroundings, went on with her work.

The interviews conducted by Miss Vivian seldom interested her in the least.

That this one was, however, destined to become an exception, struck her forcibly when the sudden sound of a piercing feminine voice on the stairs came rapidly nearer.

"... as for my name on a slip of paper, I never heard such nonsensical red-tape in my life. Why, Char's mother and I were girls together!"

Although everyone in the office was aware that Miss Vivian's baptismal name was Charmian, and that this was invariably shortened by her acquaintances to Char, it came as a shock even to the imperturbable Miss Jones to hear this more or less sacred monosyllable ringing up the stairs to Miss Vivian's very table.

"Who on earth "began Char indignantly, when the door flew open before her caller, who exclaimed shrilly and affectionately on the threshold:

"My dear child, you can't possibly know who I am, but my name is Willoughby, and when I was Lesbia Carroll your mother and I were girls together. I had to come in and take a peep at you!"

There was a sort of rustling pounce, and Grace became aware that the outraged Miss Vivian bad been audibly and overpoweringly kissed in the presence of a giggling Scout and of her own junior secretary.

CHAPTER V

MRS. WILLOUGHBY, in Miss Vivian's private office, reversed all rules of official precedent.

"Sit down again, my dear child sit down!" she cried cordially, at the same time establishing herself close to the table. "I hear you're doing wonderful work for all these dear people--Belgians and the dear Tommies and everyone--and I felt I simply had to come in and hear all about it. Also, I want to propound a tiny little scheme of my own which I think will appeal to you. Or have you heard about it already from that precious boy John, with whom, I may tell you, I'm simply madly in love? I'm always threatening to elope with him!"

"I'm afraid," said Char, disregarding her visitor's pleasantry, "that I can really hardly undertake anything more. We are very much understaffed as it is, and the War Office is always--"

"I can turn the whole War Office round my little finger, my dear," declared Mrs. Willoughby. "There's the dearest lad there, a sort of under-secretary, who's absolutely devoted to me, and tells me all sorts of official tit-bits before anyone else hears a word about them. I can get anything I want through him, so you needn't worry about the War Office. In fact, to tell you rather a shocking little secret, I can get what I want out of most of these big official places just a little tiny manipulation of the wires, you know. [Cherchez la femme though I oughtn't to say such things to a girl like you, ought I?"]

Char looked at Mrs. Willoughby's large, heavily powdered face, at her enormous top-heavy hat and over-ample figure, and said nothing.

But no silence, however subtly charged with uncomplimentary meanings, could stem Mrs. Willoughby's piercing eloquence.

"This is what I want to do, and I'm told at the camp here that it would be simply invaluable. I want to get up a Canteen for the troops here, and for all those dear tilings on leave."

"There are several Y.M.C.A. Huts already."

"My dear! I know it. But I want to do this all on my little own, and have quite different rules and regulations. My Lewis, who's been in the Army for over fifteen years, poor angel, tells me that they all from the Colonel downwards think it would be the greatest boon on earth, to have a lady at the head of things, you know."

"My time is too much taken up; it would be quite out of the question," said Char simply.

"Darling child! Do you suppose I meant you a ridiculously young thing like you? Of course, it would have to be a married woman, with a certain regimental position, so to speak. And my Lewis is second in command, as you know, so that naturally his wife... You see, the Colonel's wife is an absolute dear, but an invalid more or less, and no more savoir faire than a kitten. A perfect little provincial, between ourselves. Whereas, of course, I know this sort of job inside out and upside down literally, my dear. The hours I've toiled in town!"

"But I'm afraid in that case you oughtn't to leave--"

"I must! I'm compelled to! It's too cruel, but the doctor simply won't answer for the consequences if I go back to London in my present state. But work I must. One would go quite, quite mad if one wasn't working thinking about it all, you know."

"Major Willoughby is--er--in England, isn't he?"

"Thank God, yes!" exclaimed Lesbia, with a fervour that would have startled her husband considerably. "My heart bleeds for these poor wives and mothers. I simply thank God upon my knees that I have no son! When one thinks of it all! England's life-blood--"

Char did not share her mother's objection to eloquence expended upon the subject of the war, but she cut crisply enough into this exaltee outpouring.

"One is extremely thankful to do what little one can," she said, half-unconsciously throwing an appraising glance at the files and papers that were littered in profusion all over the table.

"Indeed one is!" cried Lesbia, just as fervently as before. "Work is the only thing. My dear, this war is killing me simply killing me!"

Miss Vivian was not apparently prompted to any expression of regret at the announcement.

"As I said to Lewis the other day, I must work or go quite mad. And now this Canteen scheme seems to be calling out to me, and go I must. We've got a building that big hall just at the bottom of the street here and I'm insisting upon having a regular opening day so much better to start these things with a nourish, you know and the regimental band, and hoisting the Union Jack, and everything. And what I want you to do is this."

Lesbia paused at last to take breath, and Char immediately said:

"I'm afraid I'm so fearfully busy to-day that I haven't one moment, but if you'd like my secretary to--"

"Not your secretary, but your entire staff, and your attractive self. I want you all down there to help!"

"Quite impossible," said Char. "I wonder, Mrs.

Willoughby, if you have any idea of the scale on which this Depot is run?"

"Every idea," declared Lesbia recklessly. "I'm told everywhere that all the girls in Questerham are helping you, and that's exactly why I've come. I want girls to make my Canteen attractive all the prettiest ones you have."

"I'm afraid my staff was not selected with a view to--er--personal attractions," said Miss Vivian, in a voice which would have created havoc amongst her staff in its ironical chilliness.]

"Nonsense, my dear Char! I met the sweetest thing on the stairs--a, perfect gem of a creature with Titian-coloured hair. Not in that hideous uniform, either."

Miss Vivian could not but recognize the description of her typist.

"I don't quite understand," she said. "Do you want helpers on your opening day, or regularly?"

"Quite regularly from five to eleven or thereabouts every evening. I shall be there myself, of course, to supervise the whole thing, and I've got half a dozen dear things to help me: but what I want is girls, who'll run about and play barmaid and wash up, you know."

"Couldn't my mother spare Miss Bruce sometimes?"

"Is Miss Bruce a young and lively girl?" inquired Mrs. Willoughby, not without reason. "Besides, I need dozens of them."

"Yes, I see," said Char languidly. She was tired of Mrs. Willoughby, and it was with positive relief that she heard her telephone-bell ring sharply.

There was a certain satisfaction in leaning back in her chair and calling "Miss--er--'Jones!"

Miss Jones moved quietly to answer the insistent bell.

"I'm afraid this rather breaks into our consultation," said Char, deftly making her opportunity, "but may I write to you and let you know what I can manage?"

"I shall pop in again and commandeer all these delightful young creatures of yours. I'm marvellous at recruiting, my dear; every man I met out of khaki I always attacked in the early days. White feathers, you know, and everything of that sort. I had no mercy on them. One lad I absolutely dragged by main force to the recruiting office, though he said he couldn't leave his wife and babies. But, as I told him, I'd had to let my Lewis go he was on the East Coast then and was proud to do my bit for England. I dare say the wretch got out of it afterwards, because they wouldn't let me come in with him while he was actually being sworn, or whatever it is. Such redtape!"

Char paid small attention to these reminiscences of Lesbia's past activities.

"What is it, Miss Jones?" "TheD.G.V.O. is here."

"The Director-General of Voluntary Organizations," said Miss Vivian, carelessly tossing off the imposing syllables, with the corner of her eye, as it were, fixed upon Mrs. Willoughby. "In that case, I'm afraid I must ask you to forgive me."

"I must fly," said Lesbia in a sudden shriek, ignoring her dismissal with great skill. "Some of those boys from the camp are lunching with me, and they'll never forgive me if I'm late."

"Ask the Director-General of Voluntary Organizations to come up, Miss Jones," drawled Char. "And show Mrs. Willoughby the way downstairs."

"Good-bye, you sweet thing!" cried Lesbia gaily, agitating a tightly gloved white-kid hand. "I shall pop in again in a day or two, and you must let me help you. I adore Belgians positively adore them, and can do anything I like with them."

Mrs. Willoughby's enthusiasm was still audible during her rustling progress down the stairs.

Char paid full attention to her interview with the opportunely arrived Director-General of Voluntary Organizations, because she wished him to think her a most official and business-like woman, entirely capable of accomplishing all that she had undertaken; but when the dignitary had departed she gave serious consideration to the scheme so lightly propounded by Mrs. Willoughby.

The visit of this enthusiast had ruffled her more than she would have owned to herself, and it was almost instinctively that she strove to readjust the disturbed balance of her own sense of competence and self-devotion by waving aside all Miss Delmege's proposals of lunch.

"I'm afraid I haven't got time for anything of that sort to-day. I've had a most interrupted morning. No, Miss Delmege, thank you, not even a bun. You'd better go to your own lunch now."

"I'm not in any hurry, Miss Vivian."

"It's one o'clock," Miss Vivian pointed out, quite aware that her secretary would now seek her cold mutton and milk-pudding with an absolute sense of guilt, as of one indulging in a Sybaritic orgy while her chief held aloof in austere abstention.

Miss Delmege, in fact, looked very unhappy, and said in low tones to her colleague at the other end of the room: "Miss Jones, if you care to go to lunch first, I'll take my time off between two and half-past instead, at the second table."

The second table for lunch was never a popular institution, the mutton and the milk-pudding having lost what charms they ever possessed, and, moreover, the time allowed being abridged by almost half an hour. Miss Delmege, in virtue of her seniority and of her own excessive sense of superiority, always arranged that Grace should take the second luncheonhour, and Miss Jones looked surprised.

"Do you mind, because really I don't care when I go?"

"I'd rather you went first," repeated Miss Delmege unhappily.

"Thank you very much. I'm very hungry, and if you really don't mind, I shall be delighted to go now," said Grace cheerfully, in an undertone that nevertheless penetrated to Miss Vivian's annoyed perceptions.

It was evident that Miss Jones had no qualms as to enjoying a substantial lunch, however long her overworked employer might elect to fast, and the conviction was perhaps responsible for the sharpness with which Char exclaimed: "For Heaven's sake don't chatter in the corner like that! You're driving me perfectly mad--a day when one simply doesn't know which way to turn."

Miss Delmege sank into her chair, looking more overwhelmed than ever, and Grace said gently, "I'm sorry, Miss Vivian," disregarding or not understanding Miss Delmege's signal that apologies were out of place in Miss Vivian's office.

Char drew pen and ink towards her, purely pour la forme, and began to make mechanical designs on the blotting-paper, while her mind turned over and over the question of Mrs. Willoughby's proposed canteen.

Char thought that her staff's time was fully employed already, as indeed it was, and had no wish to arouse any possible accusation of overworking. At the same time, she had hitherto succeeded in taking over the management of almost every war organization in Questerham and the district, and was by no means minded to allow a new Canteen, on a large scale, to spring into life under no better auspices than those of Mrs. Willoughby.

If she allowed her staff to go down to the Canteen in instalments, Char decided it would have to be definitely understood that the organization of the Canteen was entirely in the hands of the Midland Supply Depot. She surmised shrewdly that such details of practical requirements as a boiler, tea-urns, kitchen utensils, and the like, had not yet crossed the sanguine line of vision of Mrs. Willoughby. It would be easy enough for Char to assume command when she alone could supply all such needs at a minimum of expenditure and trouble. The staff, she decided, should be sent down in shifts of five or six at a time, five nights a week.

Then, Char reflected considerately, no one could have more than one night in the week, whereas she herself would always put in an appearance, even if only for a few minutes. It would encourage her staff, and would also show Mrs. Willoughby quite plainly the sort of position held by the Director of the Midland Supply Depot.

That afternoon she sent for Miss Collins and dictated a short letter to Mrs. Willoughby, in which she declared, in the third person singular, that the Director of the Midland Supply Depot had considered the proposed scheme for the opening of a Canteen in Pollard Street, and was prepared to help with the practical management of it. She would also supply six voluntary workers between the hours of 7 and 11 p.m. for every night in the week, Saturday except ed. As she took down these official statements, Miss Collins's light eyebrows mounted almost into the roots of her red hair with surprise and disapproval.

Char, being observant, saw these symptoms of astonishment, as she was meant to do, but few thoughts were further from her mind than that of consulting the views of her stenographer on any subject. She even took a certain amount of satisfaction in dictating a rather imperiously worded document, which informed each department in the office that those workers who lived in Questerham would be required to report for duty one night a week for emergency work (7 to 11 p.m.) at the new Canteen which would shortly be opened in Pollard Street under the direction of Miss Vivian and Mrs. Willoughby. Followed a list of names, with a corresponding day of the week attached to each group of six.

"Cut a stencil and roll off six copies for each department and two or three extra ones for filing," commanded Miss Vivian. "You can add at the end: '(Signed) Director of the Midland Supply Depot.'"

"Yes, Miss Vivian."

Miss Collins went away with her eyebrows still erect.

The new field of enterprise was loudly discussed by the staff, as they took the usual half-hour's break in the afternoon at tea-time.

"Isn't Miss Vivian wonderful?" said Tony excitedly. "She'd take on anything, I do believe."

"And make a success of it, too!" "Yes, rather."

Hardly anyone grumbled at the extra four hours of hard work coming at the end of the day, and there was a general feeling of disapproval when Mrs. Bullivant at the Hostel said timidly: "If you're to be down there at seven, it'll be rather difficult to arrange about supper. Cook won't like having to get a meal ready for half-past six, and, besides, you'll be so hungry by eleven o'clock."

"I'm afraid we can't think of that, Mrs. Bullivant," observed Miss Delmege severely. "Not when we remember that Miss Vivian practically never gets her supper till long after ten every night, and she doesn't get much lunch, either. In fact, sometimes she simply won't touch anything at all in the middle of the day."

And Mrs. Bullivant looked very much rebuked, and said that she must see what she could do. "Anyhow, it won't be just yet awhile," she exclaimed with Irish optimism.

"Things move very quickly with Miss Vivian."

"I think they mean the Canteen to open some time in December," said Grace. "That's not so very far off."

"Time does fly," sighed Miss Plumtree, wishing that the Monthly Averages were divided from one another by a longer space of time.

"Never mind, Sunday is all the nearer."

Sunday was the day most looked forward to by the whole Hostel, although an element of uncertainty was added to the enjoyment of it by the knowledge that the arrival of a troop-train might bring orders to any or every member of the staff to report for duty at the station at half an hour's notice.

One or two of the girls were able to go out of Questerham home, or to their friends, for the weekend, but the majority remained in the Hostel. Mrs. Bullivant tried to make the day "bright and homey" at the cost of pathetic exertions to herself, for Sunday was her hardest day of work.

A certain laissez-aller marked the day from its earliest beginnings.

Almost everyone came down to breakfast in bedroom slippers, even though fully dressed.

"A girl here before you came, Gracie," Miss Marsh told her room-mate, "used to come down in a kimono and sort of boudoir-cap arrangement. But I must say nobody liked it just like a greasy foreigner, she was. All the sleeves loose, you know, so that you could see right up her arms. Myself. I don't call that awfully nice not at the breakfast-table."

"It would be very cold to do that now," said Grace x shivering. She disliked the cold very much, and the Hostel was not warmed.

"Yes, wouldn't it? It's a comfort to get into one's own clothes again and out of uniform, isn't it, dear? That's what I like about Sundays dainty clothes again," said Miss Marsh, fiercely pulling a comb backwards through her hair so as to make it look fluffy.

"I like you in uniform, though," said Miss Jones, who had received several shocks on first beholding the Sunday garbs known to the Hostel as "plain clothes."

"Very sweet of you to say that, dear. You always look nice yourself, only your plain clothes are too like your uniform just a white blouse and dark skirt you wear, isn't it?"

"I'm afraid it's all I've got," said Grace apologetically; and Miss Marsh at once thought that perhaps poor little Gracie couldn't afford many things, and said warmly:

"But white blouses are awfully nice, dear, and crepe de Chine always looks so good."

Then she thrust her stockinged feet into her red slippers and shuffled across the room. "How lucky you are! you never have to back-comb your hair, do you?"

"I never do back-comb it, because it's so bad for it," said Grace seriously. She had a book open on the dressing-table in front of her, but was characteristically quite as much interested in Miss Marsh's conversation as in her own reading.

"' Daniel Deronda '? "said Miss Marsh, looking over her. "Never heard of him. How fond you are of reading, Gracie! I love it myself, but I don't ever have time for it here."

The plea, being one which never fails to rouse the scorn of every book-lover, Grace remained silent. Her solitary extravagance was the maximum subscription to the Questerham library.

"There's the bell," said Miss Marsh; "I must come up and make my bed afterwards. Thank goodness, there's no hurry to-day."

They went down together, Miss Marsh's heelless slippers clapping behind her on every step.

In the sitting-room after breakfast the girls clustered round the tiny smoking

fire. "It's going to rain all day. How beastly!" said Tony. "Who's going to

church?"

"I shall probably go to evensong," remarked Miss Delmege, upon which several people at once decided that they would risk the weather and go to the eleven o'clock service.

There was only one church in Questerham which the Hostel thought it fashionable to attend.

The day was spent in more or less desultory lounging over the fire. Miss Delmege wrote a number of letters and Tony darned stockings. Grace Jones read "Daniel Deronda "to herself.

Lunch was protracted, and Mrs. Bullivant, to mark the day, exerted herself and made some rather smoked coffee, which she brought to the sitting-room triumphantly.

"Isn't there going to be any music this afternoon?" she inquired.

Everyone declared that music was the very thing for such an afternoon, but no one appeared very willing to provide it.

"Do sing, somebody," implored Miss Henderson. "Plumtree?"

Miss Pluintree had a beautiful deep voice, utterly untrained and consequently unspoilt. She stood up willingly enough and sang all the songs that she was asked for. The taste of the Hostel was definite in songs. "A Perfect Day "and "The Rosary "were listened to in the absolute silence of appreciation, and then someone asked for a selection from the latest musical comedy.

Grace played Miss Plumtree's accompaniments, and loved listening to her soft, deep tones. She tried to make her sing "Three Fishers," but Miss Plumtree said no: it was too sad for a Sunday afternoon, and it was someone else's turn.

Musical talent in the Hostel was limited, and the only other owner of a voice was Miss Delmege, the possessor of a high, thin soprano, which, she often explained, had been the subject of much attention on the part of "a really first-rate man in Clifton."

It might remain open to question whether the energies of the really first-rate man could not have been turned into channels more advantageous than that of developing Miss Delmege's attenuated thread of voice. Whatever the original organ might have been, it was now educated into a refined squeak, overweighted with affectations which to Miss Delmege represented the art of production. She sang various improvident love-songs in which Love high F, attained to by a species of upwards slide on E and E sharp was all, When eventide should fall slight tremolo and a giving out of breath rather before the accompanist had struck the final cord.

"You should take the finale, rather more a tempo, dear," said the singer, in a professional way which finally vindicated the first-rateness of the man at Clifton.

Everyone thanked Miss Delmege very much, and said that was a sweetly pretty song; and then Grace Jones played the piano while Tony and Miss Henderson made toast for tea and put the largest and least burnt pieces aside for her. Tea, with the aid of conversation and the making of innumerable pieces of toast over the least smoky parts of the fire, could almost be prolonged till supper-time.

"I must say, I do enjoy doing nothing," said Miss

Henderson, voicing the general sentiment at the end of the day of rest.

"Poor Mrs. Potter is on the telephone. How cold she'll be, sitting there all the evening!"

"I hope she saw to Miss Vivian's fire," said Miss Delmege solicitously. "I particularly reminded her to build up a good fire in Miss Vivian's room. She does feel the cold so."

"Perhaps she didn't come this afternoon," said Grace. "There was nothing left over in her basket last night."

"Oh, she always comes," Miss Delmege said quickly and rather resentfully. "I've never known her miss a Sunday yet. Besides, I know she was there to-day. I saw the light in her window as I came back from church."

"I do believe," said Tony in a stage whisper, "that Delmege goes to evening church on purpose to look up at the light in Miss Vivian's window as she comes back."

But the joke was received silently, as being in but indifferent taste, and verging on irreverence almost equally as regarded church and the Director of the Midland Supply Depot.

CHAPTER VI

THE new Canteen in Pollard Street was opened before Christmas.

Lesbia Willoughby, in an immense overall of light blue-and-white check, stood behind a long buffet and demanded stridently whether she wasn't too exactly like a barmaid for words, and Char's consignment of helpers worked for the most part briskly and efficiently, only the unfortunate Miss Plumtree upsetting a mug of scalding tea over herself at the precise moment when Miss Vivian, trim and workmanlike in her dark uniform, entered the big hall and stood watching the scene with her arrogant, observant gaze. She did not ask Miss Plumtree whether her hand was scalded, but neither did she rebuke her very evident clumsiness.
She moved slowly and imperially through the thick tobacco-laden atmosphere, speaking to several of the men, and silently observing the demeanour of her staff.

The following week she issued an office circular in which the precise direction which the activity of each worker was to take was inexorably laid down.

Miss Plumtree was banished a perpetuite to the pantry, to wash up at full speed over a sink. She worked at the Canteen on Mondays, always the busiest evening. In the same shift were Mrs. Potter and Miss Henderson, to each of whom was appointed the care of an urn, Grace Jones, Miss Delmege, and Miss Marsh. Miss Delmege stood behind the buffet, which position, she said, seemed very strange to her from being so like a counter in a shop, and the other two took orders at the various small tables in the hall, and hurried to and fro with laden trays.

No one would have dreamed of disputing thia arbitrary disposal of energies, but it struck Grace as extremely unfortunate that Miss Marsh and Miss Delmege should select their first Monday together at the Canteen for the form of unpleasantness known as "words." Miss Jones became the medium by which alone either would address the other.

"I'm sorry, dear, but Delmege has really got on my nerves lately, and you can tell her I said so if you like. When it comes to suggesting that I don't do sufficient work, there's simply nothing more to be said. You heard her the other night, saying some people were so lucky they could always get off early when they liked. Just because I'd cleared up by six o'clock, for once in a way!"

"But she didn't say she meant you," urged Miss Jones, who was far too sympathetic not to take any grievance confided to her at the teller's own valuation, and foresaw besides an extremely awkward evening at the Canteen.

"Some people aren't straightforward enough to say what they mean right out, but that doesn't prevent others from seeing the point of the sort of remarks they pass," declared Miss Marsh cryptically.

"If she told you she really hadn't meant anything personal, wouldn't it be all right?"

But Grace did not make the suggestion very hopefully, and her room-mate merely repeated gloomily that Delmege had really got on her nerves lately, and though she did not think herself one to bear malice, yet there were limits to all things.

Grace's success with Miss Delmege on their way down the street at seven o'clock that evening, was even less apparent.

"It's all very well, dear, but I've always been most sensitive. I can't help it. I know it's very silly, but there it is. As a tiny tot, mother always used to say of me, ' That child Vera is so sensitive, she can't bear a sharp word.' I know it's very silly to be thin-skinned, and causes one a great deal of suffering as one goes through life, but it's the way I'm made. I always was so."

This complacent monologue lasted almost to the bottom of Pollard Street, when Grace interrupted desperately: "Do make it up with her before we start this job. It's so much nicer to be all cheerful together when we've got a hard evening in front of us."

"I'm quite willing to be friendly, when Miss Marsh speaks to me first. At the present moment, dear, as you know, she's behaving very strangely indeed, and doesn't speak to me at all. Of course, I don't mind either way in fact, it only amuses me but I don't mind telling you, Gracie, that I think her whole way of carrying on is most strange altogether."

Grace felt a desperate certainty that affairs were indeed past remedy when Miss Delmege had to resort so freely to her favourite adjective "strange "to describe the manners and conduct of Miss Marsh.

She entered the hall rather dejectedly. It was very tiring to hurry about with heavy trays at the end of a long day's work, and the atmosphere seemed thicker than ever to-night and the noise greater. Grace hung up her coat and hat, and hastily made room on the already overcrowded peg for Miss Marsh's belongings , as she heard Miss Delmege say gently "Excuse me," and deliberately appropriate to her own use the peg selected by her neighbour.

"Did you see that?" demanded Miss Marsh excitedly. "Isn't that Delmege all over? After this, Gracie, I shall simply not speak to her till she apologizes. Simply ignore her. Believe me, dear, it's the only way. I shall behave as though Delmege didn't exist."

This threat was hardly carried out to the letter. No one could have failed to see a poignant consciousness of Miss Delmege's existence in the elaborate blindness and deafness which assailed Miss Marsh when within her neighbourhood.

Miss Delmege adopted a still more trying policy, and addressed acid remarks in a small, penetrating voice to her surroundings.

"I must say the state of some trays is like nothing on earth!" she said to Grace, when Miss Marsh had spilt a cup of cocoa over her tray-cloth and brought it back to the counter for a fresh supply. "How the poor men stand it! I must say I do like things to be dainty myself. Give me a meal daintily served and I don't care what it is! All depends what one's been used to, I suppose."

"I should be awfully obliged, Gracie, if you could get hold of a clean tray-cloth for me," said Miss Marsh furiously. "There doesn't seem to be anybody notwhat-I-call-capa&Ze here."

Grace looked appealingly at Miss Delmege, but the pince-nez were directed towards the roof, and Miss Delmege's elegantly curved fingers were engaged in swiftly unloading a tray of clean plates.

"A clean cloth for this tray, please," said Gracie rapidly. "There's been a spill."

Miss Delmege, appearing quite capable of seeing through the back of her head, still kept her back turned to the infuriated Miss Marsh, and said coldly: "How very messy, dear! But I'm sure you're not responsible for that. Some people are so strange; their fingers seem to be all thumbs."

"I can't stand here all night, Gracie!" exclaimed Miss Marsh, recklessly tipping all the dirty crockery from the tray on to the counter. "You wouldn't let me have your cloth, I suppose, would you, dear?" At the same time she skilfully disproved her own supposition by rapidly possessing herself of Grace's clean tray-cloth.

"Of all the coolness! Here, dear; I'll give you another one. What's your

order?" "Cup of tea, sausage and mashed, roll of bread."

Miss Delmege gave the short mirthless snigger with which she always acclaimed such orders, so as to make it clear that she did not take anything so vulgar as a sausage and mashed potatoes seriously, and further exclaimed, "They are quaint, aren't they?" as she telephoned through to the kitchen.

"Miss Jones," said Char's cool voice behind her, "I've been watching you for the last five minutes. Kindly ask for what you want a little more quickly. You seem to forget that the man is waiting for his supper."

She waited while the order was being rapidly executed from the kitchen, watching the two girls. Miss Delmege coloured faintly, and moved about restlessly under the scrutiny of which she was obviously conscious, but Grace's smal], pale face had not altered, and she stood by the counter waiting for her tray, gazing quite interestedly at a small group of new arrivals.

Mrs. Willoughby stood at the door, eagerly ushering in visitors whom she had obviously invited to survey the scene of her activities.

"This is my little job plenty of the dear fellows here to-night, you see. Aren't they dears, and don't they look too delightfully at home for words? I must fly back to my barmaid's job now; you'll see me behind the counter in another minute, Joanna. I find I have the most wonderful talent for chaff the men love it so, you know. Do come in, John you're my chief asset here to-night; the men will simply love your Military Cross. I want you to come round and tell one or two of my special pets exactly how you won it."

Only the secret pressure of his Cousin Joanna's hand on his arm and the mirthful gleam in her blue eyes prevented Captain Trevellyan, with his Military Cross, from taking an instant departure.

Lady Vivian raised her lorgnette. "Where's Char?"

"Much too busy on her high official horse even to see me," cried Lesbia with a sort of jovial spite. "Now, Joanna, I insist upon your getting into an overall at once, and helping me. I'D commandeer one."

Grace Jones went past them with her laden tray, and Mrs. Willoughby grasped her arm.

"I want you to find me an overall for this lady before you stir another step," she shrieked emphatically.

"Nonsense, Lesbia!" interposed Lady Vivian brusquely. "I don't suppose there is such a thing to spare, and, besides, I don't want one."

She wore the plainest of dark coats and skirts and a soft silk shirt. Grace looked at her with composed admiration and a sense of gratitude. She did not wish to be further delayed with the heavy tray on her hands.

"There's my dear Lance-Corporal!" exclaimed Lesbia, and hurled herself in the direction of a burly form which appeared strongly impelled to seek cover behind the piano as she advanced.

Captain Trevellyan gently took the tray from Miss Jones. "Where shall I take it?"

"Thank you very much," said Grace thankfully, dropping her aching arms. "That table over there, right at the end, if you will. It's very kind of you."

She turned to Lady Vivian rather apologetically. "I'm afraid I ought not to have let him do that, but we're rather behindhand to-night. Are you come to help?"

She supposed that this tall, curiously attractive new-comer was the wife of one of the officers from the camp.

"Yes, if you'U tell me what to do."

"If you'd carry trays? One of our workers is is impeded to-night," said Grace, conscientiously selecting a euphemism for the peculiar handicap under which Miss Marsh was labouring.

For the next two hours Lady Vivian worked vigorously, in spite of a protest from John, who took the view of feminine weakness peculiar to unusually strong men.

"These trays are too heavy for any woman to carry! It's monstrous! I shall tell Char so."

"By all means tell her. I certainly think it's very bad for these girls, and at the end of a long day's work, too. But as for me, you know I'm as strong ae a horse, Johnnie, and I enjoy the exercise. It warms me!"

Her face was glowing and her step elastic. John realized, not for the first time, that Sir Piers's slow, rambling walks round the grounds and still slower evening games of billiards formed the major part of his Cousin Joanna's physical activities. He stood watching her thoughtfully.

Char stopped in his immediate vicinity, and gave a couple of orders in her slow, despotic drawl. She rather wanted Johnnie to see how promptly and unquestioningly they were received.

Johnnie, however, appeared to have his thoughts elsewhere, and Char rather vexedly followed his gaze.

"How I wish my mother wouldn't do this sort of thing!" she said under her breath. "It's most tiring for her, and besides--"

"Besides?" inquired Trevellyan, always courteous, but never of the quickest at catching an inflection.

"I'm afraid I think it infra dig. Darting about with all these girls, when she's capable of such very different sort of work if only she'd do it!" u My dear Char, what on earth do you want her to do?" demanded Trevellyan, to whom it came as a shock that anyone who was privileged to live near Joanna should think her anything but perfect.

"She is an extremely capable woman of business; why shouldn't she take up some big work for the Government? They are crying out for educated women."

"She couldn't possibly leave your father alone at Plessing."

"She could do a certain amount of work at home even without that. The truth is, Johnnie, that neither she nor my father have realized there's a war on at all. They've no sons out there in the trenches, and it hasn't hit them materially; they've not felt it in any single, smallest way. I shouldn't say it to anyone but you, but there are times at Plessing when I could go mad. To hear my father talk on and on about whether some tree on the estate needs cutting or not, just as though on the other side of a little strip of sea--"

She broke off with a shudder that was not altogether histrionic.

"And mother she wouldn't even knit socks, because it interfered with his billiards in the evenings! I don't understand her, Johnnie. She must know what it all means, yet it's all shoved away in the background. Brucey tells me that she's under standing orders not to discuss the news in the papers at breakfast, and mother won't have a single war-book in the house not even a war-novel, if she can help it. It's as though they were deliberately trying to blind themselves. I can't understand it."

Trevellyan did not feel sure that he understood it, either, but, unlike Char, there was in his mind no shadow of criticism for that which he did not understand. The limitation, Trevellyan always felt, was entirely his.

But he was able to look sympathetically also at Char's vexed

bewilderment. "You're not at Plessing very much, nowadays, yourself."

"No. I don't think I could bear it, Johnnie. Of course they say I'm doing too much, but, after all, I'm of an age to decide that for myself, and to my mind there's simply no choice in the matter. Thank Heaven one can work!"

"Your undertaking is a colossal thing, in its way. It's wonderful of you,

Char!" She looked pleased.

"It's running well at present. Of course, I know what a tiny part of the whole it is really, but--" She broke off quickly as Lady Vivian joined them.

"Who is the little dark-haired girl I've been working with, Char? The one at that table...."

"Oh, a Miss--er--Jones," said Char languidly.

"You never told me you had anyone of her sort here. I want to ask her out to Plessing. Couldn't we take her back in the car to-night?"

"My dear mother!" Char opened her eyes in an expression of exaggerated horror. "One of my staff?"

"Well?" queried Lady Vivian coolly, stripping off her borrowed overall.

"Quite out of the question. You don't in the least realize the official footing on which I have to keep those women."

"I should have thought you needn't be any the less official for showing some friendliness to a girl who's come all the way from Wales to help you."

"She's my under-secretary, mother."

"What! sub-scrub to the genteel Miss Delmege? She's got ten times her brains, and is a lady into the bargain."

It infuriated Char that her mother's cool, tacit refusal to acknowledge the infallibility of the Director of the Midland Supply Depot could always make her feel like a little girl again.

She rallied all her most official mannerisms together.

"It's quite impossible for me to differentiate between the various members of the staff, or to make any unofficial advances to any of them."

"Very well, my dear. As, thank Heaven, I'm not a member of your staff, I can remain as unofficial as I please, and have nice little Miss Jones out to see me."

"Mother," said Char in an agony, "it's simply impossible. The girl would never know her place in the office again; and think of all the cackling there'd be at the Questerham Hostel about my asking anyone out to Plessing. Johnnie, do tell her it's out of the question."

Trevellyan looked at Joanna with a laugh in his blue eyes. He realized, as Char would never realize, that her assumption of officialdom always provoked her mother to the utterance of ironical threats which she had never the slightest intention of fulfilling.

She shrugged her shoulders slightly at her daughter's vehemence, and crossed over to where Grace Jones was putting on her coat and hat again.

"Good-night. I hope you're not as tired as you look," she said with a sort of abrupt graciousness.

"Oh no, thank you. It's been an extra busy night. It was so kind of you to help."

"I wish I could come again," said Lady Vivian rather wistfully, "but I don't know that I shall be able to."

Lesbia Willoughby, dashing past them at full speed, found time to fling a piercing rebuke over her shoulder.

"There's always a will where there's a way, Joanna. Look at me!"

Neither of them took advantage of the invitation, and Joanna said irrelevantly: "I should like you to come and see me, if you will, but I know you're at work all day. I must try and find you next time I come into Questerham."

"Thank you very much," said Grace in a pleased voice. "I should like that very much indeed. Goodnight."

"Good-night," repeated Joanna, and went back to where her daughter, with a rather indignant demeanour, was waiting for her.

"Well?" asked Char, rather sullenly.

Lady Vivian, who almost invariably became flippant when her daughter was most in earnest, said provokingly: "Well, my dear, I've made arrangements for all sorts of unofficial rendezvous. You may see Miss Delmege at Plessing yet."

"Miss Delmege is a very good worker," said Char icily. "She's very much in earnest, always ready to stay overtime and finish up anything important."

"I'm sure Miss Jones is good at her job, too," said Trevellyan, supposing himself to be tactful.

"Fairly good. Not extraordinarily quick-witted, though, and much too sure of herself. I can't help thinking it's rather a pity to distinguish her from the others, mother; she's probably only too ready to take airs as it is, if she's of rather a different class."

"Fiddlesticks!" declared Lady Vivian briskly. "Put on your coat, Char, and come along. I can't keep the car waiting any longer. Rather a different class indeed! What has that to do with it? The girl's most attractive an original type, too."

"Of course, if mother has taken one of her sudden violent fancies to this Jones child, I may as well make up my mind to hear nothing else, morning, noon, or night," Char muttered to John Trevellyan, who replied with matter-of-fact common sense that Char wasn't at Plessing for more than an hour or two on any single day, let alone morning, noon, and night.

"Char," said Lady Vivian from the car, "if you don't come now I shall leave you to spend the night at the Questerhain Hostel, where you'll lose all your prestige with the staff, and have to eat and sleep just like an ordinary human being."

The Director of the Midland Supply Depot got into her parent's motor in silence, and with a movement that might have been fairly described as a flounce.

The members of the staff walked up the street towards the Hostel.

"Who was the lady in black who helped with the trays?" asked Grace. "She was so nice."

"My dear, didn't you know? That was Miss Vivian's mother!"

"Oh, was it?" said Grace placidly. "I didn't know that. Miss Vivian isn't very like her, is she?"

"No. Of course, Miss Vivian's far better looking. I'm not saying it because it's her," added Miss Delmege with great distinctness, for the benefit of Miss Marsh and

Mrs. Potter, walking behind, from one of whom a sound of contemptuous mirth had proceeded faintly. "It's simply a fact. Miss Vivian is far better looking than Lady Vivian ever was. Takes after her father Sir Piers Vivian he is, you know."

Miss Delmege had only once been afforded a view of the back of Sir Piers Vivian's white head in church, but she made the assertion with her usual air of genteel omniscience.

At the Hostel Mrs. Bullivant was waiting for them. It was past eleven o'clock, and the fire had gone out soon after eight; but in spite of cold and weariness, Mrs.
Bullivant was unconquerably bright.

"Come along; I'll have some nice hot tea for you in a moment. The kettle is on the gas-ring. I am sorry the fire's out, but it smoked so badly all the evening I thought I'd better leave it alone. Sit down; I'm sure you're all tired."

"Simply dead," exclaimed Miss Marsh. "So are you, aren't you, Plumtree, after all those awful plates and dishes? I must say your washing-up job is the worst of the lot."

"I'm going to bed. I can't keep on my feet another minute, tea or no tea. If I don't drag myself upstairs now I never shall. It's fatal to sit down; one can't get up again."

"That's right," assented Miss Marsh. "I'll bring up your tea when I come,

dear." "Angel, thanks awfully. Good-night, ladies and gentlemen."

Miss Plumtree left the sitting-room with this languidly facetious valediction.

"That girl does look tired. I hope she gets into bed quickly," observed Mrs. Potter, pulling off her hat and exposing a rakishly decoiffe tangle of wispy hair.

"Not she she'll dawdle for ages," prophesied Miss Marsh. "Still, it's something if she gets into her dressing-gown and bedroom slippers, out of her corsets, you know."

Miss Delmege put down her cup of tea.

"Rather a strange subject we seem to be on for meal-time, don't we?" she remarked detachedly to Grace.

"Meal-time?" exclaimed Miss Henderson derisively.

"That's what I said, dear, and I'm in the habit of meaning what I say, as far as I know."

"I really don't know how you can call it meal-time when we're not even at table. Besides, if we were, there's nothing in what Marsh said absolutely nothing at all."

"Oh, of course, some people see harm in anything," burst out Miss Marsh, very red. "The harm is in their own minds, is what I say, otherwise they wouldn't see any,"

"That's right," agreed Miss Henderson, but below her breath.

Miss Delmege turned with dignity to her other neighbour.

"I may be peculiar, but that's how I feel about it. I imagine that you, as a married woman, will agree with me, Mrs. Potter?"

Mrs. Potter did not agree with her at all, but something in the appeal, some subtle hint of the dignity of Mrs. Potter's position amongst so many virgins, caused her to temporize feebly.

"Really, Miss Delmege, you mustn't ask me. I I quite see with you but at the same time 'there wasn't anything in what Miss Marsh said, now, was there? I mean, really. Simply corsets, you know."

Nearly everyone had by this time forgotten exactly what Miss Marsh had said, and only retained a general impression of licentiousness in conversation.

"We're all girls together," exclaimed Miss Marsh furiously.

"Gentlemen in the room would be a very different thing," Miss Henderson supported her.

"I'll take a second cup, Mrs. Bullivant, if you please," said Miss Delmege with dignity.

"There!" exclaimed Miss Henderson

Miss Marsh had suddenly begun to cry.

Mrs. Bullivant hastily poured out more tea, and said uncertainly: "Come, come!"

"There's no call for anyone to cry, that I can see," observed Miss Delmege, still detached, but in a tone of uneasiness.

"The fact is, I'm not myself to-day," sobbed Miss Marsh.

"What is it?" said Gracie sympathetically. She slipped a friendly hand into her room-mate's.

"I had a letter which upset me this morning. A great friend of mine, who's been wounded a boy I know most awfully well."

"Why didn't you tell me, dear?" asked Miss Henderson. "I didn't even know you had a boy out there."

"Oh, not &feawncy only a chum," said Miss Marsh, still sniffing. "Is he bad, dear?"

"A flesh-wound in the arm, and something about trench feet."

"That's a nice slow thing, and they'll send him to England to get well," prophesied Grace. Miss Delmege rose from her seat. "I'm sorry you've been feeling upset," she said to Miss Marsh. "It seems rather strange you didn't say anything sooner, but I'm sorry about it."

"Thank you," Miss Marsh replied with a gulp. "If I've been rather sharp in my manner to-day, I hope you won't think I meant anything. This has rather upset me."

Miss Delmege bowed slightly, and Grace, fearing an anti-climax, begged Miss Marsh to come up to bed.

The final amende was made next morning, when Miss Delmege, in a buff-coloured drapery known as "my fawn peigmvaw," came to the door and asked for admittance.

Grace opened the door, and Miss Delmege said, in a voice even more distinct than usual: "I know Miss Marsh was tired last night, dear, so I've brought her a cup of our early tea."

CHAPTER VII

"MOTHER, are you coming to the Canteen again to-morrow? You remember what a rush it was last Monday, and it'll be just as bad again."

"No, Char, I am not," was the unvarnished reply of Lady Vivian.

Char compressed her lips and sighed. She would have been almost as much disappointed as surprised if her mother had suddenly expressed an intention of appearing regularly at the Canteen, but she knew that Miss Bruce was looking at her with an admiring and compassionate gaze.

Sir Piers, who substituted chess for billiards on Sunday evenings because he thought it due to the servants to show that the Lord's Day was respected at Plessing, looked up uneasily.

"You're not going out again to-morrow, eh, my dear? I missed our game sadly the other night."

"No, it's all right; I'm not going again."

Joanna never raised her voice very much, but Sir Piers always heard what she said. It made Char wonder sometimes, half irritably and half ashamedly, whether he could not have heard other people, had he wanted to. The overstrain from which she herself was quite unconsciously suffering made her nervously impatient of the old man's increasing slowness of perception.

"And where has Char been all this afternoon? I never see you about the house now," Sir Piers said, half maunderingly, half with a sort of bewilderment that was daily increasing in his view of small outward events. "I've been at my work," said Char, raising her voice, partly as a vent to her own feelings. "I go into the office on Sunday afternoons always, and a very good thing I do, too. They were making a fearful muddle of some telegrams yesterday."

"Telegrams? You can't send telegrams on a Sunday, child; they aren't delivered. I don't like you to go to this place on Sundays, either. Joanna, my dear, we mustn't allow her to do that."

Char cast up her eyes in a sort of desperation, and went into the further half of the drawing-room, where Miss Bruce sat, just hearing her mother say gently: "Look, Piers, I shall take your castle."

"Brucey," said Char, "I think they'll drive me mad. I know my work is nothing, really such a tiny, infinitesimal part of a great whole but if I could only get a little sympathy. It does seem so extraordinary, when one has been working all day, giving one's whole self to it all, and then to come back to this sort of atmosphere!"

Miss Bruce was perhaps the only person with whom Char was absolutely unreserved. In younger days Miss Bruce had been her adoring governess, and the old relations still existed between them. Char knew that Miss Bruce had always thought Lady Vivian's management of her only child terribly injudicious, and that in the prolonged antagonism between herself and her mother Miss Bruce's silent loyalty had always ranged itself on Char's side.

"It's very hard on you, my dear," she sighed. "But I have been afraid lately have you noticed, I wonder?"

"What?"

"Sir Piers seems to me to be failing; he is so much deafer, so much more dependent on Lady Vivian."

"He's always that," said Char. "I think it's only the beginning of the winter, Brucey. He always feels the cold weather."

But a very little while later Miss Bruce's view received unexpected corroboration.

Three Sundays later, when the weather had grown colder than ever, and Char was, as usual, spending the afternoon and evening at the Depot, Mrs. Willoughby paid a call at Plessing.

She was followed into the room, with almost equal unwillingness, by her husband and a small, immensely stout Pekinese dog, with bulging eyes and a quick, incessant bark that only Mrs. Willoughby's voice could dominate.

"Darling Joanna!" she shrieked. "Puffles, wicked, wicked boy, be quiet! Isn't this an invasion? But my Lewis did so want I shall smack 'oo if 'oo isn't quiet directly. Do you mind this little brown boy, who goes everywhere with his mammy? I knew you'd love him if you saw him but such a noise! Lewis, tell this naughty Puff his mother can't hear herself speak."

"Down, sir!" said Lewis, in tones which might have quelled a mastiff with hydrophobia.

Puff waddled for refuge to his mistress, who immediately gathered him on to her lap as she sank on to the sofa.

"Did 'oo daddy speak in a big rough voice, and frighten the poor little manikin?" she inquired solicitously. "Isn't he rather twee, Joanna?"

"I've not seen it before," said Joanna, in tones more civil than enthusiastic.

"It!" screamed Lesbia. "She calls 'oo it, my Puffles! as though he wasn't

the
sweetest little brown boy in the whole world. It! You've hurt his little feelings too dreadfully, my dear look at him sulking!"

Puff had composed himself into a sort of dribbling torpor.

"That dog doesn't get enough exercise," said Major Willoughby suddenly, fixing his eyes upon his hostess.

"Surely it he is too small to require a great deal," said Lady Vivian languidly. Lap-dogs bored her very much indeed, and she turned away her eyes after taking one rather disgusted look at the recumbent Puff through her eyeglasses.

"Train up a dog in the way it should go. Now, this little fellah you'd hardly believe it, Lady Vivian, if I were to tell you the difference in him after he's had a good run over the Common."

"Lewis!" cried Lesbia, opening her eyes to an incredible extent, as was her wont whenever she wished to emphasize her words. "I can't have you boring people about Puff. Lewis is a perfect slave to Puffles, and tries to hide it by calling him ' the dog ' and talking about his training."

Lewis looked self-conscious, and immediately said: "Not at all; not at all. But the dog is an intelligent little brute. Now, I'll tell you what happened the other day."

Major Willoughby gave various instances of Puff's discrimination, and Lesbia kissed the top of Puff's somnolent head and exclaimed shrilly at intervals that "it was too, too bad to pay the little treasure so many compliments; it would turn his little fluffy head, it would."

Lady Vivian reflected that she might certainly absolve herself from the charge of contributing to this catastrophe. The language of compliment had seldom been further from her lips; but in any case her visitors left her little of the trouble of sustaining conversation.

It was evident that Puff was a recent acquisition in the Willoughby menage.

"Where's your dear girl?" Lesbia presently inquired fondly of her hostess. "In Questerham, at the Depot."

"Now, Joanna, I'm going to be perfectly candid. You won't mind, I know after all, you and I were girls together. What Char needs, my dear, is flogging." Lady Vivian was conscious of distinct relief at the thought that her secretary did not happen to be within earshot of this startling expression of opinion.

"You are certainly being perfectly candid, Lesbia," she said dryly. "What has poor Char been doing to require flogging, may I ask?"

"You ask me that, Joanna! Lewis, hark at her!"

Lewis, thus appealed to, looked very uncomfortable, and said in a non-committal manner: "H'm, yes, yes. Hi! Puff! good dog, sir!" thus rousing the Pekinese to a fresh outburst of ear-piercing barks.

When this had at length been quelled by the blandishments of Lesbia and the words of command repeatedly given in a martial tone by her husband, Lady Vivian repeated her inquiry, and Mrs. Willoughby replied forcibly: "My dear, nothing but flogging would ever bring her to her senses. The way she's treating you and poor dear Sir Piers He's looking iller and older every day, and tells me himself that he never sees her now; it's too piteous to hear him, dear old thing. It would wring tears from a stone wouldn't it, Lewis?"

"Down, sir, down, I say!" was the reply of Major Willoughby, addressed to the investigating Puff.

"Oh, naughty boy, leave the screen alone. Now, come here to mother, then. What was I telling you, Joanna? Oh, about that girl of yours. War-work is all very well, my dear, but to my mind home-ties are absolutely sacred, and more than ever before in such a time as this, when we may all be swept away by some ghastly
air-raid in a night. It's simply a time when homes should cling together. I always tell my Lewis it's a time when we should cling more than ever before don't I, Lewis?"

Lewis looked at Puff with a compelling eye, but Puff was again quiescent, and gave him no opening.

Lady Vivian said, very briskly indeed: "Char is not at all a clinging person, Lesbia, and neither am I. We can each stand very comfortably on our own feet, and I'm proud of the work she's doing in Questerham. Now, do let me give you some tea."

"Joanna, I know perfectly well you're snubbing me and telling me to mind my own business, but Lewis can tell you that I'm perfectly impervious. I always say exactly what I want to say, and if you won't listen to me, I shall talk to your good man. I can hear him coming."

The entrance of Sir Piers Vivian was the signal for a frantic uproar from Puff, who hurled a shrill defiance at him from the hearth-rug, which he so exactly matched in colour as to be indistinguishable from it.

"Bless me, Joanna, what's all this?" inquired the astonished Sir Piers, looking all round him in search of the monster from which so much noise could proceed.

He failed to perceive it, and stumbled heavily over the hearth-rug.

There was a howl from Puff; Lesbia cried, "Oh, my little manikin, is 'oo deaded?" Major Willoughby exclaimed in agonized tones to his host, "By Jove! the dog got in your way, sir, I'm afraid;" and to Puff, "Get out of the light, sir; what are you doing there?" and Lady Vivian gave a sudden irrepressible peal of laughter.

So that Lesbia, taking her departure half an hour later, remarked conclusively to her Lewis that the strain of this dreadful war was making poor dear Joanna Vivian positively hysterical.

She repeated the same alarming statement for Char's benefit next time she saw her at the Canteen. "I shouldn't say it, my dear child, but that your darling mother and I were girls together, and it's simply breaking my heart to see how broken up your father is, and no one to take any of the strain of it off her." Mrs. Willoughby spoke in her usual penetrating accents, and without any regard for the fact that at least three members of Miss Vivian's staff were well within earshot.

"No one can be keener than I am about doing one's bit for this ghastly war, but I do think, dear, that your place just now is at home at least part of each day. You won't mind an old friend's speaking quite, quite plainly, I know."

Char minded so much that she was white with annoyance.

"I can't discuss it here," she said, in a voice even lower than usual, in rebukeful contrast to Lesbia's screeching tones. "I should be only too thankful if I could get my place satisfactorily filled here, but at present it's perfectly impossible for me to leave even for an hour or two. I very often don't get time even for lunch nowadays."

"Simply because you enjoy making a martyr of yourself!" said Mrs. Willoughby spitefully.

Char, dropping her eyelids in a manner that gave her a look of incredible insolence, moved away without replying.

For the next week she worked harder than ever, multiplying letters and incessant interviews, and depriving herself daily of an extra hour's sleep in the morning by starting for the Depot earlier than usual, so as to cope with the press of business. It was her justification to herself for Mrs. Willoughby's crude accusations and the unspoken reproach in Sir Piers's feeble bewilderment at her activities.

Miss Plumtree fell ill with influenza, and Char took over her work, and arranged with infinite trouble to herself that Miss Plumtree should go to a small convalescent home in the country, because the doctor said she needed change of air. She was to incur no expense, Char told her, very kindly, and even remembered to order a cab for her at the country station. Miss Plumtree, owning that she could never have afforded a journey to her home in Devonshire, cried tears of mingled weakness and gratitude, and told the Hostel all that Miss Vivian had done.

Everybody said it was exactly like Miss Vivian, and that she really was too wonderful.

Then the demon of influenza began it's yearly depredations. One member of the staff after another went down with it, was obliged to plead illness and go to bed at the Hostel, and inevitably pass on the complaint to her room-mate.

"I'm afraid Mrs. Potter won't be coming to-day," Miss Delmege announced deprecatingly to her chief, who struck the table with her hand and exclaimed despairingly:

"Of course! just because there's more to be done than ever! Influenza, I suppose?" "I'm afraid it is."

"That's five of them down with it now or is it six? I don't know what to do."

"It does seem strange," was the helpless rejoinder of Miss Vivian's secretary.

Char thought the adjective inadequate to a degree. She abated not one jot of all that she had undertaken, and accomplished the work of six people.

Miss Delmege several times ventured to exclaim, with a sort of respectful despair, that Miss Vivian would kill herself, and Char knew that the rest of the staff was saying much the same thing behind her back. At Plessing Miss Bruce remonstrated admiringly, and exclaimed every day how tired Char was looking, throwing at the same time a rather resentful glance upon Lady Vivian.

But Joanna remained quite unperceiving of the dark lines deepening daily beneath her daughter's heavy eyes.

She was entirely absorbed in Sir Piers, becoming daily more dependent upon her.

The day came, when the influenza epidemic was at its height in Questerham, when Miss Bruce exclaimed in tones of scarcely suppressed indignation as Char came downstairs after the usual hasty breakfast which she had in her own room: "My dear, you're not fit to go. Really you're not; you ought to be in bed this moment. Do, do let me telephone and say you can't come to-day. Indeed, it isn't right. You look as though you hadn't slept all night."

"I haven't, much," said Char hoarsely. "I have a cold, that's all."

"Miss Vivian was coughing half the night," thrust in her maid, hovering in the hall laden with wraps.

"You mustn't go!" cried Miss Bruce distractedly. "You really aren't fit, Miss."

Lady Vivian appeared at the head of the stairs.

"What's all this?"

"Oh, Lady Vivian," cried the secretary, "do look at her! She ought to be in bed."

Char said "Nonsense!" impatiently, but she gave her mother an opportunity for seeing that her face was white and drawn, with heavily ringed eyes and feverish lips.

"You've got influenza. Char."

"I dare say," said Char in tones of indifference. "It would be very odd if I'd escaped, since half the office is down with it. But I can't afford to give in."

"It would surely be truer economy to take a day off now than to risk a real breakdown later on," was the time-worn argument urged by Miss Bruce.

Char smiled with pale decision.

"Let me pass, Brucey. I really mean it." Vivian!" wailed tjie secretary, Joanna

shrugged her shoulders. She, too, looked weary.

"Be reasonable, Char."

"It's of no use, mother. I shouldn't dream of giving in while there's work to be done."

Miss Bruce gave a sort of groan of mingled admiration and despair at this heroic statement. Char slipped her arms into the fur coat that her maid was holding out for her.

Lady Vivian stood at the top of the stairs looking at her with an air of detached consideration, and left Miss Bruce to make those hurried dispositions of
foot-warmer, fur rug, and little bottles of sulphate and quinine which, the secretary resentfully felt, a more maternal woman would have taken upon herself.

But Lady Vivian's omissions were not destined to provide the only one, or even the most severe, of the shocks received by Miss Bruce's sensibilities that morning.

As Char extended her hand for the last of Miss Bruce's offerings, a small green bottle of highly pungent smelling salts, Lady Vivian's incisive tones came levelly from above.

"You'd better stay the night at Questerham, Char. It will be very cold driving back after dark."

"Oh no, mother. Besides, I don't know where I could go. I hate the hotel, and one can't inflict an influenza cold on other people."

"You can go to your Hostel. Surely there's a spare bed?"

The ghost of a smile flickered upon Lady Vivian's face, as though in mischievous anticipation of Char's refusal.

"It's quite out of the question. The Hostel is for my staff, and it would be very unsuitable for me, as

Director of the Midland Supply Depot, to go there too."

"Bless me! are they as exclusive as all that?" exclaimed Joanna flippantly. "Well, do as you like, but if you come back here, you're not to go near your father, with a cold like that."

Miss Bruce, almost before she knew it, found herself exchanging a glance of indignation with Char's maid, but she was conscious enough of her own dignity to look away again in a great hurry.

"You will certainly want to go straight to bed when you come in," she said to Char, pointedly enough. "We will have everything ready and a nice fire in your room."

"Thank you, Brucey."

Char bestowed her rare smile upon the little agitated secretary, and moved across the hall.

She felt very ill, with violent pains in her head and back, and shivered intermittently.

Leaning back in her heavy coat, under the fur rug, Char closed her eyes. She reflected on the dismay with which Miss Delmege would greet her, and wondered rather grimly whether any further members of her staff would have succumbed to the prevailing illness. She knew that only a will of iron could surmount such physical ills as she was herself enduring, and dreaded the moment when she must rouse herself from her present torpid discomfort to the necessity of moving and speaking.

As she got out of the car, Char reeled and almost fell, in an intolerable spasm of giddiness, and her progress up the stairs was only made possible by the remnant of strength which allowed her to grasp the baluster and lean her full weight upon it as she dragged herself into her office.

She was, however, met with no wail of condolence from the genteel accents of Miss Delmege.

Grace Jones, composedly solid and healthy-looking, said placidly: "Good-morning. I'm sorry to say that Miss Delmege is in bed with influenza."

"In bed!"

"She had a very restless night and has a temperature this morning." "She was

all right yesterday."

"She had a sore throat, you know," remarked Grace, "but she didn't at all want to give in, and is very much distressed."

Char raised her heavy eyes.

"You all seem to me to collapse like a pack of cards, one after another. I think my bed would prove a bed of thorns while there's so much work to do, and so few people to do it. In fact, I can't imagine wanting to go there."

She made an infinitesimal pause, shaken by one of those violent, involuntary, shivering fits. Miss Jones gazed at her chief.

"I think I can manage Miss Delmege's work," she observed gently.

"Oh, I shall have to go through most of it myself, of course," was the ungrateful retort of the suffering Miss Vivian.

The day appeared to her interminable. The air was damp and raw; and although Miss Jones piled coal upon the fire, it refused to blaze up, and only smouldered in a sullen heap, with a small curling column of yellow smoke at the top. A tractionengine ground and screamed and pounded its way up and down under the window, and each time it passed directly in front of the house the floor and walls of Char's room shook slightly, with a vibration that made her feel sick and giddy.

There were no interviews, but letters and telephone messages poured in incessantly, and at about twelve o'clock a telegram marked fct Priority "was brought her. With a sinking sense of utter dismay, Char tore it open.

"A rest-station for a troop-train at five o'clock this afternoon. Eight hundred. Miss Jones, please let the Commissariat Department know at once. The staff should be at the station by three. I'll make out the list at once, and you can take it round the office."

By four o'clock a fine cold rain was falling, and Char's voice had nearly gone.

As she hurried down to her car, which was to take her to the station, she heard an incautiously raised voice: "She does look so ill! Of course it's flu, and I should think this rest-station will just about finish her off."

"Not she! I do believe she'd stick it out if she were dying. No lunch to-day, either, only a cup of Bovril, which I simply had to force her to take."

Char recognized the voice of Miss Henderson, who had received her order for lunch in place of Miss Delmege, and had ventured to suggest the Bovril in tones of the utmost deference.

She smiled slightly.

The troop-train was late.

"Of course!" muttered Char, pacing up and down the sheltered platform with the fur collar of her motoring coat turned up, and her hands deep in its wide pockets.

In the waiting-rooms, given over to the workers for the time being, the staff was active.

Sandwiches were cut, and heavy trays and urns carried out in readiness, while orderlies from the hospitals put up light trestle tables at intervals along the platform.

Char paused, turned the handle of the waiting-room door, and stood for a moment on the threshold.

Everyone was talking. Trays piled with cut and stacked sandwiches were ranged all round the room; tin mugs, again on trays, stood in groups of twelve; and the final spoonfuls of sugar were being scooped from a tin biscuit-box into the waiting bowl on each tray. Even the cake was already cut, sliced up on innumerable plates.

They had been working hard, and had more work to come, yet they all looked gay and amused, and were talking and laughing as though they did not know the meaning of fatigue. And Char was feeling so ill that she could hardly stand.

Suddenly someone caught sight of her, there was a sort of murmur, "Miss Vivian!" and in one moment self-consciousness invaded the room. Those who were sitting down stood up, trying to look at ease; little Miss Anthony, who had been manipulating the breadcutting machine with great success all the afternoon, at once cut her finger with it, and someone else suddenly dropped a mug with a reverberating clatter.

"Miss Cox!"

She sprang forward nervously.

"Yes, Miss Vivian?"

"How many sandwiches have you got ready?"

"Sixteen hundred, Miss Vivian. That'll be two for each man, and they're very

large." "Cut another hundred, for reserve."

"Yes, Miss Vivian."

They began to work again, this time speaking almost in

whispers. Char turned away.

Her personality, as usual, had had its effect.

Nearly twenty minutes later the station-master came up to her on the platform.

"She'll be in directly now, Miss Vivian. Just signalled."

Char wheeled smartly back to the waiting-room and gave the word of command.

Within five minutes the urns and trays were all in place on the tables, and each worker was at her appointed stand. Char had indicated beforehand, as she always did, the exact duties of each one.

"That's a smart bit of work," the station-master remarked admiringly.

"Ah, well, you see, I've been at the job some time now," said Miss Vivian, pleased. She never pretended to look upon her staff as anything but a collection of pawns, to be placed or disposed of by a master hand.

And it was part of that strength of personality that lay at the back of all her powers of organization, which had given the majority of her staff exactly the same impression as her own of their relative positions with regard to the Director of the Midland Supply Depot.

CHAPTER VIII

CHAR moved up and down the length of the train.

She never carried any of the laden trays herself, but she saw to it that no man missed his mug of steaming tea and supply of sandwiches and cake, and she exerted all the affability and charm of which she held the secret, in talking to the soldiers. The packets of cigarettes with which she was always laden added to her popularity, and when the train steamed slowly out of the station again the men raised a cheer.

"Three cheers for Miss Vivian!"

Her name had passed like lightning from one carriage to another. "Hooray-ay."

They hung out of the window, waving their caps, and Char stood at the end of the platform, heedless of the rain now pouring down on her, and waved until the train was out of sight.

"Start washing up and packing the things at once." "Yes, Miss Vivian."

The waiting-room was already seething and full of steam from the zinc pans of boiling water into which mugs and knives were being flung with deafening clatter.

"Here, chuck me a dry cloth! Mine's wringing."

"Oh, look out, dear! You're splashing your uniform like anything."

"I've got such a lot of work waiting for me when I get back to the office."

"Poor fellows, they did look bad! Did you see one chap, quite a young fellow, too, with his poor leg and all..."

Char turned away impatiently.

Thank Heaven, there was nothing further for her to do at the station.

The work at the office would be heavy enough, but at least ehe had not to stand amongst that noisy crew of workers round the big packing-cases and wash-tubs, each one screaming so as to make herself heard above the splashing water and clattered crockery.

It did not occur to her, as the car took her swiftly back to the office, also to be thankful that neither had she to walk back, as they had, in the streaming rain and cold of the dark evening.

She swallowed one of Miss Brace's quinine tablets with her hot tea, but was unable to eat anything, and sat over her letters with throbbing temples and a temperature that she felt to be rising rapidly. She poured over each simplest sentence again and again, unable to attach any meaning to the words dancing before her aching, swimming eyes.

Soon after half-past six Grace Jones came back from the station, her pale face glowing from the wind and rain, unabated vigour in her movements.

"Have you only just got back?"

"I had some tea downstairs. I've been in about ten minutes."

Char raised her eyebrows with an expression that would have caused Miss Delmege ostentatiously to refrain from tea every day for a week, had it been directed towards herself.

But Miss Jones only said tranquilly: "Is there anything that I can do for

you?" "No. Yes. You can answer that telephone."

The bell had suddenly sounded, and Char felt no strength to exert the swollen, aching muscles of her throat.

Grace took up the receiver.

"They want to speak to you from Plessing."

Char checked an exclamation of impatience. If only Brucey wouldn't fuss so! She might know by this time that it was of no use.

"Please say that I can't take a private call from here. Ask if it's on business."

She waited impatiently.

"It's not on business it's important. Lady Vivian is speaking." Char almost snatched the receiver.

"What is it?" she asked curtly.

"Is that you, Char?" came over the wires.

"Miss Vivian speaking," returned Char officially, for the benefit of Miss Jones.

"Your father is ill. He has had a very slight stroke, and I want you to bring out Dr. Prince in the car."

"How bad is he? Have you had anyone?"

"Yes. Dr. Clark came up from the village, but he suggested sending for Dr. Prince at once. He is unconscious, of course, and there isn't any immediate danger; he may get over it altogether, but this is the first minute I've had I am going back to him now. Come as soon as you can, Char, and bring the doctor. I can't get him on the telephone, but you must get hold of him somehow."

"Yes yes. Is there anything else?"

"Nothing now, my dear. By great good luck John is here, and most helpful. He carried your father upstairs. Only don't delay, will you?"

"No. I'll come at once. Good-bye." "Good-bye."

Char replaced the receiver, feeling dazed. Involuntarily her first sensation was one of injury that anyone should be more ill than she was herself, and able to excite so much stir.

The next moment she regained possession of herself. "Miss Jones, ring up the

garage and tell them to

Bend my car round immediately. Sir Piers Vivian has been taken ill, and I am going out to Plessing at once. Tell them to hurry."

Grace obeyed, and Char began feverishly to make order amongst the pile of papers on her table.

"I'm leaving a lot undone," she muttered, "but I suppose I shall be here to-morrow morning. I must be."

Ten minutes later the car was at the door.

"Miss Jones, see that all these go to-night," Char rapidly instructed her secretary. "The letters I haven't been able to sign must be held over till to-morrow. By the way, didn't the--er--your Hostel Superintendent say that she wanted an appointment with me this evening?"

"Mrs. Bullivant? Yes. She was coming at eight."

"Then, please tell her what's happened, and say that I will arrange to see her some time to-morrow. That's all, I think."

"I hope Sir Piers Vivian will be better by the time you get back." "I hope so. Thank you. Good-night, Miss Jones."

Char hurried downstairs, hoping that the tone of her voice had put Miss Jones into her proper place again. She did not encourage personal amenities between herself and her staff.

It was nearly nine o'clock before she got to Plessing. It had taken a long while to find Dr. Prince, and the chauffeur drove with maddening precautions through a thick wet mist along the sodden, slippery roads.

"A broken leg or two would delay us worse," said the doctor philosophically.

He was a bearded, hard-working man, with a reputation that extended beyond the Midlands.

After finding out from Char that she knew little or nothing of her father's state of health, he asked her with a quick look: "And yourself, Miss Charmian? You look rather washed out."

Char gave a short, hoarse cough, semi-involuntary, at this unflattering description.

"I'm afraid I'm in the midst of an influenza attack. My staff have all been down with it, more or less. However, I can't afford to give way to that sort of thing now; there's far too much work to be done."

"You ought to take six months' holiday," said the doctor decidedly, and relapsed into silence.

Char wondered if he were meditating an appeal to her. It must outrage his professional instincts to see anyone looking as she did still upon her feet. The doctor, however, who had been up since two o'clock that morning, was merely trying to snatch some sleep. He had known Char Vivian all her life, and had no thought whatever of wasting appeals upon her. At Plessing, Trevellyan met them in the hall. "Good-evening, Char," he greeted her. "Sir Piers is much the same. Not conscious. Will you go up, doctor? They'll have some dinner ready by the time you come down. I'm afraid you've had a cold drive."

"Freezing," answered Char, with a violent shiver. "Better go to bed," said the doctor, without looking at her, as he went upstairs.

Char, still in her fur coat, hung over the fire. "Tell me what's happened, Johnnie."

"Cousin Joanna says that he was very restless and low-spirited last night talked about the war, you know, and this last air-raid. And when he came down this morning he suddenly turned giddy and fell across the hall sofa. Lucky it wasn't on the floor. Cousin Joanna was with him, and they got him flat on the sofa, and sent for Clark. I got here about the same time as he did, by pure chance came over for a day's shooting, you know and between us we carried him upstairs. By Jove! he's no light weight for a man of his years, either."

"What does Dr. Clark think?"

"That he'll probably recover consciousness in a day or two. But even then--don't be frightened, Char; it's only what generally happens in these cases his his words probably won't come quite right, you know. He may speak, but not quite normally."

Char smiled a little at her cousin's look of anxious solicitude for the effect of his surmises upon her.

"I'm not without hospital experience, you know," she said gently. "It's the left side of the brain, then? Is his right side paralyzed?"

"I'm afraid so arm and hand, you know. We shall see what Prince says."

There was a pause, and Char said hoarsely: "I wonder if I ought to go up?"

"Is that you, Miss Vivian?" came the voice of Miss Bruce from the stairs.

Char turned and went slowly up to her. Trevellyan did not see her again that evening, and Miss Bruce told him later, with rather a reproachful look, that poor Miss Vivian was not fit to be up. "It was a shock to her, I'm afraid."

"Yes oh yes; but she really was dreadfully ill when she went out this morning. She ought never, never to have been allowed to leave the house."

"You don't mean to say she's going to be ill too?" exclaimed TreveDyan in tones of dismay.

He was thinking that Joanna had enough anxiety as it was; but Miss Bruce attributed his tones entirely to concern on behalf of her adored Miss Vivian, and looked at him more amiably.

"I'm afraid it's influenza, but a couple of days in bed will make all the difference, and now that, of course, there's no question of her leaving the house, she'll be able to take care of herself for once."

"There she is," said Captain Trevellyan, and strode across the hall to meet his Cousin Joanna and the doctor.

Miss Bruce waited to hear Dr. Prince's verdict, and then went quietly up to Char's room, with offers of service that aroused the unconcealed wrath of Char's devoted maid.

"I don't want anything," Miss Vivian declared wearily. "As soon as I know whether I may see my father, I can go to bed or go up to him, as the case may be. But I suppose my mother means to come down to me some time?"

There was more than a hint of resentment in her wearied voice. "Shall I tell her

ladyship you're here, miss?" asked the maid gently.

"She knows it," said Char shortly. "I brought Dr. Prince."

The zealous Miss Bruce slipped silently from the room and down into the hall again.

Lady Vivian, oblivious of her daughter's claims, was discussing Dr. Prince's verdict in lowered tones with Captain Trevellyan.

Miss Bruce felt a sort of melancholy triumph in beholding this justification for Char's obvious sense of injury.

"Miss Vivian is in her room, and waiting for you most anxiously," she said reproachfully. "She thought you were still with Sir Piers. She won't go to bed until she knows whether she may see him."

"Poor child, it wouldn't do her any good to see him," said Joanna. "There's no sign of returning consciousness yet, though Dr. Prince thinks he may come to himself almost any time, and then everything depends upon his being kept absolutely quiet. But I'll go up to Char."

She went upstairs, but came down again much sooner than Miss Bruce approved.

"I've told her to go to bed," she placidly informed the secretary. "She can't do anything, and she looks very tired."

"She is far from well, I'm afraid," stiffly remarked Miss Bruce.

"Well, I leave her to you, Miss Bruce. I know you'll take the most devoted care of her. Let her sleep as long as she can in the morning."

"Cousin Joanna, is there anything I can do?" asked Trevellyan

wistfully. "I don't think so, Johnnie. You'll come round to-morrow?"

She was smiling at him quite naturally.

"The first thing. You're sure there's nothing I can do to-night sit up with him, or anything?"

"My maid and I are going to do it between us. We shall have a nurse down from London by midday to-morrow, I hope."

"Let me sit up instead of you." She smiled again.

"Certainly not. I'm only going to take the first half of the night much the easiest. Then I shall probably go to sleep, unless there's any change, when, of course, they'll fetch me. But Dr. Prince doesn't think there will be yet, and I shall take all the rest I can. I'm much more likely to be wanted at night later on."

Miss Bruce went upstairs again, much more nearly disposed to wonder at such reasonableness than to admire it.

Her ideals were early Victorian ones, and although she knew that she could not hope for hysterics from Lady Vivian, she would have much preferred at least to hear her declare that sleep would be utterly impossible to her, and that she should spend the night hovering between her unconscious husband and her prostrate daughter.

But Lady Vivian went to bed at half-past twelve, and did not even insist upon merely lying down in her dressing-gown, nor did she reappear in Sir Piers's room until eight o'clock on the following morning.

There had been no change during the night.

Char slept heavily until ten o'clock, then woke and rang her bell rather indignantly.

Miss Bruce, who had been hovering about anxiously since seven that morning, appeared instantly at the door.

"There is no change whatever, my dear. Now, do, do lie down again and keep warm. There is nothing that you can do."

Char complied rather sullenly. She was still feeling ill, and violently resented her own involuntary physical relief at this enforced inaction.

"What on earth will happen at the office?" she muttered. "Have you told them that I'm not coming?"

"I telephoned myself," said Miss Bruce proudly. "What did you say?"

"That you were in bed yourself with influenza, and quite unfit to move; and also that we are in great anxiety about Sir Piers."

"That's the only reason I can't go in to Questerham as usual," said Char coldly. "It was quite unnecessary to mention my having influenza, Brucey. That would never constitute a reason for my staying away from my work."

Miss Bruce looked very much crestfallen.

"You'd better telephone again, please, a little later on, with a message from me. Say that I must be rung up without fail when my secretary has gone through the letters, and I'll come to the telephone and speak to her myself."

"The draughty hall!" moaned Miss Bruce, but she dared not offer any further remonstrance.

Char's conversation on the telephone with Miss Jones

Was a lengthy one, and Miss Bruce, wandering in the background in search of imaginary currents of air, listened to her concluding observations with almost ludicrous dismay. "The departments must carry on as usual, of course, but don't hesitate to ring me up in any emergency. And no letters had better leave the office to-night in fact, they can't, since there'll be nobody to sign them. What's that?... No, certainly not. How on earth could I depute such a responsibility to anyone in the office. I shall have made some arrangement by to-morrow. Sir Piers may remain in this state indefinitely, and I can't have the whole of the work held up in this way.... That's all. Remember, nothing is to leave the office for the present. You can ring me up and report on the day's work at seven o'clock this evening. Goodbye."

As Char replaced the receiver, her mother entered the hall. They had already exchanged a few words earlier in the morning, and Lady Vivian only remarked dispassionately: "I thought you were in bed. By the way, Char, I'm sorry, but we shall have to have the telephone disconnected. The house must be kept quiet, and that bell can be heard quite plainly from upstairs. We can ring other people up, but they won't be able to get at us. Did you want to talk to your office?"

"I must," said Char. "Things are absolutely hung up there; no one who can even sign a letter."

"Why not? Have they all got writer's cramp all of a sudden?"

Char, never very graciously disposed towards her parent's many small fleers at her official dignity, thought this one particularly ill-timed, and received it by a silence which said as much.

Lady Vivian looked at her, and said rather penitently: "Well, well, I mustn't keep you here when you ought to be in bed. My dear child, do you mean to say you're wearing nothing but your dressing-gown under that coat? Do go upstairs again."

"I want to speak to you, mother."

"I'll come up in five minutes. I'm going to give an order to the stables."

Lady Vivian walked briskly down the drive, her uncovered head thrown back to catch the chilly gleams of winter sunlight.

There were dark lines under her blue eyes, but the voice in which she gave her orders was full and serene as usual, even when she answered the chauffeur's respectful inquiries by the news that Sir Piers still remained unconscious.

Five minutes later Lady Vivian's secretary had the gratification of seeing her enter Char's bedroom and establish herself on a chair at the sufferer's bedside

That afternoon Miss Bruce received a further satisfaction when Lady Vivian sought her in consultation.

"It's about Char, Miss Bruce. She's fretting herself into fiddlestrings about that office of hers. She thinks all the work is more or less held up while she's not there to see to it. And yet she may be kept here indefinitely. It's quite possible that Sir Piers may ask for her when he comes to himself again, so there can be no question of her going in to Questerham at present, even if she were fit for it, which she most decidedly isn't."

"That consideration by itself would never keep her from her work," said Miss Bruce loyally.

Lady Vivian waived the point.

"Well, as she won't do the" only sensible thing, and transfer her authority to some responsible member of the staff, she'd better have one of them out here every day to go through the work with her and take back her instructions. The car is bound to be going in at least once a day."

"It won't be the rest for Charmian that one had hoped," said the secretary dismally.

"But it will be better for her to do a little work than just to sit and worry about her father and the office though, upon my word," said Lady Vivian warmly, "I think she's a great deal more anxious about the Depot than about his illness."

Miss Bruce, not inconceivably, thought so too, but she was very much shocked at hearing such an idea put into words, and said firmly: "Then, would you like me to write to Questerham and tell Miss Vivian's secretary that it has been arranged for her to come out here daily for the present?"

"Dear me, you're as bad as Char, Miss Bruce. Anybody would think they were all machines, to be dragged about without any will of their own. No, no! Ring up the office and get hold of the secretary, and give her a polite message, asking if she can manage it, if we send her in and out in the car."

Miss Bruce obeyed, and triumphantly told her employer that evening that all was arranged, and Miss Jones would come to Plessing on the following morning to receive Miss Vivian's directions.

"Miss Jones? You don't mean to say that the genteel Delmege has abdicated in favour of Miss Jones? What a piece of luck for us!" cried Lady Vivian.

"Miss Delmege is in bed with influenza."

"Excellent!" said Joanna callously. "I shall be delighted to see Miss Jones. I wanted to ask her here, but Char nearly had a fit at the idea. She'll certainly think I've done it out of malice prepense, as it is. She's got a most pig-headed prejudice against that nice Miss Jones."

"Lady Vivian!"

Lady Vivian laughed.

"You'll have to break it to her, Miss Bruce, that it's Miss Jones who is coming. And don't let her think I did it on purpose!"

"I am sure she would never think anything of the sort."

"Perhaps not. But Char does get very odd ideas into her head, when she thinks there's any risk of lese-majeste to her Directorship. I must say," observed Joanna thoughtfully, preparing to go upstairs for her night watch, "I often wish that when Char was younger I'd smacked some of the nonsense out--"

But before this well-worn aspiration of Miss Vivian's parent, Miss Bruce took her indignant departure.

CHAPTER IX

"RATHER strange, isn't it?" said Miss Delmege in tones of weak despondency. "If it hadn't been for this wretched flu, *I* should have been going out to Plessing every day with the work, I suppose, as Gracie is doing now."

"Yes, I suppose you would," agreed Miss Henderson blankly.

She sat on the foot of the bed, which was surrounded by a perfect wilderness of screens.

Miss Delmege reclined against two pillows, screwed against her back at an uncomfortable-looking angle. The room was not warmed, and the invalid wore a small flannel dressing-jacket, rather soiled and very much crumpled, a loosely knitted woolly jersey of dingy appearance and an ugly mustard colour, and over everything else an old quilted pink dressinggown, with a cotton-wool-like substance bursting from the cuffs and elbows. Her hair was pinned up carelessly, and her expression was a much dejected one.

Miss Henderson was knitting in a spasmodic way, and stopping every now and then to blow her nose violently. She had several times during the afternoon ejaculated vehemently that a cold wasn't flu, she was thankful to say.

"It's probably the beginning of it, though," Miss Delmege replied pessimistically.

"You're hipped, Delmege, that's what you are regularly hipped. Now, don't you think it would do you good to come downstairs for tea? There's a fire in the sitting-room."

"Well, I don't mind if I do. It'll seem quite peculiar to be downstairs again. Fancy, I've been up here five whole days! And I'm really not a person to give way, as a rule. At least, not so far as I know, I'm not."

"It's nearly four now. Look here, I'll put a kettle on, and you can have some hot water."

"Thanks, dear," said Miss Delmege graciously, "but don't bother. My hot-water bottle is still quite warm. I can use that."

"All right, then, I'll leave you. Ta-ta! You'll find me in the sitting-room. Sure you don't want any help?"

"No, thanks. I shall be quite all right. I only hope you won't be in bed yourself to-morrow, dear."

"No fear!" defiantly said Miss Henderson, at the same time sneezing loudly.

She went away before Miss Delmege had time to utter any further prognostications.

In the sitting-room she busied herself in pushing a creaking wicker arm-chair close to the fire which for once was a roaring one, owing to the now convalescent Mrs. Potter, who had been crouching over it with a novel all day lit the gas, and turned it up until it flared upwards with a steady, hissing noise; said "Excuse me; do you mind?" to Mrs. Potter; shut down the small crack of open window, and drew the curtains.

"Delmege is coming down, and we'd better have the room warm," she explained. "She's just out of bed."

By the time Miss Delmege, now wearing her mustardcoloured jersey over a thick stuff dress, had tottered downstairs, the room was indeed warm.

"Now, this," said Mrs. Bullivant cheerfully, when she came in to see how many of her charges wanted tea "now this is what I call really cosy."

&he lpoked ill, and very tired, herself. The general servant had given notice because of the number of trays that she had been required to carry upstairs of late, and had left the day before, and the cook was disobliging and would do nothing beyond her own immediate duties. Mrs. Bullivant was very much afraid of her, and did most of the work herself.

She had written to the Depot in accordance with the official Hostel regulations, stating that a servant was required there for general housework; but no answer had come authorizing her to engage one, and Miss Marsh had explained to her that in Miss Vivian's absence such trifling questions must naturally expect to be overlooked or set aside for the time being. So little Mrs. Bullivant staggered up from the basement bearing a tray that seemed very large and heavy, and put it on the table in the sitting-room, very close to the fire, with a triumphant gasp.

"There! and it's a beautiful fire for toast. None of the munition girls are coming in for tea, are they?"

"Hope not," said Miss Henderson briefly. "I ought to be at the office now. I said I'd be back at five, but I shouldn't have had the afternoon off at all if Miss Vivian had been there."

Miss Delmege drew herself up. "Miss Vivian never refuses a reasonable amount of leave, that I'm aware of," she said stiffly.

"Oh, I mean we're slacker without her. There's less to do, that's all."

"Well, Grace Jones will be back presently, and I suppose she'll have work for all of us, as usual. I wonder how Miss Vivian is," said Mrs. Potter.

"And her father."

"Grace will be able to tell us," said Miss Delmege, not without a tinge of acrimony in her voice. "It does seem so quaint, her going to and from Plessing in Miss

Vivian's car, like this, every day. It somehow makes me howl with laughter."

She gave a faint, embittered snigger, and Miss Henderson and Mrs. Potter exchanged glances.

"I hear the car now," said Mrs. Bullivant. "She'll be cold. I'll get another cup, and give her some tea before she goes over to the office. I do hope she's got Miss Vivian's authority for me to find a new servant."

They heard her outside in the hall, making inquiry, and Grace's voice answering in tones of congratulation.

"Yes, it's quite all right. I asked Miss Vivian most particularly, and told her what a lot of work there was, and she said: Get someone as soon as you could. I came here before going to the office so as to tell you at once."

"Well, that was nice of you, dear, and now you shall have a nice cup of hot tea before you go out again. Just a minute."

"I'll fetch it, Mrs. Bullivant. Don't you bother."

"It's all right, dear, only a cup and saucer wanted; the rest is all ready."

In a few minutes Grace came into the sitting-room carefully carrying the cup and saucer.

When she saw Miss Delmege she said in a pleased way: "Oh, I'm so glad you're better. Miss Vivian asked after you. She was up herself this afternoon, and looking much better."

"And how's her father?"

"They are much happier about him since he recovered consciousness. He can talk almost quite well, and Dr. Prince is quite satisfied about him. And they've got a nurse at last. You know, they couldn't get one for love or money; none of the London places had any to spare."

"I should have thought they could get one from one of the Questerham hospitals."

"I think Lady Vivian meant to, if everything else failed, but Miss Vivian didn't think it a very good plan; she was afraid the hospitals couldn't spare anyone, I suppose, and, anyhow, most of the people there are only V.A.D.s."

"And is there any hope of seeing her back at the office?" asked Mrs. Potter, rather faintly.

"I don't know," replied Grace thoughtfully. "You see, poor Sir Piers may remain at this stage indefinitely, or may have another stroke any time. They don't really know..."

"And Miss Vivian goes on with the work just the same!" ejaculated Miss Henderson. "She really is a marvel."

"I'm sure she'd come to the office if it wasn't for poor Lady Vivian," said Miss Delmege. "But I know her mother depends on her altogether. I don't suppose she could leave her, not as things are now."

Miss Delmege's assumption of an intimate and superior knowledge of the menage at Plessing was received in silence. Miss Henderson, indeed, glancing sharply at Grace, saw the merest quiver of surprise pass across her face at the assertion; but reflected charitably that, after all, Delmege had had a pretty sharp go of flu, and probably wasn't feeling up to the mark yet. Her mis-statements, however irritating, had better be left unchallenged.

"Do you ever see anything of Lady Vivian when you're at Plessing?" Miss Delmege inquired benevolently of Grace, but the benevolence faded from her expression when Miss Jones replied, with more enthusiasm than usual in her voice, that she always had lunch with Lady Vivian, and sometimes went round the garden with her before going up to Miss Vivian's room for the afternoon's work.

"Dear me! I shouldn't have thought she'd have much time for going round the garden. But she's not thorough-going, like Miss Vivian is, of course.

It's quite a different sort of nature, I fancy. Strange, too, being mother and daughter."

Miss Henderson decided rapidly within herself that, influenza or no, Delmege was making herself unbearable.

"You're getting tired with sitting up, aren't you, dear?" she inquired crisply.

There was a moment's silence, and then Miss Delmege said in pinched accents: "Who is it you're referring to, dear? Me, by any chance?"

Grace knew the state of tension to which those aloof and refined tones were the prelude, and exclaimed hurriedly that she must go.

She did not want to hear Miss Henderson and Miss Delmege having "words," or to listen while Miss Delmege talked with genteel familiarity of Sir Piers and Lady Vivian.

Pulling on her thick uniform coat, she went out, and slowly crossed the street.

She was thinking of Lady Vivian, who had roused in her an enthusiasm which she could never feel for Char, and who had talked to her so frankly and warmly, as though to a contemporary, that afternoon in the garden at Plessing. For all her quality of matter-of-factness, there was a certain humblemindedness about Miss Jones, which made it a matter of surprise to her when she found herself on the borders of friendship with the woman whom she thought so courageous and so lovable.

She hoped that Miss Vivian would require her to go out to Plessing every day for a long while; then reflected that the privilege rightly belonged to Miss Delmege, who would certainly avail herself of it at the earliest possible moment.

She knew, and calmly accepted, that Miss Delmege's services would certainly be preferred to her own by the Director of the Midland Supply Depot; but she did not think that Lady Vivian proffered her liking or her confidence lightly, and felt a certain placid security that their unofficial intercourse would somehow or other continue. Then, with characteristic thoroughness, she dismissed the question from her mind and went into the office and to her work.

That evening Grace went to the Canteen. Only Miss Marsh, Miss Anthony, and Miss Henderson accompanied her.

"We shall have to work like blacks to make up for the absentees," groaned

Tony. "Never mind; it isn't quite so cold to-night. Isn't the moon nice?"

"Lovely. Just the night for Zeppelins."

Miss Henderson spoke from the pessimism of approaching influenza, but it happened that she was right. The first air-raid over Questerham took place that night.

The work was rapidly lessening towards eleven o'clock, when Captain Trevellyan came into the hall. He stood for an instant gazing round him reflectively, then said to Grace: "Who is in command here?"

"Mrs. Willoughby, when Miss Vivian isn't here." "I see, thank you."

Looking very doubtful, he sought Lesbia, who was preparing to discard her overall and to take her departure with the Pekinese.

"Johnnie! How too sweet of you to turn up just in time to see me home! My Lewis hates my going back alone in the dark; we've very nearly quarrelled over it already."

"The fact is," said Trevellyan, wondering if Mrs. Willoughby were the sort of person to have hysterics, "that there's been a telephone warning to say an air-raid is on, just over Staningham. They're heading this way, so we may hear a gun or two, you know; some of our machines are in pursuit,"

He gazed anxiously at Lesbia, whom he characteristically supposed to be about either to burst into tears or to threaten a fainting fit.

The ideas of Captain Trevellyan were perhaps not much more advanced than those of Lady Vivian's secretary.

But Mrs. Willoughby discounted his solicitude, at least on one score, in a moment.

"Zepps!" she screamed excitedly. "How too thrilling! Can I possibly get on to the roof, I wonder! I've never seen one yet."

"Stop!" said the astonished Trevellyan. "You don't realize. They'll be over here in a few minutes, and our machines may be firing at them, besides the guns on the hill; there'll be shrapnel falling."

Mrs. Willoughby tore off her overall and snatched up Puff.

"I must, must see it all!" she declared wildly. "Have you got a pair of field-

glasses?" Trevellyan restrained her forcibly from dashing to the door.

"Mrs. Willoughby, we've got to consider that there are a number of people here, and that they are all in a certain amount of danger not so much from bombs, though goodness knows they may very well drop one, but from our own shrapnel. Is there a basement?"

"You can't send us to the cellar? My dear boy, I, for one, refuse to go. We're not children, and we're not afraid. We're Englishwomen!"

On this superb sentiment Mrs. Willoughby swept into the middle of the hall and announced in penetrating accents that a Zepp raid was on, and had anyone got a pair of field-glasses?

There was a momentary outbreak of exclamations all round, and then Captain Trevellyan raised his voice: "Please keep away from the windows. There may be broken glass about,"

"Is it dangerous? What are we to do?" gasped Tony, next him. She was rather white.

At the same moment the very distant but unmistakable reverberation of guns became audible.

Trevellyan took instant advantage of the sudden cessation of sound in the room.

"If there is a basement, it would be as well for everybody to go down there, please just for precaution's sake. And then I'm going to put out these lights." His hand was on the nearest gas-jet as he spoke.

"Nothing will induce me to stir while there's any danger. I can answer for every woman here!" cried Lesbia, with a gesture of noble defiance.

Grace Jones came into the middle of the room. "Hadn't we better obey orders?" she asked gently. "There is a basement beyond the kitchen."

She held out her hand to Miss Anthony, and they went through the door into the kitchen.

After an instant's hesitation, the other women followed. Trevellyan saw that they had lit a candle, and in a moment he heard them beginning to talk quietly amongst themselves.

A few soldiers in the hall had congregated together, and were talking and laughing. The others made a dash for the door as the firing grew louder, and simultaneously exclaimed: "Here they are!"

The sound of the huge machines far overhead was unmistakable. They could see the shrapnel bursting, and the guns on the hill boomed heavily and intermittently.

"Look!" shrieked Lesbia, almost hurling herself out of the door. "They've got one of them! I can see it blazing!"

Far away, a red spot began to glow, then suddenly revealed the cigar-shaped form in flames, dropping downwards,

"They've got it!" echoed Trevellyan. "Look! it's coming down. Miles away, by this time. I wonder how many of ours are giving chase."

The air was full of whirring, buzzing wings, and very far away a red light in the sky seemed to tell of fire.

Occasional sparks and flashes told of the bursting of shrapnel, but the sounds were dying away rapidly.

"It's over, and, by Jove, we've got him!" shouted Trevellyan, dashing back into the kitchen. Everyone was talking at once, Mrs. Willoughby's voice dominating the rest.

"I saw the whole thing too perfectly! At least five of the brutes, and two, if not three, of them in flames! I saw them with my own eyes!" she proclaimed, with more spirit than exactitude. "And where are those poor creatures hiding like rats in the cellar?"

"The noise was awful!" said Tony, shuddering. "It felt as though it were right over our heads. But," she added valiantly, "I do wish we'd seen it all!"

Trevellyan turned to her apologetically. "I'm so sorry. But I really couldn't help it. They sent me down on purpose to see that this place was warned. It was really perfectly splendid of you to go down like that and miss all the fun."

"I was very frightened," she told him honestly, "though I do awfully wish I'd seen it. They must have had a splendid view from the Hostel at the top of the street."

"There was a splendid view from here," said Lesbia cuttingly. "*I* saw everything there was to be seen."

Trevellyan was looking for Miss Jones.

"Thank you so much for giving them the lead you did," he said to her gratefully. "It was very good of you. I felt such a brute for asking you to do it; but there really is danger, you know, especially from the windows, if shrapnel shatters the glass."

"Oh yes, I know. I wonder," said Grace thoughtfully, "whether they heard it much at Plessing."

"I know. I was thinking of that all the time. Not that she'd be nervous, you know, except on his account."

"It would be dreadful for Sir Piers. Oh, I do hope they didn't hear much of it," said Grace.

One of the men approached her. "If you please, Sister, could you come down into the kitching 'alf a minute?"

Grace went.

Trevellyan watched them all disperse, and escorted Mrs. Willoughby to her tram, wondering if he ought not to see her home.

But Lesbia refused all escort, declaring gallantly that she did not know the meaning of fear, and, anyway, Puffles would protect his missus from any more dreadful, wicked Zepps.

He left her entertaining her tram conductress with a spirited account of all that she had seen, and much that she had not seen, of the raid.

As he turned down Pollard Street again, a soldier with his hand bound up lurched out of the open door of the deserted Canteen.

"Is there anyone in there to shut the place up?" Trevellyan asked him.

"One of the ladies is still in there, sir. Beg pardon, sir; she's a bit upset like."

Trevellyan thought of little Miss Anthony, who had owned, with a white face, how much the sound of the guns had frightened her.

He went into the hall. It was dark, but there was a light in the

kitchen. "Who's there?" said John.

"I am. It's all right," replied an enfeebled voice; and he went into the kitchen.

Grace Jones was half leaning and half sitting against the sink, her small face haggard, her hands clutching the only support within reach, the wooden top of a roller-towel.

"I'm afraid you're ill," exclaimed Trevellyan, looking desperately round him for a chair.

"It's all right; please don't wait."

"But it's over now. They brought the brute down. It's miles away by this

time." He multiplied his reassurances.

"No, no; it's not that," gasped Miss Jones, looking whiter than ever.

"There were certainly no casualties over here. We should have seen signs of fire somewhere if they'd dropped a bomb."

"It's not that!" Grace told him desperately.

Trevellyan gazed at her helplessly, and repeated in an obtuse manner: "It's all over now 'absolutely safe.'"

Grace gazed back at him with a wan smile.

"Would you mind going?" she asked him feebly. "I shall be all right in a minute. It's very tiresome, but the sight of of blood always upsets me like this, and that man had cut his finger rather badly, and I had to do it up. It's only that."

She put her hands up to her damp forehead as though the effort of speech had brought back the sensation of nausea.

"You're going to faint!" exclaimed Trevellyan. "Let me get some water for

you." "No, I'm not. Oh, do go!"

"I can't leave you like this," protested the bewildered John.

Grace staggered to her feet, and stood holding on to the edge of the

sink. "I'm afraid I'm only going to be sick," she said with difficulty.

Ten minutes later they locked up the Canteen and went up Pollard Street,

"You see, it had nothing to do with the raid," Grace told him gently. "It was just that poor man bleeding. I've always been like that; it's the only way I'm delicate, because I'm never ill, and I don't ever have nerves. But it is very tiresome. That's why I couldn't go and work in a hospital. I did clerical work in the hospital at home for a little while, but it wasn't any good."

"Bad luck!"

"It is, rather. I hate anybody's knowing about it; that's why I said I'd stay behind and lock up. I knew it was going to happen, and I didn't want anyone to be there."

"I'm sorry. I thought it was the raid that had upset you, and that you might be going to faint."

"Nothing so romantic," said Miss Jones regretfully.

But her regrets were as nothing to those of the Hostel when they learnt what had happened.

It was impossible to conceal it from them, since the window of the ground-floor bedroom had been open, and Mrs. Potter and Miss Marsh, leaning from it, and listening eagerly, had heard every word of Captain Trevellyan's final discourse to Miss Jones, and her repeated assurances of being now completely restored.

They flew into the hall to meet her.

"Gracie dear, what has happened to you? Tony was in such a state when she found you hadn't come in with her and the others."

"Was it that beastly raid upset you?"

Grace once more repudiated the raid with as much energy as she could

muster. "You look as white as a sheet, dear! Come into the sitting-room."

Everyone was in the sitting-room, including those first back from the Canteen, and the pseudo-invalids who, having been in bed when the raid began, felt that only tea could enable them to face the night, and had hurried down in search of it.

"Oh, Gracie, there you are! I was just going back to see what had become of you," said Tony.

"Miss Vivian's cousin brought her home!" giggled Mrs. Potter. "You know, the Staff nicer one. She's been awfully upset, poor Grace! Turned quite faint, didn't you, dear?"

"But you were so brave!" cried Tony, aghast. "You were all right all the time the raid was on. You didn't mind a bit!"

"Came over you afterwards, I expect, didn't it?" said Miss Delmege kindly. "It's often the case. I'm always perfectly cool myself when anything happens I was
to-night but I generally suffer for it afterwards. Reaction, I suppose. When I came downstairs after it was all over I was simply shaking, wasn't I, Mrs. Bullivant?"

"Now, it's a funny thing," remarked Miss Henderson, without giving anyone time to dwell upon Miss Delmege's personal reminiscences "it's a funny thing, but I simply didn't feel the least bit of fear. Not for myself, you know. I just thought, well, I hope mother doesn't see any of this she's got a bit of a heart, you know but I didn't seem to feel a bit as though I was in any kind of danger myself. Not a bit."

"Now, just sit down, child, and drink up this tea," said Mrs. Bullivant to Grace. "You've not a scrap of colour in your face."

"I'm really all right now, thank you very much," Grace told her as she took the tea gratefully. "And it wasn't anything to do with the raid."

Everybody looked rather disappointed.

"Aren't you well, then, dear? I do hope it isn't another case of influenza."

"I bet I know!" suddenly cried Tony. "It was doing up that man's hand upset you, wasn't it? He cut himself somehow in the excitement and was bleeding like a fountain, poor fellow! I thought you looked rather squeamish while you were doing it, poor thing! but I never thought of it's bowling you over like this. Are you one of those people who faint at the sight of blood?"

"I didn't faint," said Grace mildly.

"Jolly near it, I expect, judging by your face now," said Tony critically. "Poor old dear!"

"Did Miss Vivian's cousin come back to find you?" asked Miss Delmege sharply.

"He came into the kitchen while I was still there, and afterwards he helped me to lock up."

"Afterwards?"

A tinge of colour crept into Miss Jones's face.

"I'm afraid you won't think I rose to the occasion at all," she said deprecatingly. "It always does make me rather ill to see blood, though I know it's idiotic, and it was the soldier's hand, not the air-raid a bit. I didn't mind that at all."

"What happened? Were you hysterical?" demanded Miss Delmege, with an inexplicable touch of umbrage in her refined little voice.

"Certainly not," said Grace emphatically. "If you really want to know, I was just sick over the sink."

Miss Jones's damaging revelation horrified the Hostel no less than the crude manner of its avowal.

"Well," said Miss Henderson, "you really are the limit, Gracie and a bit over."

"Poor child!" said Mrs. Bullivant kindly. "How dreadful for you! Miss Vivian's cousin and all, too! But, still, it was better than an absolute stranger, perhaps."

"I don't see how you're ever going to face him again, though really I don't," giggled Tony.

"Poor man! so awful for him, too," minced Miss

Delmege. "He must have been too uncomfortable for words."

"Not he," Miss Marsh told her with sudden defiance. "He brought poor Gracie home, and delighted to have the chance. Come on, Gracie, let's go to bed. You look done for."

She had grown very fond of her room-mate, in spite of all that she regretfully looked upon as an absence of propriety in her conduct; and when they were outside the sitting-room door, she said, without troubling to lower her voice: "Don't you mind their nonsense, dear. You couldn't help it, and that Delmege has only got the pip because she hadn't the chance of being brought home by Miss Vivian's cousin herself."

And when they got upstairs she "turned down" Gracie's bed for her, and put her kettle on to the gas-ring, and brought her an extra hot-water bottle.

"There! Good-night, dear, and don't you worry. I think it was splendid of you to tell the truth. Lots of girls would have fibbed, and said they'd fainted, or something high-faluting of that nature. I should myself."

"Thank you so much. You are nice to me," said Grace warmly. She did not look upon the affair herself as being more than a merely unfortunate incident, but she knew that Miss Marsh regarded it as an overwhelming scandal, and was proffering consolation accordingly.

Miss Marsh bent over the bed and tucked her in. "I'll turn out the gas, and you must go straight to sleep. It's frightfully late. And look here, Gracie, when we're alone together up here, I'd like you to call me Dora, if you will. It's my name, you know."

CHAPTER X

"THAT settles it," said Char. "If this sort of thing is going to happen, I must be there. With no definite organization, there might be a panic next time an air-raid takes place. According to Mrs. Willoughby, everyone made a dash for the basement, as it was. Women are such fools when one leaves them to themselves!"

It was part of Char's policy always to disparage her own sex. It threw into greater relief the contrast which she knew to exist between herself and the majority of women-workers.

She was speaking to Miss Bruce, but, rather to her annoyance, Lady Vivian came into the room in time to overhear her.

"Surely the basement was the most sensible place to dash for?" she inquired, never able to resist an opportunity of attacking her offspring's arrogantly expressed opinions. "As for your being there, in my opinion, it's a very good thing you weren't. You'd only have drilled the poor things out of their senses, which would have taken up more valuable space in the basement."

"I should not have been in the basement," returned Char superbly.

"Then you might have been blown into bits, my dear, unless, as Director of the Midland Supply Depot, all enemy aircraft has orders to respect your person?"

Joanna was jeering quite good-humouredly, as she generally did, and even Miss Bruce saw some exaggeration in the white, tense silence with which Char received these indifferent pleasantries.

"I hear the car," said the secretary, anxious to create a diversion.

"Miss Jones. Mother, I'm going through the work with her in here this morning. There's no fire in the morning-room."

"Very well, Char. You won't disturb me in the least."

"I thought you were going to sit with father."

"Not yet. Besides, I want to see Miss Jones."

Char sighed patiently. At Plessing only the faithful Miss Bruce gave her work that consideration to which she had become accustomed at the office. She was finding Plessing almost intolerable. There were no interviews, the telephone-bell was not allowed to ring, no one urged her not to neglect the substantial meals which were served for her with the greatest regularity, and Miss Jones daily assured her, with perfect placidity, that the whole work of the office was progressing with complete success without her.

The Director of the Midland Supply Depot was completely shorn of her glory.

And what was she doing, Char indignantly asked herself, while the organization which she had practically made was thus abandoned to its own resources?

Nothing.

She paid a purely perfunctory visit, morning and evening, to Sir Piers, who hardly ever heard what she said to him, and had the rest of the day at her own disposal. She had no share in the work of nursing, which was divided between Lady Vivian and the professional nurse who had come from London, and when she rather indignantly demanded of Dr. Prince whether he did not think that he had better utilize her hospital experience at Plessing, the doctor merely replied dryly: "Hospital experience, as you call it, acquired on paper only, won't help you much here, or anybody else either. Nurse Williams can do all that's necessary, and Sir Piers doesn't want anyone but Lady Vivian when he's awake."

"That's perfectly true," said Char sharply, "and that's why I can't help thinking it's rather waste of time for an able-bodied woman with a certain amount of brains to remain here unoccupied when there is so much to be done elsewhere."

"You can take your mother for a walk every day. She is wise enough to take an hour's exercise every afternoon, and Miss Bruce can't be much of a companion. Besides," maliciously added the doctor, who had suffered considerably under the Central Depot's arbitrary interference with his Hospital work, "it'll do you a lot of good to keep quiet for six months or so. You've been suffering from overstrain, whether you know it or not, and your work will be all the better for some relaxation. I assure you, we haven't had a wrong enclosure sent us from the office since you left."

Dr. Prince walked off very triumphantly after this parting gibe.

"Serve her right!" he thought to himself. "Conceited monkey! Perhaps I shall get station transport for my cases properly put through now, without her interference. Hospital experience, indeed!"

"Of course," said Char to Miss Bruce, "a country doctor is naturally jealous of the R.A.M.C. men who've come to the fore. He's never forgiven me for getting his Hospital run on a proper military basis."

"I'm sure he really admires your splendid work, dear, as anybody must, but he's known you ever since you were tiny, so I suppose he allows himself a certain amount of freedom."

Char supposed so too. sombrely enough, and prepared herself to extract from Miss Jones an account of panic at the Canteen on the occasion of the air-raid which should justify her in returning to her post, even in the eyes of Dr. Prince.

Needless to say, Miss Jones was unsatisfactory.

"Oh no; there wasn't any sort of panic at all. Captain Trevellyan was there, and asked us to go to the basement, and we just went."

"John tells me that they were perfectly splendid, all of them, and that you set the first example," said Joanna cordially.

"The whole thing didn't last ten minutes," Grace told them. "We heard all the noise, but didn't see anything. The men did, of course. They saw the Zeppelin come down in the far distance. But by the time we came out there was nothing. It was all over."

"What a shame!" exclaimed Joanna.

"I must institute a proper drill for air-raid alarms," said Char, unsmiling. "That sort of haphazard sauve qui pent is most unofficial. I shall see about it directly I get back."

Joanna put up her lorgnon and looked at her daughter.

She did not speak, but something in her expression made Char exclaim very decisively: "I can't desert my post at a time like this. Everybody must see that unless I had any extremely definite call elsewhere, my place is at the Depot. The work is suffering horribly from this piecemeal fashion of doing things."

She indicated Grace and her sheaf of bulging envelopes with a gesture of condemnation.

Lady Vivian glanced from her daughter's set face to Grace Jones, whose eyes were cast down. Then she left the room without speaking.

Char looked at her secretary, and said, very slowly and stiffly: "I shall probably be back at the office to-morrow or Monday, Miss Jones. You may tell the staff. Sir Piers's condition is not likely to alter at present, and, in any case, the work comes before any personal considerations at a time like this."

There was silence.

"Miss Jones!" said Char sharply.

Miss Jones lifted her great grey eyes and looked straight at the Director of the Midland Supply Depot.

She was not at all an eloquent person, but perceptions much less acute than those of Char Vivian could have felt the intense, almost violent hostility with which the atmosphere vibrated.

Then Grace dropped her eyes and said gently and coldly, in a tone as remote as it was impersonal: "Yes, Miss Vivian."

The encounter had been a wordless one, and, indeed, Char knew that she would never have allowed it to become anything else. The relative positions of the Director of the Midland Supply Depot and one of her staff were far too clearly defined in her mind for that. But it left in her a sort of cold, still anger, as well as an invincible determination.

That night Trevellyan dined at Plessing.

Lady Vivian did not come downstairs until dinner was over and they were in the drawing-room. Then she took out some needlework. Sir Piers had always liked to see her pretty hands working at what he generically called "embroidery."

She sat down under the big standard lamp.

Disquiet was in the air, and Char knew that only the unperceptive Trevellyan was unaware of an impending crisis. Miss Bruce fidgeted with the fireirons, dropped them, and apologized. As though a spell had been broken, Joanna looked up and spoke.

"Char, I don't know if you realize that there can be no question of your returning to the office to-morrow or at all, for the present."

The attack had opened.

Char was glad of it, although a flare of resentment passed through her mind that her mother should have sought a cowardly protection from a possible scene in the presence of John Trevellyan.

"Why not?" she added quietly. "My father is no worse?"

"He is exactly the same. But I am not going to risk any shock or vexation to him. He asked me this afternoon if you were at home, and was glad when I said yes. You know he never liked your doing this excessive amount of work."

"He never forbade it."

"He is not likely to forbid it. When has he ever forbidden you anything? But he thinks that your place now is at home which it very obviously is."

"To do what?" asked Char, with rising bitterness, which she did not try to keep out of her voice. "Does he ever ask for me? Am I of the slightest use?"

"He sees you every day, and he might ask for you at any time. He wishes you to remain at home for the present."

"It's not fair, it's not reasonable. I do nothing here. I am of no use. It's not as though he really wanted me. It's simply because you and he won't be reminded of the war of the ghastly horrors going on all round us won't think of the war, or let it be mentioned. You want to shirk it all--"

"Don't, Char!" said John suddenly. "Don't say things you'll be sorry for afterwards." "No. I shall not be sorry for speaking the truth. You know it's true, Johnnie."

"True!" said Joanna. "What if it is true? Do you suppose that if I can give him one little hour's comfort by ignoring the war, and keeping every thought of it away from him, I wouldn't do so at any cost? The war isn't your responsibility or mine your father is."

She rose, and paced rapidly up and down the length of the room. Char had never seen her mother give way to such impetuous agitation before. She eyed her coldly, but strove to speak gently.

"Mother, if it was anything else I'd give in. But I am doing work in Questerham real, absolutely necessary work and here why, I'm not even justifying my existence."

"You're working here. You do a lot every day, going through all those letters and things with Miss Jones," Trevellyan pointed out.

Joanna threw him a quick glance of gratitude.

"Work here, Char, as much as you like," she exclaimed eagerly. "You can have anyone you please out here so long as they don't make a noise," she added hastily.

The expression was infelicitous.

"You talk as though I were a child, and wanted to have other children out here to play with me. Good heavens, mother! do you realize that my work is for the nation, neither more nor less?"

"If I don't, it's not for want of being told," said her mother with sudden dryness.

"It's easy to say that sort of thing, to accuse me of self-complacency in the tiny little part I contribute to an enormous whole."

"It's not that, Char!" cried Joanna hastily. "I don't care if you have megalomania in its acutest form "Miss Bruce bounded irrepressibly on her chair "but I will not have your father distressed. That's my one and only concern. Johnnie, help me to make her understand."

"I do understand, mother," said Char. "You would sacrifice everything to the personal question women always do. But I can't see it like that. The broader issue lies there, under my very eyes, and I can't shirk it."

"Johnnie!" said Joanna despairingly. "Tell her that she's blinding herself."

"Can't you give it up, Char?" he asked her gently. "You can do work here, you know, and let someone else carry on at Questerham."

"Yes, yes, a deputy. Someone who'll be under your orders," breathed Miss Bruce eagerly.

She cordially wished her contribution to the discussion unuttered, however, when it evoked from Johnnie the inspired suggestion: "Miss Jones! Make her your deputy, Char, and the whole thing will go like a house on fire."

Joanna, still pacing the room, gave a quick, short laugh, which made Trevellyan look at her in wondering surprise, and Char in sudden anger.

"May I suggest--" Miss Bruce began timidly, and paused. "Anything!" said Joanna

brusquely.

"Couldn't Dr. Prince tell us whether there is any reason anything to fear any danger," faltered Miss Bruce, becoming terribly involved.

Trevellyan came to her rescue.

"You mean whether there is likely to be any immediate change, for worse or for better, in Sir Piers's condition?"

"Of course I couldn't go if my father was in immediate danger," quoth Char impatiently. "But he's not. We've already been told so. He may go on in this state for months and months. And at the end of a telephone! Why, I could be sent for and be back here within an hour."

"I'm not discussing the question from that point of view at all," Joanna told her. "The point is not that you should be at hand in case of any crisis, but simply that he should not be vexed. Your insensate hours of work at the Depot vex him."

The words sounded oddly trivial, but no one doubted that Joanna was angry, angrier than they had, any of them, ever seen her.

"Look here, Cousin Joanna, can't we settle this later on? There can be no need to arrange it to-night," said John. "Suppose we let the Doctor give the casting vote, as Miss Bruce suggested?"

He felt pretty sure that no vote of Dr. Prince's would ever be exercised in favour of Char's immediate return to the Midland Supply Depot.

"Dr. Prince is coming here to-night," said Lady Vivian. "He ought to be here any minute now, if it's after nine."

"Ten past," said Miss Bruce, glancing at the clock.

"Neither he nor anyone else can convince me that I ought to remain in idleness when every worker in England is needed," said Char.

"My dear Char, you can't run any risks with Sir Piers in his present condition," said John unexpectedly. "That's what we want Dr. Prince to tell us whether there is any danger to him if you persist in going against his wishes."

Something of condemnation, such as Char had never yet heard in her easy-going cousin's voice, silenced her. She felt bitterly that everyone was against her, no one understood.

Then Miss Bruce's hand came out timidly and patted her on the shoulder. Dear old Brucey! Char recognized her fidelity in a sudden spasm of most unwonted gratitude. Brucey at least knew that a real struggle was in progress between Char's sense of patriotism and the pain that it naturally gave her to resist the wishes of the parents whose point of view she could not share.

For the first time since she was a child, Char felt moved to one of her rare demonstrations of affection towards the faithful Miss Bruce. She smiled at her, pain and gratitude mingling in her gaze, and let her hand lie for a moment on the little secretary's.

Trevellyan leant against the chimney-piece, his hands in his pockets, and looked at Joanna with inarticulate, uncomprehending loyalty and admiration in his gaze.

She was pacing up and down the long room with a sort of restrained impatience, the folds of her black dress sweeping round her tall figure as she moved. In the silence, broken only by the rustling of Joanna's gown, the approach of Dr. Prince's small, old-fashioned motor-car was plainly audible.

Miss Bruce gave one timid look at Lady Vivian, then got up and went to the door.

They heard her speak to the servant in the hall, and then she came back again and took up her place close to Char.

"Did you ask him to come in here?"

"Yes, Lady Vivian. At least, I told them to show him in

here." Joanna resumed her restless pacing.

Then the drawing-room door opened and closed again upon the doctor, entering with the stooping gait of a hard-worked, tired man at the end of the day.

"Good-evening, Dr. Prince," said Joanna abruptly. "Will you give us the benefit of your advice?"

"On whose account?" demanded the doctor, glancing sharply from one to another of the group.

"It's just this," said Char's cool, incisive tones. "My mother wishes to persuade me that my father is not in a fit state for me to take up my work at Questerham again.

That I ought to remain here, doing practically nothing, while there's work crying out to be done."

"Sir Piers is in no immediate danger," said the doctor slowly. "In fact, there is every reason to hope that he is getting better. Otherwise, I suppose, you would hardly contemplate leaving home."

"But she's not suggesting leaving home!" cried Miss Bruce. "It's only a case of going backwards and forwards every day."

The doctor shrugged his shoulders and glanced at Lady Vivian.

"Sir Piers doesn't wish it," said Joanna curtly. "Surely that's reason enough. It distressed him very much, even before he was ill, that she should go and do this office work."

"I see. Yes. The ideas of the present day are not very easily assimilated by our generation," said the doctor gently.

He had often thought himself that Miss Vivian of Plessing had better have worked with her needle or amongst the poor, as had done the great ladies of his own generation, instead of in a Questerham office. But he had also been rather ashamed of his thoughts, and would not for the world have had them guessed by his pushing, good-natured wife, who was proud to let her two daughters help at the Depot.

"We live in abnormal times," Char said. "I'm not doing the work for my own pleasure, but because the need for workers is desperate. I can do the job I've undertaken, and so far as I can see, there is no adequate reason, unless my father gets very much worse, for me to desert it."

"It's not," said Miss Bruce judicially, "as though anyone could take her place at the Depot."

"For the matter of that," Trevellyan remarked, with unexpected logic, "it's not as though anyone could take her place here."

"But that's just it!" cried Char. "I don't do anything at all here. Dr. Prince, you know perfectly well that I don't; we spoke of it the other day. Can you conscientiously tell me that my absence during the day is going to make the slightest difference to my father's case?"

"No. Speaking professionally, I can't," said the doctor.

Joanna stopped in her walking and looked at him, but it was evident that the doctor had not finished. He cleared his throat and faced Char.

"But if you're trying, which you obviously are, to bamboozle me into justifying you in taking your own way, Miss Charmian, then I'll tell you something else. It's not the work you want to get back to, young lady; it's the excitement, and the official position, and the right it gives you to interfere with people who knew how to run a hospital and everything connected with it some twenty years or so before you came into the world. That's what you want. I can't tell you, as a matter of medical opinion, that it will bring on a second stroke, if you vex and disappoint your good father by monkeying about in a becoming uniform and a bit of gold braid on an office stool while he desires you to stay at home; but I can and I do tell you that you're playing as heartless a trick as any I ever saw, making patriotism the excuse for bullying a lot of women who work themselves to death for you because you're of a better class, and have more personality than themselves, and pretending to yourself that it's the work you're after, when it's just because you want to get somewhere where you'll be in the limelight all the time."

There was perfect silence, while the doctor took out a large handkerchief and wiped his forehead.

At last Joanna said dryly: "Well, I don't know that I should have said it myself, but upon my word, Char, I believe you've got the case in a nutshell."

"No!" cried Miss Bruce. "It's unjust!"

Char looked at her, white and smiling.

"Yes, it's unjust enough," she said slowly. "But, as my mother has just implied, it is her own opinion, apparently, as well as Dr. Prince's."

"No! no!" cried Joanna quickly, moving towards her daughter. "Not altogether, Char. Only I can't have your father vexed indeed, I can't."

"You are making it very hard for me. But my choice is made. I cannot, and will not, let a personal consideration come before the work."

"You mean to go back?"

"On Monday the day after to-morrow."

For a moment Char looked at them, superbly alone. Then she moved towards the door. Miss Bruce, looking half frightened and half admiring, crept after her, and Joanna made a sudden movement that caused Trevellyan to put out his hand towards her.

"No, I'm not going to touch her. But if you go, Char, you'll stay in Questerham. I won't have you coming back and disturbing the house and waking him at all hours. I won't have you here at all, unless he asks for you."

Char made a gesture of acquiescence, and went without a word from the room.

"Oh!" cried Joanna, her blue eyes dark and her voice shaking, but unconquerably colloquial in the midst of her pain and anger. "Oh, why in Heaven's name didn't I whip Char when she was younger?"

CHAPTER XI

"ENTER Edith Elizabeth Plumtree, restored to health and happiness. Loud cheers from the spectators."

"Hurrah! How nice to see you back, dear! You look a different girl."

"I feel it," declared Miss Plumtree, exchanging vigorous handshakes with everybody.

"What with her being in plain clothes, and having gone up about a stone in weight," said Tony, "I simply didn't know her at the station. Gracie and I tore down on our bicycles to meet her, and thought of commandeering two orderlies and a stretcher to bring her up from the station. Instead of which she's so much stronger than we are that she pushed both bikes up the hill without turning a hair, while Gracie and I panted in the rear!"

"Doesn't she look well?" cried Grace. "I've never seen her look so well and isn't it becoming?"

Everybody laughed. Personal remarks of any but a markedly facetious order were known by the Hostel to be indelicate; but it was generally conceded that Gracie Jones was so nice it didn't matter what she said, since she probably couldn't help being unlike other people.

Miss Delmege eyed Miss Plumtree's fair round face and plump figure with approval.

"I like that costume," she observed critically. "New, isn't it, dear?" "No, dyed. It's

my last year's grey."

"You don't mean to say it's turned that sweet saxe? Well, you have done well with it! I must commence seeing about my own winter costume, I suppose. I'd been thinking of mole or nigger."

Miss Delmege possessed an almost technical vocabulary of descriptive adjectives which she applied prodigally and exclusively to matters of wardrobe.

She proceeded to elaborate her favourite theme, although unable to command a better audience than Grace, since everyone else immediately became more absorbed than ever in Miss Plumtree.

"Of course, blue's my colour, you know, being fair. Not sky, I don't mean, but royal or navy. But, then, one sees so many of those shades about, and I do like something distinctive."

"You should get some patterns."

"I have done already. You must help me to choose, Gracie. There's a shade of elephant that I rather liked; it would look nice with my cream blouse, I thought."

"Yes, very," Grace agreed cordially, and perhaps not without a hope that this would now close the discussion.

"Then there's the style." Miss Delmege pursued her reflective way. "I thought of a pleat down the centre, being tall, you see; I always think one must be tall to carry things off. Unless, of course," she added hastily, "one has a really perfect figure, like Miss Vivian."

Miss Plumtree turned round.

"How's Miss Vivian? Didn't someone tell me she was back at the office? I suppose her father's better."

"Very much the same," Miss Delmege told her sadly. "Of course, it's perfectly wonderful of her--"

"Oh," said Miss Marsh maliciously, "if you want news about Plessing, Greengage, you must ask Gracie, she's been out there every day in the car, so as to go through the letters with Miss Vivian."

"I say! Really?"

"Yes, rather. She had lunch with Miss Vivian's mother nearly every day." "I rather envied her the motor ride," said Miss Delmege languidly, with the implication that no other consideration could have moved her to jealousy for a moment. "But, as a matter of fact, I couldn't manage to go myself laid up with this wretched flu, you know. I simply wasn't fit to stir. Of course, Miss Vivian knew that; she was awfully sweet about it. But, then, I always say, the attractive tiling about her is that she's so desperately human, when once you get to know her."

"And is she back at the office?" inquired Miss Plumtree, turning a deaf ear to these descriptive touches.

"Comes back to-morrow morning, Monday. Someone from Plessing rang up yesterday afternoon when I was on telephone duty and said so."

"That would be Lady Vivian's secretary, Miss Bruce."

"Yes," said Miss Delmege reflectively. "She's been with them for years, and is perfectly devoted to Miss Vivian. She's too sweet about her Miss Vivian, I mean. I've heard her telephoning sometimes; she calls her Brucey."

"Frightfully human!" was Tony's enthusiastic comment. "Yes, isn't it?"

A moment's thoughtful silence was consecrated to the consideration of Miss Vivian's humanity, and then Miss Plumtree was escorted upstairs to take off her hat.

"Really, that girl looks a different creature!" Mrs. Potter exclaimed.

"Doesn't she? She ought to be most awfully grateful to Miss Vivian. You know Miss Vivian arranged the whole thing? With all she's got to think of, too! But that's Miss Vivian all over. Never lets slip a chance of doing a kindness. I've seen her go out of her way..."

But Miss Delmege's anecdote was not fated to meet with attention. Mrs. Bullivant

walked into the sitting-room looking awestruck. "Girls, who do you think is coming

to sleep here to-morrow night?"

"There isn't room for anyone else, is there?" mildly inquired Mrs. Potter, who slept in a bedroom which contained four beds.

"We shall have to manage somehow. I've just had a note Miss Vivian is coming here."

"She isn't!"

There was a chorus of astonishment; then Miss Delmege's attenuated little tones contrived, as usual, to make themselves audible: "Well, I'm not altogether surprised, do you know? I'd rather suspected something of the kind. Plessing has to be kept quiet on account of Sir Piers; and she's been ill herself, and isn't fit to come backwards and forwards in this cold. I thought something of the kind would be arranged, and I had a very shrewd suspicion as to what it would be "

It need not be added that nobody made the faintest pretence of believing in this prescience.

"Well, I'm blessed!" said Miss Henderson emphatically. "Where is she going to sleep? There isn't a single room in the house, is there?"

"She must have my room," said Mrs. Bullivant simply. "I think I can make it nice and bright for her before to-morrow night. It'll just need fresh curtains and a bit of carpet or two, and I thought you'd let me have the looking-glass out of your room, Miss Jones dear. Mine is such a cracked old tiling."

"Yes, of course. But where are you going to sleep yourself, Mrs. Bullivant?"

"That's another thing, dear. Your room is absolutely the only one where there's an inch of space for a spare bed. Would you and Miss Marsh mind very much....?"

"No," said Miss Marsh emphatically, "of course not. But wouldn't it be more comfortable for you to have a bed in your own sitting-room? There'd just be room behind the door, I think."

"Ah, yes, dear; but, then, I must have somewhere for Miss Vivian's meals. I can't send her down to the basement for supper very well, can I?"

"Hardly!" exclaimed Miss Delmege, with a slight, superior laugh at so outrageous a suggestion.

"I'm sure I hope she'll be fairly comfortable. It's only for a few nights, till she's made other arrangements."

"I can tell you one thing," Miss Delmege remarked authoritatively. "The one thing Miss Vivian hates is a 'fuss. I happen to know that. She'll simply want everything to go on as usual, and to be let alone."

"That's all very well, but it's easier said than done!" even gentle Mrs. Bullivant was constrained to exclaim. "It'll mean an upset for the whole house, with extra meals and everything. I mean, dear, one really can't help seeing that it will. I don't know what cook and Mrs. Smith will say, I'm sure."

"Considering that it's Miss Vivian who pays them their wages, they won't say much, unless they want to be dismissed," Miss Delmege retorted.

Mrs. Bullivant went away looking very much harassed.

"Do let's help her to turn out of her rooms!" exclaimed Grace, "It'll be much easier for her to do it to-night, with us to help her, than to-morrow, when she's sure to be busy all day."

"Good egg! Come on, girls!" cried Tony.

Miss Marsh and Miss Plumtree responded to the summons. They helped Mrs. Bullivant to take her crumpled blouses and limp black skirts from behind the torn curtain where they were huddled against the wall; and Grace mended the curtain while Tony and Miss Plumtree put away the clothes in a big cardboard dress-box, where Mrs. Bullivant said they would do very well for the time being.

"What about that stain on the wall where the damp came through so badly?" Miss Marsh asked doubtfully.

"Pin up a copy of an Army Council Instruction as a delicate attention. Then she can learn it by heart while she gets up in the morning," was Tony's facetious suggestion.

"Put up a map of the Midlands, with a red-ink line round every affiliated depot."

"Don't be silly, girls! You're so foolish I can't help laughing at you," declared Mrs. Bullivant. "No; but I think we might put up a picture or something. Now, I wonder what we've got."

"There are Kitchener and Lord Roberts in the sitting-room," suggested Miss Marsh. "I'll fetch them up."

She ran down, and came back triumphantly with the large framed photogravures. It was found that Lord Roberts would successfully mask the stain on the wall, and Miss Plumtree and Mrs. Bullivant made themselves very dusty by clambering on to chairs and affixing a nail, hammered in with the heel of Miss Plumtree's shoe, from which the picture was finally suspended.

"It looks quite nice and bright, doesn't it?" Mrs. Bullivant asked them. "Not Like Plessing, perhaps but, then, Miss Vivian won't expect that. Now, is there anything else up here?"

"We might put in a kettle," Grace said. "I'm sure she won't have one of her own." So Grace's own kettle, which was a pretty little brass one, was left upon the washing-stand, and Miss Marsh said that Gracie and she would share hers. They went downstairs congratulating one another upon their forethought, and upon the renovated appearance of the tiny bedroom.

Just before supper Miss Delmege, coming upstairs with a graceful, bending gait indicative of still recent convalescence, encountered Grace.

"You've made the rooms look quite sweet, dear, and Miss Vivian is sure to appreciate it. She's one of those people who always notices little things."

Grace was tired, and had run up and down stairs a number of times, for the most part with her hands and arms full.

"I wanted to help Mrb. Bullivant, that was all," she said curtly.

"There's no call to get annoyed, dear!" exclaimed Miss Delmege,

amazed. Grace looked up penitently.

"I know there isn't. I don't know why I sounded so cross. I think perhaps I'm a little tired of the sound of Miss Vivian's name, that's all."

"Well! Of all the peculiar things to say! Upon my word, dear," said Miss Delmege scathingly, "if I didn't know you so intimately, I should sometimes consider your manner downright strange!"

This conviction remained with Miss Delmege. She went into the sitting-room to await the supper-bell, which Mrs. Bullivant generally rang some quarter of an hour after the appointed time, and remarked in a detached voice: "Poor Grace Jones seems rather upset to-night. What I should almost call sort of on edge. I suppose she doesn't like the idea of having to go back to the ordinary office routine to-morrow, after going in and out from Pleasing in the way she has done."

"I didn't notice anything wrong with her, I must say!" exclaimed Miss Marsh, who was both fond of Grace and anxious to miss no opportunity for contradicting Miss Delmege.

"No, dear? Well, perhaps you wouldn't. There's none so blind as those that won't see, and we all know that love is blind," was the gentle response of Miss Delmege, as she sank into the chair nearest the fire.

Miss Marsh could think of no better retort than "I'm sure I don't know what you mean by that, Delmege, and I shouldn't think you did yourself, either."

"There's the bell," said Tony.

They trooped down to the basement, and everyone said how nice it was to see old Plumtree back in her place again, and Mrs. Bullivant triumphantly announced that there would be sausages, because Miss Plumtree liked them, to celebrate her return.

"Not two for me, really, please," Miss Delmege protested elegantly, and manipulated the extreme ends of her knife and fork with the merest tips of her exclusively curved fingers, as a protest against the great enthusiasm displayed by several of her neighbours.

On the same principle, when the sausages were followed by a loaf of bread and a pot of marmalade, Miss Delmege cut up her bread into small, accurately shaped dice, and said, "Pass the preserve if you will, please, dear," between two very small sips at her cup of cocoa. She sat at the foot of the table, and the chairs on either side of her generally remained vacant. Grace came down late, and apologized. One might be, and almost inevitably was, late on week-days, owing to the exigencies of the office, but Sunday supper was something of a ritual.

"So nice and homelike, all sitting down together with no one in a hurry," Mrs. Bullivant always said. But she smiled a welcome at Grace.

"I've kept your supper nice and hot, dear," she said, uncovering a plate next to her own. "Come and sit down here, won't you? You look tired to-night."

Miss Delmege shot a triumphant glance at Miss Marsh, who pretended not to see it, and did not fail to observe that, tired or not, Grace made her usual excellent supper.

"I wonder if anyone has any cigs?" Tony suggested wistfully.

"Yes," said Grace promptly. "Luckily, I have a whole box."

"Oh, you angel! How lovely! I do hate Sundays without a cigarette. Somehow, on other evenings there never seems to be time to smoke, or else one's too tired and goes straight to bed."

In the sitting-room Grace produced her box of cigarettes.

It was almost a matter of course at the Hostel that such things should be treated as belonging more to the community than to the individual.

"Thanks awfully, Gracie."

"Really? Are you sure? Well, then, thanks so much, if I may just one." "Delmege?

Oh, you don't smoke, though, do you?"

"No, thank you. I dare say I seem old-fashioned, but it's the way mother brought us all up from children, and I must say I always feel that smoking is--well, rather unwomanly, you know."

In the face of this commentary Miss Marsh struck a match, and passed it round the room.

The atmosphere became clouded.

"You know," Grace said rather mischievously to Miss Delmege, "that Miss Vivian smokes?"

"She doesn't!"

"Indeed she does. Didn't you know that? Why, I've often noticed the smell of tobacco when she hangs up her coat in the office. It's unmistakable."

"That might mean anything!" hastily exclaimed Miss Delmege. "Tobacco does cling so. Very likely it hangs all round the house at Plessing, you know, with a man in the house and people always coming and going, probably."

"You forget that Gracie knows all about Plessing," cried Miss Marsh instantly. "Of course, she's seen Miss Vivian at home."

"And does she really smoke?" asked Tony.

"Yes, she does. Quite a lot, I think."

"Ah, well, that's different, isn't it?" Miss Delmege's serenity remained quite unimpaired. "One can understand her requiring it. I believe it really is supposed to be soothing, isn't it? Of course, working as she does, her nerves probably require it. What I mean to say is, she probably requires it for her nerves."

"I dare say. I wonder where she'll smoke here?"

"In Mrs. Bullivant's sitting-room, I suppose. Not that she'll be here much, I don't suppose. Only just for her meals, you know, and then to go straight to bed when she gets in."

"I do hope that her sleeping in Questerham isn't going to serve her as an excuse for working later than ever!" exclaimed Miss Delmege, in the tones of proprietary concern with which she always spoke of Miss Vivian's strenuous habits.

"Yes, I see what you mean," Mrs. Potter agreed. "With her car waiting, she simply had to come away sooner or later."

"Exactly; and she's always so considerate for her chauffeur, and everyone. I really do think that I've never seen anyone and I'm not saying it because it is Miss Vivian, but speaking quite impersonally anyone who went out of her way, as she does, to think of other people."

"Look at what she did for me even ordered a cab each way for me!" cried Miss Plumtree, very simply.

"That," said Miss Delmege gently, "is just Miss Vivian all over."

Miss Marsh bounced up from her chair, rudely severing the acquiescent silence that followed on this well-worn cliche.

"I'm going up to get my knitting. I simply must get those socks done for Christmas. I suppose no one will be shocked at my knitting on Sunday?"

"Gracious, no! Especially when it's for the Army. When's he coming on leave, Marshie?"

"Oh, goodness knows! The poor boy's in hospital out there. Can I fetch anything for anyone while I'm upstairs?"

"My work-basket, if you wouldn't mind," said Grace.

"I say," asked Mrs. Potter, as the door slammed behind Miss Marsh, "is she engaged?"

"Oh no. She has heaps of pals, you know," Miss Henderson explained. "She's that sort of girl, I fancy. Haven't you noticed all the letters she gets with the field postmark? It isn't always the same boy, either, because there are quite three different handwritings. And her brothers are both in the Navy, so it isn't them."

"Well," said Miss Delmege, with the little air of originality so seldom justified by her utterances, "they say there's safety in numbers."

"Here's your basket, Graoie," said Miss Marsh, reappearing breathless. "How extraordinarily tidy you are! I always know exactly where to find your things that is, if mine aren't all over them!"

"What are you going to make, Gracie?"

"Only put some ribbon in my things. The washing was back last night, instead of to-morrow morning, which will be such a saving of time during the week. I wish it always came on Saturday," said Grace, serenely drawing out a small folded pile of linen from her capacious and orderly basket.

Everyone looked rather awestruck.

"Do you put in ribbon every week?"

"Isn't it marvellous of her?" Miss Marsh inquired proudly, gazing at her room-mate. "She has such nice things, too."

Grace uncarded a length of ribbon, and began to thread it through the lace of the garment known to the Hostel as a camisole.

"I can't say I take the trouble myself. My things go to the wash as they are, ribbon and all. The colour has to take its chances," said Miss Plumtree.

"Are we going to have any music to-night?" inquired Miss Delmege, with a sudden effect of primness.

The suggestion was received without enthusiasm.

"Then," Miss Delmege said, with a glance at Grace, who had completed the adornment of her camisole, and was proceeding to unfold yet further garments, "I think I shall go to bed."

"Do, dear," Mrs. Bullivant told her kindly. "I hope anyone will go early who's

tired." Miss Delmege smiled cryptically.

"Well," she said gently, "underwear in the sitting-room, you know!"

"Oh dear!" cried Grace in tones of dismay. "Is that really why she's gone

upstairs?" "No loss, either," Miss Marsh declared stoutly.

"But it's only my petticoat bodice."

"I suppose she didn't know what might be coming next."

Grace, guiltily conscious of that which might quite well have been coming next but for this timely reminder, hastily completed her work and put it away again.

She leant back in the wicker chair, unconsciously adjusting her weight with due regard to its habit of creaking, and gazed into the red embers of the dying fire.

Her mind was quite abstracted, and she was unaware of the spasmodic conversation carried on all round her.

Her thoughts were at Plessing.

How could Miss Vivian be coming to stay at the Hostel when her father was so ill, and Lady Vivian alone at Plessing? Grace remembered the expression on Joanna's face when her daughter had said that she could no longer stay away from the office at Questerham.

She supposed that a consent had been extorted from her by Char, unless, indeed, Miss Vivian had not deemed even that formality to be necessary. Grace wondered, with unusual despondency, when or if she should see Lady Vivian again. She felt quite certain now that never again would any pretext induce Char to let her return to Plessing, and was not without a suspicion that she might be made to feel, in her secretarial work, that the Plessing days had not been a success in the eyes of Miss Vivian.

"Never mind; it was quite worth it," thought Grace, and it was characteristic of her that the idea of seeking work elsewhere than with the Director of the Midland Supply Depot never occurred to her.

"A penny for your thoughts, Gracie."

"Oh, they're not worth it, Mrs. Potter. They weren't very far away."

"Perhaps they were just where mine have been all the evening with poor Miss Vivian. She'll be feeb'ng it to-night, poor dear, knowing she's got to leave to-morrow, and Sir Piers so ill. I do think she's wonderful."

"I must say, so do I," Miss Henderson said thoughtfully. "When she used always to refuse me the afternoon off, or any sort of leave, and say that she couldn't understand putting anything before the work, I used to resent it sometimes, I must own. But, really, she's lived up to it herself so splendidly that one can't ever say another word."

"Isn't Sir Piers any better?" asked Miss Plumtree pityingly.

"Not a bit, I think. But he's not exactly in immediate danger, either. Only the house has to be kept quiet, so I suppose she can't come backwards and forwards like she used, and it's a choice between her leaving home or giving up the work altogether."

"Well, I do think it's splendid of her!"

"Because, of course," Tony said, "nobody could take her place here. And I suppose she can't help knowing that. It will seem extraordinary having her in the Hostel, won't it?"

"It won't really be comfortable for her after Plessing, I'm afraid. I wish I could think of some better arrangement..." murmured Mrs. Bullivant to herself.

"Oh, Mrs. Bullivant!" cried Grace Jones. "You couldn't do more than give up your own bedroom and your own sitting-room to her!"

Then, because the heretical words "And that's more than she deserves," were trembling on her tongue, Grace went upstairs to bed.

Her sense of loyalty to her chief did not allow her to throw any doubt on the glory of her return to work under such circumstances.

Moreover, the Hostel's point of view on the subject was as adamantine as it was universal.

CHAPTER XII

THE next morning Char came back to the office. She found her table loaded with violets and a blazing fire on the hearth. Miss Delmege greeted her with an air of admiring wonder, suffused by a tinge of respectful pity, and ventured to hope that Sir Piers Vivian was better.

No one else was sufficiently daring to approach so personal a topic, but little Miss Anthony, blushing brightly, turned round at the door just as she was leaving the room with her work, and said stammeringly that it was so nice to see Miss Vivian back in the office again.

Char smiled.

She was still looking ill, and she knew that her departure from Plessing had been a severe strain on her barely recovered strength. The effort of giving her attention to the arrears of work which required it taxed all her powers of determination.

"Is this all the back work, Miss

Delmege?" "Yes, I think so, Miss Vivian."

"There are several tilings here which ought to have been brought to

me." "I suppose Miss Jones didn't know."

"But she ought to have known. It was most annoying having to leave so much to her. She hasn't the necessary experience for one thing, and is far too fond of acting on her own initiative."

It gave Char a curious satisfaction to say this, in the cool and judicial tones of complete impartiality.

"I shall have a fearful amount to do with these back numbers. Bring me the Hospital files, and the Belgian file, and W.O. letters and--yes, let me see Colonial Officers. That will do for the moment; and send for Miss Collins, please."

The stenographer entered the room with her most degage swing, and seated herself opposite to Char, her pad poised upon her crossed knees.

"Good-morning, Miss Vivian," she said gaily. "Nice to see you back again. I hope you've quite got over the influenza?"

"Thank you," said Char icily. "Please take down a letter to the O.C. London General Hospital."

She dictated rapidly, but Miss Collins's shorthand was never at a loss, and at the end of forty minutes she still appeared tireless and quite unruffled. "That will do, for the moment." Miss Collins uncrossed her knees, and looked up. "I shall be wanting ten days' leave, Miss Vivian," was her unprecedented remark.

The scratching of Miss Delmege's pen paused for a moment, and, although she did not turn round, a tremor agitated her neat, erect back. Char looked at her unabashed typist. "There will be no Christmas leave," she said coldly, taking the resolution on the instant.

"I expect I shall want it before Christmas about the end of this week. The fact is--"

"I'm sorry, but it's quite out of the question. Naturally, one rule applies to the whole staff, and I shall not expect anyone to be absent from duty except on Christmas Day itself, which will be treated as a Sunday. As for ten days, the suggestion is absurd, Miss Collins. I consider that you've practically had ten days' holiday during my absence >and more."

"I've been here every day as usual, and cut any number of stencils, and rolled them off," Miss Collins cried indignantly.

"I'm glad to hear it. Why do you want leave now?"

Miss Collins giggled, tried to look coy, and at last said in triumphant tones, which strove to sound matter-of-fact: "I'm going to be married."

There was silence. Char was drawing a design absently on her blotting-pad.

"My friend is getting leave at the end of next week, and we've settled to be married before he goes out again. He's an Australian boy."

"Of course, that slightly alters the case," Char said at last, stiffly. "Do you wish to go on working here just the same?"

"Oh yes, Miss Vivian. What I feel is, that with him out there, I simply must be doing my bit at home.

It'll take my mind off, too, like, and as he says--

" Char interrupted her ruthlessly.

"In the circumstances, Miss Collins, you can take eight days' leave at the end of this week. But I may tell you that you have chosen a most inconvenient moment, with the Christmas rush coming on and a great deal of back work to be done." Her manner was a dismissal.

Miss Collins left the room.

"Miss Delmege, do you think that we could find someone to replace Miss

Collins?" "For the time or permanently?"

"While she's away, I meant. It would be difficult to get anyone permanently in her place, I'm afraid. Besides, she's an extremely good stenographer, and I can't afford to have one who'll make mistakes."

Char paused, and her feminine curiosity conquered official aloofness. "Did you know that she was engaged to be married?"

"I've seen her wearing a ring, but, naturally, I never come across her except officially," was the haughty response of her secretary.

But however detached she might proclaim herself to be, Miss Delmege did not keep the news of Miss Collins's wedding to herself. In less than twenty-four hours it was known all over the office. It was perhaps fortunate that the Director of the Midland Supply Depot did not know the number of departments in her office that interspersed the day's work with discussions as to what Miss Collins would wear as a wedding-dress. The interest of it almost eclipsed the sensation of Char's own inotallation at tho Hoctol.

She arrived there at nine o'clock that night. It would have been possible for her to leave the office a good deal earlier, but she was aware that the members of her staff would not expect any deviation from her usual iron rule, and were probably telling one another at that moment how wonderful it was to think that Miss Vivian should never have her dinner before half-past nine at night.

Char, tired and oddly apprehensive, was inclined to think it rather wonderful herself. The door of the Hostel stood open to the street, as usual, but since the
air-raid over Questerham all lights had been carefully shaded, and only the faintest glimmer of a rather dismal green light appeared to welcome Char as she rang the bell.

She thought that the hall looked narrow and dingy, and a large box took up an inconvenient amount of space at the foot of the stairs. Then it occurred to her, with an unpleasant sense of recognition, that the box was her own.

"Is that Miss Vivian?" came a voice through the gloom. "Won't you come in?"

Char came in, gingerly enough. Then a match was struck, and Mrs. Bullivant anxiously held up a lighted candle to guide her footsteps.

"Just down the step, Miss Vivian, and I've got supper all ready for you in my sitting-room. I thought you'd like it best there. Our dining-room is in the basement, you know."

"Thank you; this will do very well."

Char looked round the tiny room rather wonderingly. Preparations for a meal stood on a table that was obviously a writing-table pushed against the wall and covered with a white cloth.

"It'll be ready in one minute, Miss Vivian," repeated the Hostel Superintendent nervously. "I'll just go and tell the cook. I expect you must be hungry, and would rather have supper first, and then go to your room. And I'm very sorry, but we've had to leave your trunk downstairs. The stairs are rather too narrow, and the maids thought they couldn't manage it."

Mrs. Bullivant went away, as though supposing that the last word had been said upon the subject of the trunk.

Char thought otherwise.

In a few minutes Mrs. Bullivant came back with a tray, on which stood a cup of cocoa, another one of soup, and a plate with two pieces of bread. "I thought you'd like soup, as it's such a cold night," she said triumphantly. "Now, you must tell me if you have any special likes and dislikes, won't you? I do so hope you'll be fairly comfortable here, Miss Vivian. I can't tell you how very much it's impressed all the girls, your coming here like this, for the sake of the work. I'm afraid it won't be as comfortable as Blessing."

The same fear was also taking very definite possession of Char's mind.

She pulled up a low cane-seated chair to the table and began the soup and bread. The cocoa, already poured out, must, it was evident, be allowed to get cool until the arrival of a next course. This proved to be a dish of scrambled eggs, and was followed by one large baked apple.

Char felt thankful that she had refused her maid's solicitations to come with her. Preston confronted by such a meal, either for herself or for Miss Vivian, was quite unthinkable.

Char thought of Plessing and the dinner that had awaited her there every evening, with Miss Bruce hovering anxiously round the other end of the table, with something like home-sickness.

Then she derided herself, half laughing. What did food matter, after all?

But she decided that Miss Delmege must be told to find her rooms in Questerham as soon as possible. Then Preston could join her.

This last thought was prompted by Char's strong disinclination to unpack, a duty which she realized now would, for the first time, devolve upon herself.

It would not be facilitated by the prominent position given to her trunk in the hall of the Hostel.

"Mrs. Bullivant," said Char, when the Superintendent returned, "my trunk must .be taken up to my room, please."

Her tone was unmistakably, and quite intentionally, that of the Director of the Midland Supply Depot issuing instructions to a member of her staff.

"Yes, Miss Vivian," automatically replied the little Superintendent, and added desperately: "But I'm afraid that cook and Mrs. Smith won't do it not if they've once said they won't."

Char raised her eyebrows.

"If the servants don't obey your orders they must leave," she said. "But isn't there anyone else?"

"Perhaps two of the girls "Mrs. Bullivant hesitated, and then left the room.

Char heard her open the door of the next room, wlu'ch she knew must be the sitting-room, and a babel of voices, immediately became audible. She waited, rather annoyed.

Mrs. Bullivant came out into the hall, followed by quite a large group.

"This is it. Look, dears, can you manage it? Miss Henderson, dear, you're tall."

"Oh yes. It's only up one flight, and it isn't a very large box only an awkward shape. Will someone give me a hand?"

Miss Plumtree, who was sturdy, came to assist, and between them, with a great deal of straining and pulling, and many anxious ejaculations from the door-way of the sitting-room, they slowly lifted the box.

"Don't hurt yourself, now!" cried Mrs. Bullivant. "Get it from underneath, Henderson!"

"Mind the paint on the wall!"

"Mind the banisters!"

"Oh, mind what you're doing, Greengage!"

Similar helpful ejaculations resounded, as the two girls carried the box up the first flight of narrow stairs.

Just as they reached the top step, Char heard the small, clear voice of her secretary, standing in the hall.

"Can you manage, or shall I help you?"

There was a general laugh, echoed from above, as Miss Henderson's voice came briefly down to them: "Thanks, Delmege; just like you, dear, but we happen to have finished."

They all laughed again.

Char, through the half-open door, saw Miss Delmege tossing her fair head. "I'm afraid I don't quite see the point of the joke," she observed acidly.

"Now go in to the fire again, all of you," Mrs. Bullivant exclaimed. "Miss Vivian will hear you if you chatter like this in the hall. I'll tell her the box is safely upstairs."

When she returned to impart the information, Char had shut the door of her little room again.

"Wouldn't you like to come upstairs, Miss Vivian?" the Superintendent asked her timidly. "They've managed to get your box up all right, and I expect you'll be wanting to unpack."

Char wanted nothing less, but she realized that the unwelcome task must of necessity precede her night's rest, and went upstairs with Mrs. Bullivant.

The bedroom seemed to her very tiny, and, indeed, what space there was, her box and dressing-bag mainly occupied. It was also exceedingly cold.

When Mrs. Bullivant had wished her good-night, with a certain wistful air of expecting an enthusiasm which Char felt quite unable to display, she slipped on her fur coat and began to tug at the strap of her trunk.

The process of unpacking at least succeeded in warming her. But there was hardly any room to put away even the limited number of belongings that she had brought, and Char told herself rather indignantly that Mrs. Bullivant seemed to be a most incompetent manager, and might at least have provided her employer with a respectably sized bedroom in her own Hostel.

Towards ten o'clock she heard the sitting-room door opened, and a general whispering and rustling proclaimed that several people were coming upstairs. Char did not, however, at once realize the full significance of the fact that her own room adjoined the bathroom.

A thin but incessant stream of conversation began, punctuated by the loud hissing of a kettle which had overboiled upon the gas-ring. "How's the water to-night?"

"Fair to middling. I don't know who is having baths, but there won't be enough water for more than two."

"It's only tepid as it is."

"I'm so hungry," proclaimed a plaintive voice in incautiously raised tones.

"H'sh-sh! You'll disturb Miss Vivian. Why are you hungry at this hour,

Tony?"

"Well, we didn't have anything frightfully substantial for supper, did we? and I had to go after the scrambled eggs, because I was on telephone duty. So I didn't even have any pudding."

"Oh, poor kid! Couldn't Mrs. Bullivant have got you something?"

"I didn't like to ask her; she's so worried to-night, what with Miss Vivian's coming and everything. Besides "Tony's voice sounded very serious "there never is anything, you know. Only to-morrow's breakfast."

"Hasn't anyone got some biscuits?"

"I'll go down to the kitchen and find some milk for you," said the peculiarly distinct tones of Grace Jones. "I know where it's kept."

"Oh, why should you bother?"

"It isn't at all a bother. You must be starving."

Char heard Miss Jones going downstairs again, and then a triumphant voice proclaimed: "*I* know who has some biscuits! Plumtree. She brought them back from her holiday. I'll go and ask her."

"Come on!"

Evidently Tony and Miss Marsh felt an equal certainty that Miss Plumtree's biscuits could be looked upon as community goods.

There was a silence, before a voice from the next story cried urgently down the stairs: "I say, is my kettle boiling? I put it on the gas-ring ages ago, as I went upstairs. Will someone have a look?"

"It boiled over some time ago," Miss Delmege proclaimed very distinctly. "I took it off for you."

"Thanks very much. I'll come."

There was a hasty descent, evidently in bedroom slippers, and then a long whispered colloquy of which Miss Vivian heard only her own name. Evidently

Miss Delmege, at least, had not forgotten the proximity of her chief. Char several times heard her "H'sh!" her companions in a sibilant and penetrating whisper.

"You can't want to wash brushes at this hour!"

"My dear, I simply must. Just let me have the basin half a minute; I've got the water all ready."

"This your kettle?"

"Yes, dear, thank you."

"Oh, Mrs. Potter, have you actually got some ammonia in that water? I wish you'd let me do my brushes with yours."

"Of course, Miss Marsh. There's plenty of room."

"Well, good-night, girls," from Miss Delmege. "It may seem strange to you, me going to bed before ten o'clock, but it's the life. One gets tired, somehow."

"Good-nights "resounded, and one door banged after another.

There was splashing in the bathroom for a little while, and then silence.

Char realized with dismay that she had no hot water, and that the brass kettle on her washing-stand was empty. After reflection, she filled it from the jug, and decided that she must go to the bathroom where the gas-ring was.

She would not have been averse to being seen by her mother just then. War-work under these conditions could not be mistaken for anything but the grim reality that it was.

Lady Vivian, however, not being present, Char performed her domestic labours unobserved, and went shivering to her bed.

She wondered if anyone would call her in the morning. This, however, proved not to be necessary.

The walls were thin and the stairs only carpeted with oilcloth, and before seven o'clock Char was startled out of sleep by a prolonged whirring sound overhead, which she only identified as that of an alarm-clock, when footsteps hastily crossed the floor above, and it ceased abruptly.

"Who on earth wants to get up at this hour, when they none of them start work before half-past nine!" she reflected rather disgustedly.

But she remembered that Mrs. Bullivant's duties as Superintendent might include the supervision of Mrs. Smith's arrival every morning and the preparation of breakfast, when a step stole past her door, and the reflection of a lighted candle was flung for a moment on the wall.

Conversations in the bathroom were much briefer in the morning than at night. Evidently everyone was too cold, or in too much of a hurry, to talk, although there were sounds of coming and going from half-past seven onwards.

Char went to the bathroom herself at eight o'clock, selecting a moment when it appeared to be empty. She went behind the curtains that screened off the bath from the rest of the room, and found the water very cold.

"Very bad management somewhere," she reflected austerely, and wondered why it should be difficult to provide boiling water by eight o'clock in the morning.

She felt chilled, and not at all rested.

In the little sitting-room downstairs she found a rapidly cooling plate of bacon, uncovered, but solicitously placed on the floor close to the gas-fire, and some large, irregular slices of toast. Marmalade stood in a potted meat jar.

It cannot be denied that Miss Vivian flung an agonized thought to the memory of the admirably furnished breakfast-tray provided for her each morning by the agency of the invaluable Preston at Plessing.

Still very cold, and feeling utterly disinclined for the day's work, Char donned her fur coat over her uniform and went out.

She was not unconscious of the likelihood that her exit from the Hostel might be observed from the windows, and reflected that it would be incumbent on her for the present to take advantage of her new quarters by starting for the office at least an hour earlier than anyone else.

But again she found here inconveniences which she had not taken into consideration. The fire in her office was not yet lit, and the charwoman who had charge of keeping the building in order greeted her with frank dismay.

"Your room isn't done yet, miss."

Miss Vivian, exasperated, and colder than ever, set her lips together in a line of endurance.

"You can leave it for to-day, and in future I wish it to be ready for me by nine o'clock. Please light the fire at once."

The stage of lighting the fire, however, was further off than she realized, and she was obliged to sit huddled in her fur coat, opening letters with mottled, shaking hands that were turning rapidly purple, while the charwoman made an excruciating raking sound at the grate, put up an elaborate and exceedingly deliberate erection of ooal, otioko, and nowcpaper, and finally applied to it a match which resulted in a little pale, cold flame which did not seem to Char productive of anjr warmth whatever.

She sat at her table and wrote:

"DEAREST BRUCE Y,

"Will you send me every woollen garment I have in the world, please? Preston will find them. The cold here is quite appalling, and, of course, one feels the absence of proper heating arrangements at the Hostel terribly. It is, however, naturally much more convenient for me to be able to give more time to the work, which is fearfully heavy after my absence, and will probably increase every day now. I am writing from the office, having been able to get in very early. It might not be a bad plan, later on, to put in a couple of hours' work before breakfast, but please don't let the suggestion dismay you! I shall move into rooms as soon as my secretary can find some, and probably send for Preston. She could be quite useful to me in several ways.

"There is a mountain of papers on my table, all waiting to be dealt with, so I can't go on writing; but I know how much you wanted to hear if the Hostel had proved at all possible. Don't worry, dear old Brucey, as I really can manage perfectly well for the present, in spite of the bitter cold and poor Mrs. Bullivant's hopeless bad management. She had not even arranged for my box to be taken upstairs; and as for hot water, decently served meals, or proper waiting, they are simply unknown quantities. I dare say I shall have to make one or two drastic changes. You won't forget to ring me up if there is any change in father's condition, of course. I could come out at once. This anxiety underlying all one's work is heartbreaking, but I know that I was right to decide as I did, and stick to my post.

"Yours as ever,

"On. VIVIAN.

"P.S. Do as you like about reading this letter to my mother."

It was fairly certain in what direction Miss Bruce's "liking" would take her on the point, and it was not without satisfaction that Char felt the certainty of her voluntarily embraced hardships becoming known at Plessing.

Her letter to Miss Bruce somehow restored to her that sense of her own adequacy which physical conditions of discomfort, against which she had felt unable to react, had almost destroyed.

When Miss Jones came to work, a few minutes earlier than usual, she noted, with a regret that was not altogether impersonal, the cold, bluish aspect of her employer's complexion, and wondered if she dared infringe on Miss Delmege's cherished privilege of producing a foot-warmer.

But she was not aware that her own excellent circulation, quite unmistakably displayed in her face and in an unusually white pair of capable hands, formed a distinct addition to the sum of calamities that had befallen Miss Vivian.

CHAPTER XIII

"CHAR, I've come to warn you," portentously said Captain Trevellyan a week later, entering the Canteen one evening.

"That's very kind of you. Is it another air-raid?"

"No; besides, you're all quite blasees about them now. Miss Jones, single-handed, could cope with--"

"What did you want to warn me about?" interrupted Char, with more abruptness than apprehension in her voice.

"A rescue-party. Miss Bruce is so much upset about you, because she thinks the Hostel is killing you, that she's arranged a crusade to deliver you."

"Miss Bruce means very well, but surely she knows by this time that I don't admit of interference with my work. What does she want to do? "

"You'll see in a minute. I can hear the rescue-party at the door now, I think. They were close behind me."

Char swung round abruptly, and was engulfed in a furry embrace on the instant.

"My dear, pathetic martyr of a child! I've come to take you out of this at once. I hear you've been through the most unspeakable time at that Hostel!"

Char disengaged herself from Mrs. Willoughby's clasp, and endeavoured to silence the intolerable yapping sound that was going on apparently beneath her feet.

"That's Puffles wicked little boy, be quiet. He would come with me, though I told him that all good little boys went to bye-bye at this hour; but he can't bear me out of his sight, you know. Isn't that too quaint? Quiet, Puff! He understands every single word that's said to him, you know. 'Oo clever, clever little man, aren't 'oo? Everything except talk, 'oo can."

"Come, come; he makes a pretty good shot at that, doesn't he?" Trevellyan said dryly.

"Johnnie, go away and find my precious Lance- Corporal for me. He'll never forgive me if I don't go and talk to him; but you've such a crowd here to-night I can't see anyone. Besides, I want to talk to this dear thing. Can't we sit, Char? My dear, never stand when you can possibly sit. That's been my rule all my life, and so I've kept my figure. Not that I'm as slim as you are; but, then, it simply wouldn't be decent if I were, at my age. My Lewis always says that my figure is exactly right, but I dare say he's biassed. Now, dear, what about you?"

"We are particularly busy," Char said pointedly, "and I haven't a moment to call my own. I've only looked in here to-night just to see that everything's in order. Then I must go back to the office."

"Quite unnecessary, I'm perfectly certain. And your looking in here is all nonsense, dear. They all know the work perfectly, and do it far better by themselves than when you're just pottering about, getting in the way. If you put on an overall, and really turned into a perfect barmaid, as I do, it would be different, but just to stand and look on helps nobody, and tires you for nothing. You don't mind my speaking like this? But I know your dearest mother's girl couldn't mind anything, from me!"

Lesbia possessed herself of Char's unresponsive fingers and squeezed them affectionately.

"Now I want to have a real heart-to-heart chat," she proclaimed, lightly but penetratingly.

Char flung a glance round the hall.

One of the men was strumming on the piano, and a group gathered round him was singing and humming, all together, "When Irish eyes are smiling."

The atmosphere was thick with tobacco-smoke, and the demands upon the tea-urns heavier even than usual. Char saw Mrs. Potter, untidier than ever, handing steaming cups across her buffet with incredible rapidity. The noise of
clattered crockery was unceasing. But Mrs. Willoughby's voice dominated all these sounds.

"I've heard the whole story from your beloved mother, ridiculously monosyllabic though she always is, and, of course, from that poor, good creature, Miss Bruce, who is miserable about you. She says that your letters are too heartrending about the misery of that wretched Hostel, I mean. No food, no baths, no fires and in this weather, too! So, my dear child, you're simply coming straight home with me
to-night, to stay until we can find decent rooms for you, or persuade you to give up all this nonsense and go back to Plessing."

"Thank you; but I couldn't dream--"

"Lewis will be delighted. I've explained the whole thing to him, and he's quite overjoyed."

It was impossible, remembering Major Willoughby's unalterable gloom of demeanour, not to suppose that Lesbia's optimism might be overstating the case, but Char only gave a fleeting thought to this consideration.

"It's more than kind of you, but I'm afraid that poor Miss Bruce may be over-anxious--"

"Not another word, Char. Can't we send someone to put your things together at once?"

"Really, I'm most grateful, but I can't accept," said Char decisively. "It's quite true that my secretary hasn't found rooms for me yet, but meanwhile the Hostel does perfectly well, and I'm glad of the

Opportunity for being so near my work. I couldn't dream of moving."

She began cordially to wish that she had not sought to relieve her feelings by those letters to Miss Bruce, from which the little secretary would appear to have quoted so freely, and to have derived so much food for anxiety.

"Dearest girl, listen to me!" Lesbia exclaimed, raising her voice more than ever above the increasing din and clatter all round them. "I've been talking the whole thing over with your mother, and she's more than willing that I should have you. You needn't trouble about that for a moment. Poor dear Joanna was simply too sweet about it for words. 'I know you'll be a mother to my girl for me,' she said."

Lesbia gazed at Char with the air of one who believes absolutely in the pathos she exploits, and Char was forced to the conclusion that she actually imagined herself to be quoting correctly. For her own part, she attached not the slightest value to Mrs. Willoughby's flights of fancy.

Nevertheless, she was vexed and uneasy. Why could not people leave her alone? It was all very well for Miss Bruce to appreciate the stress of circumstances under which Char pursued her work, but the voluble importunity of Mrs. Willoughby was as unwelcome as it was unescapable. Char looked round her, in search of a possible channel into which to direct Lesbia's attention.

"Isn't that your Lance-Corporal?" she rather basely inquired. "Where?" shrieked

Lesbia. "You know, I'm quite, quite blind!"

This was a fiction frequently indulged in by Mrs. Willoughby, whose eye could safely be trusted to pierce the densest crowd when convenient to herself.

"*I* see him, just come in. Now, I suppose he'll make a bee-line straight for my little corner. Dear thing, he always does! It's too wonderful to hear him describe all that goes on out there, you know. He was out right at the very beginning, all through Mons and the Marne and Ypres and everything. They say the men don't like talking about it; but I've had, I suppose, more experience than any woman in London, what with one thing and another, and they always talk to me. The dear fellows in the hospital I visit simply yarn by the hour they love it and it's too enthralling for words. They're so sweetly quaint. One dear fellow always talked about a place he called Wipers, and it was simply ages before I realized that he meant Ypres! Wasn't that too priceless?"

On this highly original anecdote Mrs. Willoughby hurried away, struggling into her blue-and-white overall as she went.

Char saw her reach the side of the Lance-Corporal and break into voluble greetings, punctuated by hysterical protests from the Pekinese, wedged firmly under her arm.

"Well?" said Trevellyan's voice behind her.

"Well! Nothing will induce me to go and stay there, with that wretched little beast making its hideous noise all day and all night."

They both laughed.

"Seriously, Johnnie, I wish you'd tell Brucey that she really has exceeded her privileges. I can't have plans of that sort made over my head, as she should have known. What on earth possessed her?"

"Your letter worried her. She thought that the Hostel sounded so uncomfortable."

"So it is. But, after all," said Char, torn between a desire to show John how very much she was enduring in a good cause, and at the same time how little she heeded such external conditions, "after all the work is what really matters. It's for the sake of the work I put up with what poor Brucey thinks are hardships."

"But are they really necessary?"

"What do you mean?" said Char, displeased. "It certainly isn't possible for a house built like the Hostel to be either as roomy or as convenient as Plessing is. A certain amount of discomfort is practically unavoidable."

"Dear me! that's very hard on all of you. Don't the others find it trying? They have to be there all the time, don't they?"

"What others?" was the freezing inquiry of the Director of the Midland Supply Depot.

Trevellyan looked at her in surprise, and replied quite simply: "The other workers, of course."

"Oh, I really don't know. I naturally never see anything of them, except at the office; but, of course well, I suppose they're used to very much that sort of thing at home."

"Surely not. I was really thinking," Trevellyan remarked with some superfluity, "of Miss Jones."

"You and my mother appear to find some recondite quality in Miss Jones which I'm unable to discover!" exclaimed Char, laughing a little. "Of course she's a lady, but really, as far as work goes--which is, of course, all that matters just now I've had a great many clerks who can be of far more use than she can. It was a mistake having her out to Plessing that time."

She spoke in a reflective tone that had a conclusive quality in it, but the tactless Trevellyan ignored the hint of finality and inquired matter-of-factly: "Why?"

"Because it may make the silly girl imagine that she's on a sort of superior foothold. You know how idiotic some of them are about well, about me as Director of the Supply Depot, I mean. They can't look upon me as a human being at all."

"But you don't seem to want them to, Char. If you can live in the same house with them all and yet never see them except at the office, it's no wonder they don't look upon you as a human being."

He spoke so quietly that it was only after a moment she realized the condemnation that lay behind his words.

It hurt her more than she would have supposed possible. Like most complex organisms, she had an unreasoned craving for the approval of the very simple, and she had always thought that Johnnie, easy-going and uncritical, would accept her judgment as necessarily wider and more subtle than his own.

"I see," she said, very low. "You accept me and my work only at my mother's valuation."

"WeU, no, Char. It isn't only that."

John's voice held a certain regret, but no retractation.

"It isn't only that evening at Plessing though you know very well that I didn't see that question of your leaving home as you did but every time I see you, you say or do something that makes me understand what Dr. Prince meant that evening."

"Thank you," said Char, low and bitterly.

"Perhaps I haven't any business to say anything about it at all. Only," said Trevellyan, with his habitual extraordinarily ill-inspired candour, "you know how much I care about Cousin Joanna."

"So much that it blinds you to any point of view but hers, apparently. Don't you really think that there was anything to be said for me, John? I don't altogether enjoy giving up my whole life to this office work, you know, under conditions of great difficulty and discomfort, and with the additional pain of knowing how hopelessly misunderstood my motives are. What has my father said about my leaving Plessing.,?"

"I don't think Cousin Joanna has told him. You see, he's one of the people who would misunderstand your motives, too, isn't he? And it would upset him so much."

"It's only in theory. He doesn't really want me in the least. It's simply that he hasn't moved with the times, doesn't understand the necessity that has arisen for women's work."

"Yes, that's quite true," Trevellyan said, but there was no sound of concession in his voice.

"My mother has given in to that all the time. You know she has. I believe that if it had been possible she wouldn't have let him know there was a war at all. It's it's like helping an ostrich to bury its head in the sand."

"Don't you see," Trevellyan said, with a curious effect of reluctance, as though aware that she would not see, after all, "that all that is because she cares so much?"

"I'm afraid I don't. To me, the larger issue must always come first. It's England at stake, John, and our own petty little personal problems don't seem to count any longer."

"I suppose," he acquiesced, "that the difference between your point of view and hers is just that. She thinks that the personal problem still counts, you see."

"And you, of all people, can agree to that?"

"It's not quite the same thing for me, is it? War is my profession, so to speak. There are no other claims, so I need not balance values. It's just plainsailing for me. And for most other men, I suppose."

"Do you mean that all the women who have been giving time and trouble to serious work, all the munition-makers, the nurses, the Government workers, ought to go home again because of the old plea that home is a woman's sphere?"

"No, I don't, and you know I don't. But I think that the question of degree enters into it, and that where some women can very well afford to give their whole time and strength, others can't."

"I see. Then it's simply a matter of counting the cost, and if it comes too dear, hide behind the fact of being a woman!" said Char mockingly.

It was always easy to defeat Johnnie verbally.

He looked bewildered, and said: "You're too clever for me, Char, as you always were. I can't pretend to argue with you. And I do admire the work you're doing, more than I can say. Everybody says it's wonderful."

He looked at her wistfully, and Char felt glad that the conversation should end on a note that, on his part, was almost pleading.

She rose, smiling a little.

"It's all right, Johnnie. And you'll soothe Plessing for me, won't you?"

But Captain Trevellyan, also rising, shook his head and looked very uncompromising.

"Cousin Joanna is wonderful, but she looks very tired," he remarked, and moved away as the sound of Puffies's bark heralded Lesbia Willoughby's return.

Char, also moving out of reach as rapidly as possible, saw him making his way towards the corner where Grace Jones was wiping plates as fast as they were handed to her, steaming and dripping, from the zinc wash-tub.

She felt annoyed and almost uneasy, and thought to herself: "He can't be seriously attracted by her. Why, she isn't even pretty, as one or two of them are."

Attracted or not, Captain Trevellyan remained in conversation with Miss Jones for the rest of the evening. Char had not even the satisfaction of seeing her neglect her work, and forthwith rebuking her, for her exceedingly pretty hands never stopped their rapid, moving.

Char decided that she owed it to the uniform to inform her cousin that members of her staff, when engaged in the performance of their duty, must not enter into unofficial conversations.

She reserved this shaft, however, for later on, not wishing Trevellyan to discover the immediate workings of the law of cause and effect.

Her energies for the time being were fully engaged in avoiding the hospitable advances of Mrs. Willoughby.

"Well, my dear, sweet child," said Lesbia acrimoniously, "you are behaving like an absolute little fool (I know you won't mind your mother's greatest friend being perfectly candid with you), and I assure you that you'll regret it bitterly. As my Lewis said to me quite the other day, that girl is simply ruining her chances. Whom does she ever see, shut up with a pack of women all day and every day? Now, with us, you'd at least have civilized meals, with half the regiment always dropping in. The boys in Lewis's regiment always did come to me, from the days when he was only a Captain young things always cling to me."

"Thank you," said Char; "but I'm afraid I shouldn't be very good company. By the time I've finished work, and interviewed all the various officials and dignitaries that I'm unfortunately obliged to see on nine days out of ten, I have not very much conversation left to entertain youths from the barracks."

Mrs. Willoughby made no pretence at failing to perceive the motive inspiring these utterances.

"Yes, dear, you may drag in those moss-grown and mouldering old officials as much as you please to show me that it isn't only a pack of women, but I'm not in the least impressed. Unfortunate old dotards put into khaki which is much too tight for them, and probably thinking what a pity it is that a pretty girl should talk so much nonsense! I met Dr. Prince the other day, and I can assure you that he doesn't in the least enjoy your interference with his Hospital."

"Probably not. I've had it put on to a proper military basis, and all these country practitioners resent anything done by the R.A.M.C."

"Nothing to do with the R.A.M.C., darling," retorted Lesbia piercingly. "Don't be childish! All that lie resents and I perfectly sympathize with him is being shown his business by a chit who, as he says himself, probably would never have come into the world alive at all without his help."

Char left the honours of the last word with the outspoken Mrs. Willoughby, having, indeed, no reply ready to fit the occasion.

"Well, good-night, Char, and if you like to eat humble pie and come to me at any time, Lewis and I will be perfectly delighted. I've always longed to have a girl of my own, as I told Joanna, and I understand all young things. Don't I, my Pufflos I Now I must take 'oo home, precious one, so come along. Oh! mustn't bark naughty, naughty!"

Char turned her back on Mrs. Willoughby and the utterly unsilenced Puff, and left the Canteen.

She had meant to return to the office again, but had stayed longer than usual at the Canteen, and decided to go back to the Hostel instead. Certainly, it was uncomfortable there, and as the piercing weather continued, she found the lack of comfort ever more trying. But to return nightly to Mrs. Willoughby and Puff! She dismissed the thought with a shudder.

Besides, there were her mother and Trevellyan and Miss Bruce to convince that she was in earnest about her work, and would undergo discomfort and privation in order to carry it on successfully. Even Dr. Prince, Char reflected with some bitterness, might admit that she was prepared to make sacrifices in the attainment of her goal.

There was also the Hostel. Char knew from Mrs. Bullivant, and less directly from Miss Delmege, that her staff felt a wondering admiration and compassion at her courage in having left home and a father who was ill for the sake of patriotic work. She knew, by the sort of uncanny intuition that is generally the possession of the ultra-subtle, that when her gaze from time to time became abstracted over her work, or her attitude of set concentration relaxed for an occasional moment, Miss Delmege thought pityingly of the anxiety which must underlie all Miss Vivian's close and capable attention to the many details of her gigantic task. Miss Delmege thought her "wonderful," undoubtedly. Char told herself, with a slight smile, that she did not deserve her secretary's blind idealism of her, but at the same time she was subconsciously aware of a certain resentment that the idealism should be so utterly unshared by Miss Delmege's understudy, the matter-of-fact, eminently undazzled Miss Jones.

Char went into the Hostel still thinking of Miss Jones. The hall was quite dark, but the sitting-room door was open, and as she went upstairs Char glanced in, hearing the sound of voices. There was a circle gathered close round the fire, and for a moment she did not recognize the central figure, seated on the floor and drying a cloud of brown hair at the blaze. Then she saw that it was Miss Plumtree, and noted with surprise that the girl, with her hair on her shoulders and her round, flushed face, was very pretty.

"Perhaps Johnnie was right, and I really don't look.upon them as human beings," she thought, rather amused.

Some obscure instinct of testing herself caused her suddenly to turn and enter the sitting-room.

There was a sudden, startled silence as she stopped in the doorway, and then, almost simultaneously, the members of the staff rose to their feet.

"Oh, don't move," Char said affably.

There was an awkward pause, and then Miss Plumtree, giggling, exclaimed: "Oh, my hair! I've been washing it, Miss Vivian."

"' You're all late to-night, aren't you? I fancy I generally hear you come upstairs earlier than this."

"I do hope we don't disturb you, Miss Vivian," Miss Delmege said, in a concerned voice. "I'm so often afraid that you must hear the water going in the bathroom, and all that sort of thing."

"It doesn't matter."

There was another silence. Nobody had sat down again. Miss Plumtree had clutched at her hair with both hands and was shoving it behind her ears as though in a desperate attempt to convince Miss Vivian that it was not really loose on her shoulders.

Miss Delmege put her head on one side, and gazed at Miss Vivian with a rather concerned expression of attention.

"Well, I'm afraid I'm disturbing you."

"Oh no, Miss Vivian," they chorused politely. "Good-night."

"Good-night, Miss Vivian."

The relaxation of a strain was quite unmistakable in this last chorusing.

"Idiots!" ejaculated Miss Vivian to herself as she went to her own room. She heard voices and laughter break out again as she went up the stairs.

Obviously it was not possible to attempt any unofficial footing with her staff, even had she herself desired such a thing. To them she was Miss Vivian, a being in supreme authority, in whose presence naturalness became impossible and utterly undesirable.

John knew nothing about it.

On this summing up, Char went to bed.

Twice she heard conversations on the stairs, in which the astounding fact that "Miss Vivian came into the sitting-room, and there was Plumtree with her hair down, actually down, my dear." was repeated, and received with incredulous ejaculations or commiserating giggles. Finally, the workers from the Canteen came in, groped their way up in the dark, and were met on the landing by the hissing, sibilant whisper peculiar to Miss Delmege.

"H'sh, girls! Don't make a noise. Miss Vivian has practically told me that she can hear you in the bathroom every night. It really is too bad, you know, when she simply needs every minute's rest she can get."

"Well, so do we. Let me get past, dear." Miss Marsh's tones spoke eloquently of the tartness induced by fatigue.

"Must you go to the bathroom to-night?"

"Of course we must. What an idea! How am I to get my kettle boiled? I'm simply pining for a cup of tea; the work was awful to-night."

"Was Miss Vivian at the Canteen?"

"Just for a bit; talking to that cousin of hers--the Staff Officer one, you know."

"I know. She came into the sitting-room when she got in, and what do you think? Plumtree had been washing her hair, and it was all down her back!"

"Gracious! And Miss Vivian came in?"

"Came in, and there was Plumtree with her hair down her back!" "What did she do?"

"Nothing. There was nothing to do, you know; there she simply was, with her hair actually down her back!"

"I say, Gracie, do you hear that? Plumtree really has no luck. Miss Vivian came into the sitting-room to-night just when she'd been washing her hair, and had it actually down her back."

Char listened rather curiously to hear how Miss Jones would receive this climax. Her voice came distinctly, with a little amusement in it, and the usual quality of sympathetic interest which she apparently always accorded to anyone's crisis.

"Well, I hope she didn't mind. She has such pretty hair."

"That's hardly the point, is it?" said Miss Delmege reprovingly. "It looked rather funny, after all, for Miss Vivian coming in like that, to see her with her hair absolutely down her back."

"Even if it was funny," said Grace literally, "I dare say Miss Vivian didn't notice it. I never think she has much sense of humour. Good-night."

CHAPTER XIV.

"GOOD-MORNING, Miss Vivian."

"Good-morning, Miss Collins. Please take a letter."

The stenographer giggled and tossed her red head: "Mrs. Baker-Bridges, if you please!"

Char looked at her typist blankly for an instant, and then recovered herself, unsmiling.

"Yes. This letter is to the Town Hall Hospital, and I wish you'd remember, Miss Collins, to--"

"I haven't got used to it meself yet," Mrs. Baker- Bridges said coyly. "A double name, too, so I suppose it's harder to remember."

"Will you make me three copies of this, please?" "Yes, Miss Vivian."

Char dictated her letter very briskly, and avoided the use of her stenographer's name, not wishing to submit to further correction. It did not add to her complacency, during the busy days before Christmas, when her instructions were received with an affronted giggle and "Mrs. Baker-Bridges, please, Miss Vivian!"

Char was in rooms now, with the devoted Preston in attendance and occasional visits from Miss Bruce. She was working very hard, and the Christmas festivities indulged in by the Questerham Hospitals frequently required her presence as guest of honour.

Char still retained a vivid recollection of finding herself next to Dr. Prince on one of these occasions, both of them required to join in a rousing chorus of which the refrain was:

"All jolly comrades we!"

And the look which the doctor, singing lustily, had turned upon her, held a humorousness that Char felt no disposition to reflect in her own gaze. She was quite aware that neither of them had forgotten the doctor's peroration delivered on the night of her decision to leave Plessing, and the recollection of it still, almost unconsciously, coloured all her official dealings with him.

It was therefore with surprise that she received an announcement from Miss Jones one evening: "Dr. Prince is downstairs and wants to see you for a moment."

"At this hour? Quite impossible! It's nearly seven, and I have innumerable letters to sign."

Grace hesitated, and then said, very gently: "I think he's just come from Plessing." Char glanced at her sharply. "Ask him to come up, then."

Sudden apprehension had taken possession of her, and increased at the sight of the doctor's kind bearded face, with its lines of fatigue and anxiety.

"What is it, Dr. Prince?"

"Could you spare me a few moments?" "Certainly. Miss Jones, will you--"

Char, glancing round, saw with a slight feeling of annoyance that Miss Jones had not waited to be dismissed. Char did not relish being perpetually disconcerted by the independence of her junior secretary.

"A nice girl, that," said the doctor benevolently. Char looked utterly unresponsive, and supposed rather indignantly to herself that Dr. Prince had not come to the office at the end of a long day's work merely in order to tell her that Mioo Jonoo woo a nioo girl.

Something of the supposition was so evident in her manner that the doctor added hastily: "But I mustn't take up your time. Only I've just come from Plessing, and Lady Vivian asked me herself to come in here for a moment and and tell you ask you, you know--just suggest--only throw it out as a suggestion, since no doubt you've thought of it for yourself "

The doctor fell into a fine confusion, and looked imploringly at

Char. "Is my father worse?"

"No. I didn't mean to frighten you, Miss Vivian; I'm so sorry. He's not worse, though, as you know, he's not gaining ground as we'd hoped, and of course he's not getting any younger. But the fact is, that he's set his heart on your being at home for Christmas." Char drew her brows together.

"Of course, I can arrange to spend a couple of nights there if he wishes it. But my mother laid great emphasis on the fact that she did not wish there to be any going backwards and forwards between the office and Plessing, as you doubtless remember."

"My dear young lady, where Sir Piers's wishes are concerned, she has no will but his. You don't need me to tell you that."

"Of course," said Char musingly, "he has oldfashioned ideas as to one's spending Christmas at home."

"Yes," said the doctor, "that's it. That was our generation, though I'm twenty years younger than your father, Miss Vivian. But early Victorians, I suppose you'd call us both. He can't understand your not being at home, all together, for Christmastime. We can't disguise from ourselves that his mind is a little--a very little clouded, and he doesn't rightly understand your absence."

"I can't go over that ground again," Char told him frigidly. "I was in an exceedingly painful position, and had to choose between my home and what I conceived to be my duty. As you know, I put my country's need before any personal question just now."

"Yes, yes," said the doctor, obviously determined to stifle recollections of his Hospital in its pre-Vivian days. "I--I see your point, you know. But Sir Piers hears very little of the war nowadays, and I don't think he connects your absence with that now."

"What does he suppose, then?" Char asked sharply.

"Miss Vivian, his mind is clouded. We can't deny that his mind is clouded. I believe," said the doctor pitifully, "that he just thinks you are away because Plessing is so dull and quiet. Lady Vivian promised him that you were coming back for Christmas, and it pleased him."

"It is most unjust to me that the facts have not been explained to him."

"But you remember," the doctor reminded her gently, "that they were explained to him before he got ill. And he wanted you to stay at home, you know."

Char was silent.

"Well," said the doctor at length, "Lady Vivian suggested that I should drive you out on Christmas Eve. I shall be going to Plessing then next Thursday."

"Thank you; but I'd better hire something if they can't send the car from home. I may not get away till late. Troop-trains are pouring in, and there is a great deal to be done. There are the Hospital festivities to be considered."

The doctor repressed an inclination to say that he knew all about the Hospital festivities, and instead answered that he quite understood, but could arrange to call for Miss Vivian at any hour convenient to her.

"I will let you know, if I may."

Char, nothing if not self-possessed, rose to her feet, and it became obvious that the interview was over.

"Good-night, Dr. Prince."

The dismissed doctor hurried downstairs, muttering to himself, after his fashion when vexed and disconcerted.

At the foot of the stairs he overtook Grace Jones with her hat and coat on. She looked up at him with her ready, pleased smile.

"Good-night, doctor. I'm so glad you found Miss Vivian disengaged."

"Conceited monkey "began Dr. Prince, almost automatically, then
hastily recollected himself and said: "Yes, yes. Are you off duty now?"

"Just. I've got to go down to the station and see about a case of anti-tetanic serum for one of the hospitals, which is due by the 7.50 train, but I can take it up there
to-morrow. You know how precious it is, and we daren't trust the orderlies with it since. Coles had that smash."

"To be sure. Well, I'll drive you down in my car to get it, if you like, and then I can take it up to the Hospital. I've got to go there again to-night."

"Oh, thank you."

The doctor liked the pleased gratitude in Grace's voice.

"I want so much to know how Sir Piers Vivian is," he said presently. The doctor

shook his head.

"A question of time, you know, when there's been a stroke at that age. He doesn't rally very much, either. And the brain, Miss Jones, is clouded. We can't deny that it's clouded."

"Oh, poor Lady Vivian!"

"She knows it as well as I do. Doesn't let on, you know, but she's never been deluded from the first. And there she is all day, in the room, you know, except just when he's sleeping, reading to him, and talking quite cheerfully and trying to get him to take a pleasure in some little thing or other. I've never seen her break down, and we doctors see that sort of thing when other people don't sometimes. But she's been under a strain for a long while now oh, before he got ill and yet she carries on somehow. Ah, breeding is a wonderful thing, Miss Jones. There have been Vivians at Plessing for more generations than I can count, and she was a Trevellyan. They're from these parts, too, though it's a West Country name. I may be an old snob, Miss Jones, but I was brought up to reverence those whom God Almighty had set in high places, and the Vivians of Plessing have always stood to me for the highest in the land. A pity there isn't a son there!"

"Yes."

"There are cousins, of course. Sir Piers has a brother with children. But one would have liked the direct line and for her to leave Plessing, it seems hard. If there 'd only been a boy!"

"He would be fighting now," Grace reminded him. "To be sure, and so many only sons have gone. If Miss Charmian there had been a boy, though! I tell you frankly," said the doctor, in an outburst, "that I don't understand her. She and I have had ructions in our time, Miss Jones, and I've known her ever since she came into the world. And now, when it comes to a Hospital Return!"

The doctor nearly swerved his car into a market waggon, apologized to Grace, and said candidly: "I really hardly know what I'm at when I get on to the subject. Army Form 1864A in duplicate, indeed! And as for the Nomenclature of Diseases that we hear so much about nowadays, I rather fancy that I was at home there some twenty years before Miss Charmian's little typewritten pamphlets on the subject were issued. Telling me that conjunctivitis is a disease of the eye, and what V.D.H. stands for! War Office instructions, indeed!"

Grace laughed discreetly, and after an instant the doctor laughed too.

"Well, well, well, we're all working in a great cause," he conceded, "and I suppose she does wonders. They all tell me so. Perhaps it seems a little hard to those of us who've been trying to conquer pain and disease for a number of years to be put under military discipline by an impudent monk H'm, h'm, h'm! by a young lady in a uniform striped with gold like a zebra! But she's certainly untiring in her work; so are you all. This must be quite a new style of thing to you, Miss Jones?"

"I was in a hospital for a little while at the beginning of the war, but I can only do clerical work."

"But nothing before the war, eh?"

"Oh no. I just helped my father at home."

"I thought so," said the doctor, with an odd sound of unmistakable satisfaction in his voice. He was glad that this nice little girl who listened with such interest while he talked, and so evidently admired Sir Piers and Lady Vivian of Plessing, should have lived at home before the war and not gone dashing out in search of an independent livelihood.

"Lady Vivian asks after you very often," he told her. "You saw her every day for a time, didn't you?"

"Yes, while Miss Vivian was at Plessing. I should like to see her again. Will you give her my love?" said Grace.

"Yes, indeed I will. She's lonely out there, I often think, though young Trevellyan comes out when he can. Nice boy that, but they'll be sending him out again directly, I suppose. Now, then, Miss Jones, here's the station."

Grace despatched her business at the parcels office as quickly as possible, and came back with the neat wooden case carefully labelled all over.

"Put it there; it'll be quite safe. I wish I could take you back to Pollard Street, but they're expecting me at the Hospital and I must get on. Shall you be all right?"

"Oh yes, and thank you so much. The walk will warm me, and it isn't far. Good-night, doctor."

"Good-night," responded the doctor cordially as the car started down the hill towards the Hospital.

He wondered whether Char would accept his offer to drive her out to Plessing on Christmas Eve, and reflected rather ruefully that, if so, it would certainly be a late and cold transit. But, at all events, his mission would have succeeded.

He triumphantly told Lady Vivian next day that Char was coming to Plessing on Christmas Eve.

"I put the case diplomatically, you know just used a little tact, and she never made any difficulty at all. Delighted to come, if you ask me." said the doctor.

"Thank you so much, Dr. Prince. I've told Sir Piers that she's coming, and he's so pleased. Don't let her start too late; it's so bitterly cold and the roads are very bad. I can't send the car in for her, as you know; since the chauffeur was called up, I've no one to drive it. But if you're kind enough to bring her--"

"I'll bring her fast enough, if she'll let me," said the doctor. "Anyhow, she shall come, which is the point. She said at once that she'd come."

"Yes," said Joanna dryly. "You won't expect me to be enthusiastic at such condescension, will you?"

The doctor looked at her with concern evident in his shrewd, kindly gaze.

He had known Joanna Vivian ever since she had come to Plessing as a bride, and had never heard that note of bitterness in her voice before. He told himself sadly that the long strain of Sir Piers's illness was telling on her at last, in spite of her splendid physique. In his heart the doctor did not believe that the strain would last much longer.

"I wish you had someone here to keep you company," he said awkwardly. "Even Miss Bruce was better than no one."

"She's only with Char for a few days. She'll soon be back, probably to-morrow. And meanwhile I had an offer of companionship only this morning. Do you know Mrs. Willoughby?"

"Good Lord, yes!" said the doctor, and they both laughed.

"I should really like Char's Miss Jones to come out to me for a few days," said Joanna, rather wistfully. "She and I understood one another very well, and she's such a restful person."

"A thoroughly nice girl, and most intelligent," warmly remarked the doctor, reflecting how sympathetic Miss Jones had shown herself to be over the question of Medical Boards. "Why shouldn't I bring her out with Miss Charmian on Thursday night?"

"I only wish you would, but I don't want to throw Char into a fit."

"I'll chance that," said the doctor grimly. "She'd only tell me that fits are a disease of the nervous system, and should be shown as N.S. on all Hospital returns."

He told himself that if Lady Vivian wanted to see Miss Jones it was preposterous that she should not be allowed to have her out to Plessing. Diplomacy, the doctor reflected, could arrange the whole thing.

Believing himself to be the possessor of this attribute, Dr. Prince, on the morning before Christmas Eve, rang up the office of the Midland Supply Depot on the telephone.

"Can I speak to Miss Vivian, if you please?"

"Who is it?" inquired an attenuated voice at the other end.

"The Officer Commanding Questerham V.A. Hospital," firmly replied the

doctor. If Miss Vivian wanted officialness, she should have it.

"Can I give a message for you?"

"I'm afraid I must speak to Miss Vivian herself." "One moment, please."

The doctor waited, and presently the voice said: "I've put you through to Miss Vivian."

"Hallo!" exclaimed a weary tone. "Miss Vivian speaking."

"Good-evening," said the doctor briskly. "What time am I to call for you to-morrow afternoon?"

"Oh, is that you, Dr. Prince? But you really mustn't trouble to call for me; I can hire something."

"Not on Christmas Eve."

"Perhaps not. Well, let me see. Unless anything unforeseen occurs I think I could get away by eight."

"That will do splendidly," ruefully said the doctor, aware of sacrificing truth to diplomacy. "I suppose your office work will go on without you just the same?"

There was a pause, which the doctor interpreted as an astounded one.

"The office will treat Christmas Day as a Sunday. It will probably be necessary for me to come in during the afternoon, as I do on Sundays, but only for a few hours."

The doctor gathered himself together for a Machiavellian effort.

"Why not leave that very intelligent little secretary of yours, Miss Jones, to take your place?"

"A junior clerk? Out of the question. But I needn't trouble you with those details, of course. As a matter of fact, no one will be here on Christmas Day except the telephone clerk."

"I strongly advise you to leave Miss Jones in charge, if I may be permitted to suggest it."

"Miss Jones," said Char, very distinctly, "has none of the experience necessary for a position of responsibility, and I should not dream of entrusting her with one. She will have nothing whatever to do with the office during my absence."

The triumph of diplomacy was complete. "In that case," said the doctor in a great hurry, "your mother need have no scruple as to inviting her out to Plessing for Christmas. I know she wants to in fact, I'm charged with the invitation but it seemed incredible that you should be able to spare her from her work. But I mustn't keep you. Goodnight, Miss Vivian. At eight to-morrow I'll come for you both. Good-bye."

The triumphant doctor put back the receiver.

"Hoist with her own petard!" he muttered to himself in great satisfaction.

That afternoon he found time to call on Miss Bruce, on the verge of departure from Char's lodgings, and triumphantly charged her with a message for Lady Vivian.

"Tell her that I've arranged the whole thing, and Miss Jones is coming out to-morrow evening in the car to spend Christmas."

"At Plessing? But why?" asked the astonished Miss Bruce.

"Because Lady Vivian wants her," said the doctor stoutly. "She's taken a fancy to her, and I'm sure I don't wonder. A charming girl!"

"I had an idea that Miss Vivian never thought her very efficient," doubtfully remarked Miss Bruce.

"There are a great many people whom she doesn't think efficient, although they've been at their job more years than she's been out of long clothes; but in this case it serves our turn very well. She'll be out of that confounded office for a couple of days."

"Does Miss Vivian know this?"

"Dear me, yes," said the doctor glibly. "I talked it all over with her on the telephone this morning. That's quite all right. Now, Miss Bruce, supposing you let me give you a lift to the station? It's going to snow again."

Miss Bruce accepted gratefully, and the doctor felt slightly ashamed of his own strategy for avoiding any possible conversation between her and Char on the subject of Miss Jones's visit to Plessing.

Diplomacy was not an easy career.

Nothing now remained, however, but to tell Miss Jones of her invitation and to insure her acceptance of it.

The indefatigable doctor stopped his car at the door of the Hostel soon after half-past seven that evening.

"Would Miss Jones be good enough to speak to me for a moment?" he inquired, when Mrs. Bullivant came to the door.

"I'm sorry, but I think she's out. Some of the girls have gone to the theatre to-night. Is it a message from Miss Vivian?" the Superintendent asked anxiously.

"Not exactly," was the evasion exacted by diplomacy.

"Shall I give her any message when she gets back?"

"Yes, yes; that might be best," eagerly said the doctor, conscious of cowardice. "Would you tell her that Lady Vivian and and Miss Vivian are both expecting her at Plessing to-morrow evening, to spend a couple of days? Lady Vivian particularly wants to see her again, and it will be good for her to have someone to cheer her up. Tell Miss Jones that it's all been arranged, and I'll call for her at the office
to-morrow evening at eight o'clock and drive her out. I've got to go out there in any case, and the last train goes at four, so they must go by road."

"Well, I'm sure that will be delightful for her!" exclaimed the unsuspecting Mrs. Bullivant. "How very kind of Miss Vivian!"

"Yes. It's Lady Vivian, of course, who really suggested the idea, one day when I happened to mention Miss Jones. She likes her very much, a ad, of course, it's lonely for her now. I'm glad this should have been thought of," said the doctor, with a great effect of detachment. "Well, I mustn't keep you at the door in this cold. It's freezing to-night again, unless I'm much mistaken. Good-night."

"Good-night, doctor. I won't forget the message. I'm delighted that Gracie should have such a treat."

The doctor, as he drove away, was delighted too, with himself and with the success of his manoeuvres. He thought that Lady Vivian would be very glad to see the girl for whom she evidently felt such a sense of comradeship, and he, like Mrs. Bullivant, was glad of the pleasure for Grace; but, most of all, the doctor felt a guilty satisfaction in the knowledge of having successfully outwitted the Director of the Midland Supply Depot.

CHAPTER XV

"TELL Miss Vivian that we can't wait; we must start at once. The sleet has been falling, and the roads will be impossible in less than an hour. I don't know how the car will do it as it is."

Dr. Prince was harassed but determined.

Miss Marsh reluctantly took this message upstairs. She had already had occasion to observe during the course of the evening that Miss Vivian was in no frame of mind to welcome interruptions.

"I'm not ready."

"No, Miss Vivian."

Miss Marsh stood unhappily in the doorway.

"What the dickens are you standing there for?" cried Miss Vivian in exasperated tones.

Miss Marsh was standing there from her own intimate conviction of being placed between the devil and the deep sea, and her extreme reluctance to confront the impatient doctor with Miss Vivian's unsatisfactory reply. To her great relief, she found Grace in conversation with him.

"Well, is she coming?"

"The moment she can, Dr. Prince. She really won't be long now," was Miss Marsh's liberal interpretation of her chief's message.

"The thaw isn't going to wait for her," said the doctor grimly. "It's begun already, and after three weeks' frost we shall have the roads like a sheet of glass."

"I think I hear the telephone," said Miss Marsh, hastening away, thankful of the opportunity to escape before the doctor should request her to return with his further commands to Miss Vivian.

But presently Char came downstairs in her fur coat and heavy motoring veil, carrying a huge sheaf of papers and a small bag.

"I'm sorry you've been kept waiting. I was afraid that, as I told you, I might not be able to start punctually."

"It's this confounded change in the weather," said the doctor disconsolately. "How could one guess that it would choose to-night to begin to rain after three weeks' black frost? However, I dare say it won't have thawed yet. Come along. At any rate, it won't be quite so cold."

The little car standing at the door was a very small two-seater, with a tiny raised seat at the back.

"Where will you sit, Miss Vivian, with me in front or on the back seat?" inquired the doctor unconcernedly. "Have either of you any preference?"

"I think I'd better come in front," said the Director of the Midland Supply Depot, very coldly. She took no notice of Miss Jones.

It was very dark, and a thin, cold rain had begun to fall. The doctor groaned, and drove out of Questerham as rapidly as he dared. On the high road it was already terribly slippery. After the car had twice skidded badly, the doctor said resignedly: "Well, we must make up our minds to crawl. Lady Vivian will guess what's delayed us. I hope you had dinner before starting?"

"Yes, thank you," replied Grace serenely.

"Naturally, I haven't been able to leave the office, but then I never have dinner till about nine o'clock," Char said. "I've almost forgotten what it is to keep civilized hours."

"Then, all I can say is, that you'll be extremely hungry before we get to Plessing," was the doctor's only reply to this display of patriotism.

The car crawled along slowly. About four miles out of the town the doctor ventured slightly to increase speed. "Otherwise we shall never get up this hill," he prophesied.

"It's better here, I think," said Char. "I think it is. Now for it."

The pace of the little car increased for about a hundred yards. Then there was a long grinding jar and a violent swerve.

"Confound her! she's in the ditch!" cried the doctor. "Are you all right there, Miss Jones?"

"Yes," gasped the shaken Grace, clinging to her perch.

"Get out," the doctor commanded Miss Vivian, in tones that suggested his complete oblivion of their respective positions as regarded official dignity. Char obeyed gingerly, and stood grasping the door of the car.

"Take care; it's like a sheet of ice." The doctor slid and staggered round to the front of his car, the two front wheels of which were deeply sunken in the snow and slush of the ditch. He made a disconsolate examination by the light of the lamps.

"Stuck as tight as wax. Now, what the deuce are we to do?"

"Can't we move her?" asked Grace. "Not much chance of it, but we might as well try." Grace got down, and they strained at the car, but without any success.

"No use," said the doctor briefly. "I think you two had better stay here while I get back to Questerham we're nearer Questerham than Plessing, I fancy and bring something out. Though, good heavens! I'd forgotten it's Christmas Eve. What on earth shall I get?"

"I can authorize you to call up one of the ambulance-cars."

"That's an idea. I'm sorrier than I can say to leave you on the roadside like this," said the doctor distractedly. "Put the rug round you both, and if anything comes past, get a lift. The car will be all right. I defy the most determined thief to make her move an inch. H'm! I must take one of these lamps, and I'll make as much haste as this confounded sheet of ice will allow."

"Wait!" cried Grace. "I can hear something coming, I think."

They stood and listened. The hoot of a very distant motor-horn came to them distinctly.

"Coming towards us," was the doctor's verdict. "With any luck it'll take you both back to Questerham. It's your best chance of getting to bed to-night. Miss Vivian, you're shivering. Confound it all, it's enough to give you both pneumonia, hanging about on a night like this! What an old fool I've been!"

"It couldn't be helped, could it?" said Grace. "There were no trains running after four o'clock, and we couldn't guess the weather would change so. And it isn't nearly so cold as it has been."

"Have a cigarette?" said the doctor suddenly, lighting his own pipe. "It'll help you to keep warm."

"Smoking in uniform is entirely out of order, but for this once thank you," said Miss Vivian, with a slight laugh.

The sound of a motor-bicycle became unmistakable, and the doctor advanced cautiously into the middle of the road.

"Ahoy, there! Could you stop half a minute? We've had a spill. Two ladies here."

"Is that Dr. Prince?" came a voice that made Char exclaim: "It's John

Trevellyan!" The motor-bicycle, with its small side-car, drew up beside them.

"Have you had a telephone message?" said John.

"From Plessing? No. What's happened?" said the doctor sharply.
The two men exchanged a look.

Char came forward.

"You'd better tell me," she said in her slow, deep drawl.

"Cousin Joanna telephoned just before eight o'clock, but you must have started," John said gently. "She wanted to ask Dr. Prince to make as much haste as possible and you."

"My father?"

"I'm afraid it's another stroke, my dear."

The doctor asked a few rapid professional questions, and Grace came and stood near Char Vivian.

"When you didn't come," said John, "Miss Bruce got anxious, and felt sure there 'd been a spill. Cousin Joanna was upstairs, with him; I don't think she realized. So I brought the only thing I could get hold of. You can ride a motor-bike, doctor?"

"Of course I can. But we can't leave two young ladies planted in a ditch, with that confounded machine of mine," said the doctor, his distress finding vent in irritability.

"There's the side-car," said Grace.

"Miss Vivian must go with you, doctor." "Can't we get your machine out of

the ditch?" John suggested.

"Not unless you're a Hercules," said the doctor crossly. He began to examine the motor-bicycle.

"I can manage this all right, though no machine on earth will do anything but crawl on such a road. Miss Vivian, that will be our best plan."

"Yes," said Char, very quietly. "And, Johnnie, can you look after Miss--er-- Jones, and take her back to Questerham?"

"Get in, Char," said Trevellyan. "I shall certainly look after Miss Jones, and bring her out to Plessing somehow or other. Your mother wants her. Send anything you can to meet us, doctor."

"Right; but I'm afraid we can't count on meeting anything to-night, of all nights. Miss Jones, I'm so sorry. All right there?"

The motor-bicycle, with a push from Trevellyan, jolted slowly away along the slippery road, and John and Miss Jones stood facing one another by the indifferent light of the motor-lamps.

Grace looked at him with her direct, gentle gaze. "Please tell me whether you really meant that," she said. "Does Lady Vivian want me at Plessing just the same?"

"Yes," he answered, with equal directness. "She said so. She told me to bring you. She said she wanted you."

Grace drew a long breath, then said: "We shall have to walk, shan't we?"

"I'm afraid so at least part of the way. Unless you'd rather stay in the car, and keep as warm as you can, while I go on to Questerham and try to get hold of something that will take us both out? I'm going back there, of course. Which shall we do, Miss Jones?"

"Walk, I think. It's only about five miles, and I doubt if you could get anything to-night to go out all the way to Plessing."

"I think we can go across the fields, if you don't mind rough walking. It saves nearly a mile, and the only advantage of keeping to the road would be the chance of meeting something, which I think most unlikely. Miss Jones, you're splendid. Do you mind very much?"

"Not now that I know Lady Vivian really wants me," said Grace

shyly. Trevellyan unhooked one of the lamps.

"Shall I carry the other one?"

"It will make your hands very cold, and I think one will be enough. Have you anything that you must take?"

"My bag; it isn't heavy."

"Right. Then give it to me, and you take the lamp, if you will." Grace obeyed without any of the protestations which might have appeared suitable, and they started very cautiously down the road.

"Keep to the side," said Trevellyan; "it's not very bad there. I'm afraid you'll never get warm at this rate, but a broken leg would be awkward."

"Tell me what happened at Plessing."

He told her that Sir Piers had suddenly had a second stroke that afternoon, and was again lying unconscious. Lady Vivian had come down and spoken with Trevellyan for a few minutes, and assured him that the trained nurse would not allow her to relinquish hope.

"But it all depends upon what one means by hope," said Trevellyan. "One can hardly bear to think of his lying there day after day, unable to understand or to make himself understood and as for her "She is very brave," said Grace. There was a silence, and each was thinking of Joanna.

Presently Trevellyan spoke again.

"We shall turn off in a minute and take the short cut. Are you very

cold?" "Pretty cold, but I'm glad I had dinner before starting. Did you?"

"No, worse luck! I started from Plessing at halfpast eight, and the servants were in such a fuss. I'm fearfully hungry," said Trevellyan candidly.

"Well, wait a minute."

Grace stood still and put the lamp on the ground while she felt in her coat-

pocket. "I thought so. I've a packet of chocolate. Will you take it?"

"Thank you," said Trevellyan seriously; "it's very kind of you. Let's both have some."

Grace divided the little packet scrupulously, and they stood and ate it with their backs to the hedge, the bag and the lamp on the ground in front of them.

"Christmas Eve!" said Grace. "Isn't it extraordinary?" "Where were you last Christmas?" he asked.

"In the hospital, near my home. We were decorating the wards for Christmas, and all stayed there very late. There was a convoy in, too, I remember; the nurses stayed on long after we'd all gone home. I was only a clerk, you know."

"I remember. You told me that when you on the night of the air-raid," said the tactful Trevellyan, with a very evident recollection of the unfortunate disability which debarred Miss Jones from the nursing profession.

Grace laughed.

"Exactly. It is so idiotic and provoking, and, as a matter of absolute fact, it was because I always got ill at anything of that sort that they couldn't let me go on at the hospital any more my father and stepmother, I mean."

"I didn't know you had a stepmother."

"I've had her about four years," Grace informed him.

"Do you like her?" Trevellyan asked bluntly.

"Very much indeed. She's only a few years older than I am, and she lets me call her Marjory. She's so nice and pretty and merry."

It was evident that Miss Jones was not a person to make capital out of circumstances.

When they started again, Trevellyan said gently: "You'd better take my arm, if you will. It's heavy going along this field."

It was, and an incessant sound of splashing told Grace that she was almost in the ditch.

"I think I can manage," she said breathlessly. "I'm afraid of the light going out, and it's easier to hold in both hands."

Trevellyan said nothing, but presently Grace felt him take hold of the lamp.

"You must let me," he said quietly. "You'll want all your strength, for we're going uphill now, and the ground's very rough."

They trudged up a steep incline, Grace with both cold hands deep in her pockets and her head bent against the wet driving mist that seemed to encompass them. Her feet were like ice, and she had long since given up trying to avoid the puddles and small snowy patches that lay so plentifully on the way. Twice she stumbled heavily.

"We're just at the top," said Trevellyan encouragingly. "You're perfectly splendid, Miss Jones, and I feel such a brute for not taking better care of you.

Cousin Joanna will be very much distressed; but, you see, I know she wants you."

"I'm very glad," said Grace simply. "I never admired anyone so much as I do her."

"Nor I. She's been so ripping to me always. Even when I was a big clumsy schoolboy, with nowhere to go to for the holidays, she'd have me out to Plessing, and make me feel that she cared about having me there. She wrote to me all the time I was in India I don't think she ever missed a mail and all the time I was in Flanders last year. Some day," said Johnnie, rather shyly, "I'd like to show you her letters to me.

No one has ever seen them. But I've always felt that you knew what she really is more than other people do."

"Thank you," said Grace.

John seemed satisfied with something in the tone of the brief reply, and they went on in silence till he raised the flickering lamp.

"Wait a moment. There ought to be a fence here, and it may be barbed wire. Take care."

Grace was thankful to stand still, her aching legs still trembling beneath her from the ascent. John held up the lamp and made a cautious examination.

"There ought to be an opening here we are."

He waved the lamp in triumph; the light gave a final flicker and expired.

There was a dead silence from both, Grace speechless from dismay and fatigue, and Trevellyan from his inability to express his feelings in the normal manner in the presence of Miss Jones.

"Have you any matches?" she asked at last.

"Yes. I'm sorrier than I can say, but I'm very much afraid that the wretched thing has given out. Why on earth the doctor can't get proper electric lamps for his rotten car--"

John fumbled despairingly amongst his matches, made various unsuccessful attempts, and at last apologized again to Grace, and said that it never rained but it poured. They must go on in the dark.

"Very well. Only let's avoid the barbed wire."

"Miss Jones, I can't tell you what I think of you. Anyone else would be perfectly frantic."

"But I'm never frantic," said Grace, rather regretfully. "I often wish I was like the people in books who feel things so desperately. Maggie Tulliver, for instance. It's so uninteresting always to be quite calm."

"Always?"

"Well," said Grace, "practically always."

"It's an invaluable quality just at present, but perhaps one of these days--

" "I'm so sorry, but I think my skirt has caught in the barbed wire."

Trevellyan released her skirt in silence.

"Now, then, if we get through the gate here, the next field takes us on to the road again, and with any luck they'll have got to Plessing and sent something back to pick us up."

Trevellyan, who knew his ground and appeared able to see in the dark, pushed at the creaking wooden gate, and Grace passed through it, feeling her feet sink into an icy bog of mud and water.

"I'm afraid I can't see much. You see, I don't know the way at all."

"I know; it makes all the difference. Look here, will you let me take your hand? I know every inch of the way."

Grace put out her small gloved hand and said very sedately: "Thank you; I think that will be the best way."

They went on steadily after that, speaking very little, and Grace stumbling from time to time. Once John asked her: "Are you very tired? This is rotten for you."

"I don't mind," said Grace shyly.

After a long pause, Trevellyan said cryptically: "Neither do I."

On this assurance they reached the high road, and Grace said gently, withdrawing her hand: "I can manage now, thank you."

"It can't be long now before something meets us. I don't know what they can send; but if it's only a farm cart, it will be better than nothing."

"Luckily I'm a very good walker. I don't think that poor Miss Vivian could ever have got out to

Plessing unless we'd met you with that motor-bicycle. She dislikes walking, and is not used to it."

"I wouldn't have had this walk with Char," said Trevellyan fervently, "for any money you could offer me. She's a splendid companion, of course, on her own ground, but for this sort of thing it's only two people in a million, Miss Jones, who could do it without hating one another for ever afterwards."

"We must be very remarkable, then, for I don't think it's going to have that effect, "said Grace, laughing.

"As far as I'm concerned," said Trevellyan slowly, "it's exactly the opposite. You won't want me to tell you about it now, but perhaps some day soon you'll let me Grace."

Miss Jones walked along the muddy, slushy edge of the road with her mind in a tumult. She felt quite unable to make any reply. But Captain Trevellyan, always matter-of-fact, did not appear to expect one. He presently remarked that it was getting colder again. Was Miss Jones very wet?

"Rather wet, but the worst half must be over by now. I wonder what news we shall find when we arrive. Do you know, I can't help being selfishly thankful to be going there. It's been so hard never hearing anything about her, and knowing all the time that she was in such anxiety." "Doesn't Char tell you?"
"No; but I don't think I asked her. She likes us to be official, you know."

"I never heard such inhuman nonsense in my life!" exclaimed Trevellyan in tones of most unwonted violence.

They both laughed, and the next minute Grace said,

"Listen!" They both heard wheels.

"It's the dog-cart. I thought so. It was the only thing left, and I suppose they've got hold of a boy to drive it. Thank goodness! Miss Jones," said Trevellyan for the fourth time, "I can't tell you what I think of you; you've been simply wonderful."

"Don't! Of course I haven't."

Grace's voice was more agitated than accorded with her previous declaration of imperturbability, and something in the few shaky words caused John to put out his hand and grasp hers for a moment, while he hailed the cart.

"Here we are! Did Miss Vivian send you?"

"Her ladyship, sir. Couldn't come any faster, sir; the roads are so

bad." "They are. How is Sir Piers?"

"The same, sir still unconscious. Dr. Prince don't anticipate no immediate change, sir, but he's staying the night."

"Good! He's telephoned to Questerham, I suppose. Now, Miss Jones, let me help you. Boy, you'd better get on to the back seat; your inches are better suited to it than mine," said John firmly. He put the rug round Grace, and she sank thankfully on to the small seat of the dog-cart.

They hardly spoke while he drove cautiously along the remaining mile of high road and up the long avenue to Plessing.

Even when John helped her down at the hall door he only said: "I shall see you to-morrow. I shall never forget this Christmas Eve."

"Nor I," said Grace.

In the hall Miss Bruce greeted them with subdued exclamations.

"How tired you must be, and half frozen! Sir Piers is just the same; the doctor is still upstairs. He and Charmian got here two hours ago or more, and told us what had happened. There wasn't anytiling to send for you but the little cart. Poor dear

Charmian! such a home-coming for her! She's wonderful, of course never given way for an instant."

"Where is she?"

"Upstairs. I've sent to tell her and Lady Vivian that you've arrived at last."

"And, Miss Bruce, we should like some food if it can be managed without too much trouble."

"Of course, of course. Miss Jones, your room is ready. Wouldn't you like to change your wet shoes at once?"

Miss Bruce spoke with an odd mixture of doubt and compassion, as she looked at Grace warming her frozen hands at the hall fire. It was evident that she did not feel certain whether Miss Jones was to be regarded as a friend of Lady Vivian's, whom Captain Trevellyan had judged necessary to bring to Plessing at all costs, for Joanna's sake, or as Char's junior secretary, thrusting herself upon her chief's family at a particularly inopportune moment. But the question was solved a few instants later, when Joanna Vivian herself, coming downstairs in her black tea-gown, exclaimed softly: "You've brought her, Johnnie! Well done! No; there's no change yet. I want you to see Dr. Prince." Then she took Grace's hands in hers and said: "Thank you, my dear, for coming to me."

CHAPTER XVI

"WELL, I couldn't have believed it Christmas morning and all!" "What, Mrs.

Bullivant?"

"This letter from the office, dear."

Little Mrs. Bullivant's face was scarlet, and her voice shaking. "But what is it?"

"Miss Vivian has dismissed me. This was evidently written two days ago, and has been delayed in the post. She simply says that she has come to the conclusion that I find the Hostel rather too much for me and is making other arrangements at the New Year. Oh, my dear!"

Mrs. Bullivant dissolved into tears, and Tony, aghast, picked up the small trebly-folded sheet of crested paper that had fallen from its square envelope.

"Written by herself, too, not typed! Oh, I am sorry! But doesn't she give any reason?"

"Not any. But I suppose she wasn't comfortable when she stayed here last month. She said one or two little things at the time the hot water, you know, and the gas giving such a poor light, and then the servants. But I never knew she was thinking of this."

"I must say, I think she might have given you a reason, or asked you to go and see her at the office," said Tony, her allegiance to Miss Vivian shaken at the sight of the little Superintendent in tears.

Everyone liked Mrs. Bullivant at the Hostel, and when Tony told the others that she was to be dismissed there was a general outcry.

"But why What a shame!"

"She always works so hard, and she's so nice to everyone. It's too bad of Miss Vivian."

"It does seem very unlike her to be so inconsiderate!" Mrs. Potter exclaimed.

"I can't believe there isn't some satisfactory explanation. It's too unlike Miss Vivian."

Miss Delmege was caustically reminded by Miss Marsh that no explanation could really be satisfactory from the point of view of Mrs. Bullivant.

"Couldn't we all send round a petition, and sign it? Do let's. We can put it on her table for when she gets back to-morrow or next day."

Miss Plumtree's suggestion was acclaimed, and she and Miss Marsh spent most of the morning in composing a petition that should combine sufficiently official wording with appealing arguments in Mrs. Bullivant's favour.

"Shall we wait till Gracie gets back before fastening it up, so as to make her sign it too?"

"Why?" said Miss Delmege sharply. "Several of the others are away, too, for the week-end, and we can't wait for everyone to get back."

"Well," provokingly said Miss Marsh, "as she's Miss Vivian's own secretary, one naturally looks upon her as being important. Besides, look at the way they've had her out to stay; she's a sort of special person, isn't she?"

Everyone knew that Miss Marsh was "getting a rise out of Delmege," always a favourite form of amusement, and there was a general giggle when Miss Delmege said in a very aloof manner: "If you ask me, I think Miss Vivian thinks it just as strange as anyone else that Gracie should be asked out there now, with

Sir Piers still so ill. But Lady Vivian is quite well known to be a most eccentric person."

"I shouldn't be a bit surprised if Miss Vivian's Staff Officer cousin had got her asked. I think he admires Gracie."

"Go on, Marshie! Why, he's never seen anything of her, has he? except, perhaps, at the Canteen."

"There was that night, you know," Miss Marsh reminded

them. "What night?"

"Why, when there was the air-raid, and he brought her back here afterwards. Don't you remember?"

"Well!" Miss Delmege exclaimed, "I must say that I should have thought--"

"I'm sure I've read somewhere that those four words 'I should have thought' are responsible for more quarrels than any others in the language."

Miss Delmege disregarded Tony and her literary allusions.

"I should have thought that after the strange way Grace Jones behaved that night, the less said about it the better. It's not the kind of thing one cares to dwell upon."

"I must say," Miss Henderson agreed, "that it would have been more likely to put him off than to make him admire her. At least, so far as my experience of human nature goes."

"Well, just sign this, will you, girls?"

They all hung over Miss Plumtree's shoulder, and read the petition.

Miss Vivian's secretary put her signature down first on the list, as by rights, and decorated her "Vera M. Delmege "with an elegant flourish.

"I must say I do like what I call a characteristic signature," she remarked, hastening back to appropriate the wicker arm-chair nearest the fire.

The others cowered round, in twos and threes, gazing disconsolately at the driving hail and stormy clouds of the grey world outside.

"Rather a wretched Christmas, isn't it? I do think we might have had a week's leave, really," said Miss Henderson, shivering.

"Miss Vivian isn't taking that herself," Miss Delmege at once reminded her. "And those who live near enough have been given the week-end, after all."

"I might just have managed it if I hadn't been on telephone duty. But she wouldn't let me change with anyone else. I suppose I must go over there now and release Miss Cox," said Tony, rising reluctantly to her feet.

"Well, take the petition, dear, and leave it on Miss Vivian's table, will you? Then she'll find it when she comes. I dare say she'll be in this afternoon. Poor Mrs. Bullivant!"

They talked of Mrs. Bullivant in a subdued way at intervals during the day. The little Superintendent remained in her own room.

"Oh, isn't it wretched?" groaned Miss Marsh for the hundredth time. "I declare I'd welcome a trooptrain; it would give us something to do, and make a break."

But Miss Anthony returned from the office at four o'clock with an awed face and a piece of news.

"Girls, what do you think? It's too awful poor Miss Vivian's father is dead. He died this morning, after a second stroke yesterday. Isn't it dreadful?"

Everyone exclaimed, and echoed Miss Anthony's "dreadful!" with entire sincerity, although the announcement of Sir Piers Vivian's death had given them food for thought and conversation for the rest of the evening.

"How did you hear, Tony?"

"Gracie Jones telephoned. My dears, they've had every sort of adventure. Dr. Prince's car broke down last night, or something, and a messenger met them from Plessing to say Sir Piers had had another stroke, and Miss Vivian and the doctor were to come at once. And he never recovered consciousness, and died this morning early. Isn't it dreadful?"

"Oh, poor Miss Vivian! Did Gracie say anything about her?"

"Only that she was being very brave. Of course, that's just what she would be."

"I suppose Gracie's coming back here to-night? Rather awful for her, poor girl, to be there just now."

"That's the extraordinary thing," said Tony with great animation. "She's actually been asked to stay on."

"She hasn't!"

"She has, really. I asked her what she was doing, and she said nothing much, but that Lady Vivian wanted her to stay."

"Well, I suppose she thinks she'll be of some use to Miss Vivian, but it seems rather queer, in a way, doesn't it? I mean her not knowing them, except officially, so to speak."

"Has anyone told Mrs. Bullivant?" Miss Delmege inquired.

But official intimation came to Mrs. Bullivant. A car stopped outside the door, and Dr. Prince, looking tired and haggard, asked to speak to her. He brought a note from Miss Jones, and offered to take a small suit-case out to Plessing for her, if Mrs. Bullivant would get her things together.

"But, doctor, she isn't going to stay there now, surely?"

"She'll stay there just exactly as long as I can persuade her to," said the doctor grimly.

Mrs. Bullivant looked thoroughly bewildered, but she gazed at the doctor's tired face, and said gently: "Come into the sitting-room while I get her things packed. There's a nice fire, and the girls have got tea in there. Do come in."

"Well," the doctor yielded.

His own home was two miles out of Questerham, and his wife would not be best pleased at his having spent Christmas Eve and Christmas morning away, and might say that he must not return to Plessing that night. The doctor fully intended to do so, but he felt far too weary for argument.

The sitting-room fire was blazing, and the Hostel community greeted him eagerly, and begged him to take the strongest arm-chair. They were glad of a guest on Christmas Day, and they wanted to hear news of Plessing.

Tony brought him a cup of tea, and Miss Plumtree shyly offered him buttered toast.

"Well, well, this is very good of you all. They're expecting me up at my Hospital, I believe, and I shall have to look in there later, I suppose, but I somehow didn't feel in tune for the festivities just at the moment. It's a sad business at Plessing, though one knew it had to come."

"How is Miss Vivian?"

"Only saw her for a moment," said the doctor briefly. "She arrived in time to see him, poor girl, but he never recovered consciousness. It's a melancholy thought for her that she wouldn't do as the poor old man begged her during the last few weeks he had to live. It wouldn't have cost her so very much to give up her position here, and it wouldn't have been for long, after all."

"But did Sir Piers want her to?" asked Tony, round-eyed.

"It made him unhappy, you see," the doctor said, almost as though apologizing for a weakness which he felt himself to share. "His generation and mine, you know, didn't look upon these things in the same light, and though he was proud of her war-work at first, later on, when his mind became clouded, he couldn't understand her always being away, and it made him unhappy. Lady Vivian tried to explain it to him as far as possible, but he couldn't understand. He didn't realize all she was doing, and he wanted her to stay at home, especially after he got ill. I fancy myself that he knew pretty well how things were he didn't expect to get well."

"But Miss Vivian didn't know; she couldn't have known," said Miss Henderson quickly.

The doctor shrugged his shoulders.

"We've heard a lot about 'hospital experience' and the rest of it," he said curtly. "It doesn't take much science to know that an old man of seventy odd who has had a stroke stands a very good chance of having another one sooner or later and probably sooner. *I* don't know why she couldn't have given in to him and made his last months on earth peaceful ones. It would have spared poor Lady Vivian something, too."

"But I thought that Lady Vivian did all the nursing herself?"

"Nothing of the sort!" declared the doctor vehemently. "She followed my orders and had a trained nurse, like a sensible woman. But she was with him herself whenever he wanted her, which was practically all day and half the night, and for ever having to try and explain to him, poor thing, why Miss Charmian was away.

She's been wonderfully brave all along, but it isn't very difficult to understand why she feels bitter about it all now. In all the years I've known them both," said the doctor emotionally, "she's never had one thought apart from him. She was a young woman of about five-and-twenty, I suppose, when she first came to Plessing, and he was twenty years her senior, and always fussing about her, though God forgive me for saying so now. She was as fine a horsewoman as ever I saw, a perfect figure and a beautiful seat, but she gave up hunting because it made him nervous about her. She buried herself down here, and was just as gay as a lark, because she knew it was pleasing him that they should live at Plessing and only go up to town once in a blue moon. I don't believe she's ever had a thought beyond making him happy and keeping worry away from him."

"Oh, poor Lady Vivian!" cried Miss Plumtree. "What will she do now?"

"I don't know, indeed. It's simply the destruction of her whole world. But she's most wonderfully plucky, and I don't believe it's in her to give way.

Miss Jones is doing more for her than anyone just now. They understand one another very well, and the mere fact of having someone to talk to who isn't one of the family is a great help. Steadies everybody, you know. That nice lad, Captain Trevellyan, will be there a good deal, but he tells me that he has to go before his Board on Tuesday, and that will mean

France again to a certainty. Poor Lady Vivian was dreading that but more for Sir Piers's sake than for her own. She didn't want to have to tell him the boy had gone back to fight. Just the same with everything; she looked at it all from one angle, how it was going to affect him. That's why I can't help hoping that after a time she'll take up things from another point of view, so to speak a less personal one. She's so full of energy, and there's so much to be done now."

"Lady Vivian came in once.or twice to the Canteen, before Sir Piers got ill, and she said she liked the work there. Perhaps she'll take up some war-work later on," suggested Mrs. Potter.

"I hope so I hope so very much. Miss Jones is inclined to think so, I fancy."

"Miss Vivian herself would be the best person to provide her mother with war-work, surely," said Miss Delmege between closely-folded lips.

"Well, well, I don't know that one could altogether expect that. You see, when all's said and done, her war-work was a source of great distress and vexation to Sir Piers, and Lady Vivian can't quite forget that. But perhaps," said the doctor, looking rather anxiously at the circle of absorbed faces in the firelight, "I'm an old gossip to be talking so freely. But the Vivians of Plessing well, it's rather like the Royal Family to us ordinary folk, isn't it? That's what I always feel. And I know that you'll want me to tell Miss Vivian how much you all feel for her."

But it was only Miss Delmege who said rather elaborately: "If you will do, please, Dr. Prince."

The others mostly looked concerned and bewildered, and Miss Plumtree exclaimed with soft abruptness: "Oh, but it's Lady Vivian after what you've told us. It's so dreadful to think of! What a good thing she likes Gracie Jones so much! I'm glad she's got her out there."

"So am I," said the doctor heartily.

"I've got her things here," Mrs. Bullivant said in the doorway.

"I'll take them when I go out after dinner. I promised Miss Jones to come back and see if Lady Vivian is all right, and, to tell you the truth, I doubt if I could keep away. I've been there so much just lately, and then last night--"

"Was she with him when he died?"

"Yes. So was Miss Vivian. It's overset her altogether, poor thing, I believe; but I haven't seen her since early this morning. That little companion, Miss Bruce, is with her all the time. Well, poor child, one's very sorry for her, though she made a great mistake when she took her own way in spite of all their pleading, and I'm afraid she'll find it hard to forgive herself now."

"Do you mean," said little Miss Anthony, who looked rather dazed, "that when she came back to the office after she'd had influenza, and when he'd had the first stroke, that Miss Vivian knew her father and mother wanted her to stay at home?"

"Well," said Miss Delmege, very much flushed, and her voice pitched higher than usual, "it was just what she's always said herself. Miss Vivian puts the work before everything."

"I don't know how to believe it," Mrs. Potter said.

The doctor misunderstood her.

"Perhaps it was that. She's done very fine work, and never spared herself any more than she's spared others. And maybe there was something in being boss of the whole show, and in hearing you all say how wonderful she was human nature's a poor thing, after all."

The doctor shook his head and went out again to his little car.

In the sitting-room the members of Miss Vivian's staff looked at one another.

"Girls," said Miss Marsh slowly, "do you remember Gracie's once saying, ages ago, when she first came, that she wondered if Miss Vivian would do as much work if she were on a desert island? Well, after what Dr. Prince has been telling us, I'm rather inclined to think she was right. Miss Vivian can't be as wonderful as she wants us to think she is."

"It would be too heartless. I can't believe it of her," said Mrs. Potter again, but she spoke very doubtfully.

"She must have thought that she owed her first duty to the work, and not to her own home. But I'm sorry for her now."

"So am I. She'll make it up to her mother by staying with her now, I suppose,"

"If Lady Vivian wants her. But *I* should imagine she'd hate the sight of her,

almost." "Tony!"

"Well," Miss Anthony asseverated, almost in tears, "I mean it. I think it's the most dreadful thing I've ever heard of, and the most unkind. And to think how we've all been admiring her for coming to live here, and for going on with the work in spite of being anxious and unhappy about her father! Why, she can't have cared a bit!"

"But she was splendid, in a sort of way," Miss Henderson said, bewildered. "Look how she's worked, and never spared herself, or given herself any rest, not even proper times off for meals. She can't have liked all that."

"I suppose," said Miss Marsh grimly, "that she liked thinking how splendid she was being, and how splendid everybody thought her. It would have been much duller for her to stay at home and do nothing, just because her father asked her to."

There was silence. To hear Miss Vivian reduced by criticism and analysis to the level of an ordinary human being seemed to revolutionize the whole mental outlook of the Hostel.

When Mrs. Bullivant came into the sitting-room, she looked strangely at the disturbed faces. "Dr. Prince seems to have upset you all," she said at last.

"Did you hear what he was saying about Miss Vivian, though?"

"Some of it. He asked me in the hall just now whether he'd been indiscreet. I had to say that I was afraid we'd none of us quite realized before how very much her personal influence had been counting with us in the work."

"That's quite true," said Tony dejectedly, "and I don't believe I shall ever feel the same again. Why should we all work ourselves to death for anyone like that?"

"Oh, my dear," said the Superintendent, sinking into a chair, "I'm afraid that's just the weak point in women's work. So much of it is done from the personal point of view. We can't keep personalities out of it."

"If you ask me, that's just what Miss Vivian has been doing. I mean, bringing her own powers of personal fascination to bear all the time." Mrs. Bullivant sighed.

"It's the work one ought to think of, not the individual. Anyway, my work here is over, I'm afraid."

"There you are!" cried Miss Plumtree. "You have to leave work you care about, just because she was uncomfortable at this Hostel. Talk about personal points-of-view!"

"Well, I've been personal long enough," declared Tony. "I shall chuck the office and go to munitions. They're impersonal enough!"

She let the door bang behind her.

"Poor old Tony! She'll go to the other extreme now, and think everything Miss Vivian does is hopeless. I must say, it's a bit of a disillusionment."

Miss Delmege stood up, gulped two or three times, and at last said, rapidly and nervously: "I don't at all agree with you. We've no business to sit in judgment on her like this, and I for one shall always believe there's some satisfactory explanation to the whole thing. I'm not saying it in the least because it's Miss Vivian, but quite impartially."

"Of course," said Miss Marsh, under her breath. "Look at the way she works and all it is perfectly wonderful; and Dr. Prince probably doesn't really know anything about what Sir Piers wanted. He's always been more or less on the defensive with Miss Vivian, just because she had to get his Hospital under proper control. It's all prejudice and disloyalty.

And all I can say is, that as long as there's work to be done for Miss Vivian, I'm ready to do it, singlehanded if necessary, if all the rest of you choose to desert her, and I shouldn't have the least hesitation in repeating all I've said to her face."

Miss Delmege's peroration left her rather shrillvoiced and breathless, but her pose on the hearth-rug, chin uplifted and one slim foot slightly thrust forward, was heroic in the extreme.

No one believed for a moment in her defiant assertion that she was prepared to launch her rhetorical declaration at Miss Vivian in person; but it was left to her old enemy, Miss Marsh, to remark with an unpleasant matter-of-factness: "There's no need to get so excited, Delmege. There'll be no call for you to do the work single-handed, either. I should be sorry for Miss Vivian if you tried it on, in fact. We're all fairly patriotic, I hope, whatever we may think of Miss Vivian, and, as Mrs. Bullivant says, doing the work is the point, not the person we're working for."

"That's right," agreed Miss Henderson. "It's for the war, after all."

"Otherwise," said Miss Marsh, with an icy look at Miss Delmege, "I'm bound to say that after what we've just heard of Miss Vivian I should be very much inclined to chuck working for her straight away."

"Don't discuss it any more, girls. It won't do any good," Mrs. Bullivant declared. "You must just try and think more of the work and less of Miss Vivian. Now, I've got a treat for your supper, as it's Christmas night, and I must go and see after it. Do, someone, go and get Tony downstairs again. She can't really have meant to go to bed at this hour. She was just upset, poor child, but she'll feel better when the lamp is lit and it's all looking homely and bright."

The Superintendent hurried away.

"Isn't she ripping?" asked Miss Henderson. "Come on, Greengage, and let's fish out Tony."

"Yes, do let's try and all cheer up," begged Mrs. Potter. "It has been a depressing Christmas Day. How would it be to change for supper? It would please Mrs. Bullivant."

"All right, let's."

The girls hurried upstairs to hunt for clean blouses and small pieces of jewellery, and Miss Delmege was left alone, still standing in her attitude of defiance before the sitting-room fire.

CHAPTER XVII

"Is there any more apple-pudding?"

"Yes, my lady."

"Then I will have some," said Lady Vivian, not at all unaware of the pained expression which Miss Bruce had unconsciously assumed. The unquenchable laugh still danced in her deeply-circled blue eyes as she gazed across the luncheon-table at Grace.

"Do have some more pudding, Grace. I know you never get enough to eat at your Hostel."

Miss Bruce put down her fork with a look of resignation. The excellent appetite displayed by Lady Vivian seemed to her extraordinary enough on the part of one widowed only a week ago, but that of the still-visiting Miss Jones amounted to a scandal.

In Miss Bruce's opinion, Miss Jones should have removed herself from Plessing a week ago, in spite of the strong predilection evinced by Lady Vivian for her society. It was not decent, Miss Bruce thought, to shun one's own daughter and take so many and such lengthy walks in company of a comparative stranger of less than half one's own age.

"Un-natural, I call it," said Miss Bruce, shaking her head. Char shrugged her shoulders.

"What does it matter? I'm glad she should take an interest in anyone or anything, though I can't understand such a friendship for that trivial little girl myself. But one thing is certain enough: I shall have to ask her to resign. It would be quite impossible, since my mother has chosen to treat her as one of the family, to keep her on at the office when I go back there. Though perhaps I ought to say if I go back there."

"Oh, my dear Charmian, why? Surely there can be no reason now less than ever, I mean to say why you should not take up that splendid work at the Supply Depot again. Why, the whole thing hinges on you."

"I know," said Char dejectedly. "But there's my mother to consider. I really don't see how I'm to leave her all alone here, and I don't know if she'll care to come into Questerham with me."

Char had hardly seen her mother since Sir Piers's funeral, three days ago. Lady Vivian had refused to display any form of prostration, had discussed every necessary item of business with John Trevellyan and Dr. Prince, and when not engaged in answering innumerable letters and telegrams of condolence, had taken Grace Jones for long walks with her across the snowy fields.

"But," Char said to Miss Bruce, "we shall have to discuss business sooner or later. For all I know, we may have to leave Plessing. It was to be my mother's for her life, I believe, but she may choose to let Uncle Charles come into it at once. He has a large family of children, after all. His being in Salonika now makes it all so much more complicated."

"I dare say there will be no change just at present. Everything will be so unsettled until this dreadful war is over," Miss Bruce soothed her vaguely.

But she, too, thought that it would be necessary for Lady Vivian soon to give her daughter some outline of her future plans.

On New Year's Day, rising from the helping of applepudding which she had left unfinished as a protest, Miss Bruce after lunch said firmly to Lady Vivian: "You will want to talk to Charmian this afternoon, I feel sure. There is a fire in the library, so perhaps--"

She looked meaningly at Miss Jones, who, instead of making at least a pretence of at once following her out of the room, gazed imperturbably at Lady Vivian.

"Char," inquired Joanna mildly, "do you want to talk to me?"

"We'd better come to an understanding, hadn't we, mother? You see, I haven't the vaguest idea of your plans."

"But why should you have any, my dear? They won't interfere with your work at Questerham. If you want to know about Plessing, I can tell you in two words.

Your Uncle Charles doesn't want any change made until after the war, so that I can either let it or go on living in it, as I please."

Decorum took Miss Bruce as far as the door of the dining-room, but was not strong enough to put her outside it while Grace Jones still remained, with no apparent consciousness of indiscretion, sitting unmoved in her place, and in full hearing of this discussion, which every tradition would restrict to a family one.

Even Char said: "Hadn't we better come to the library?"

Joanna rose.

"I'm going there now, for the very good reason that Lesbia Willoughby is to be shown in there in half an hour's time. I shall have to see her some time, and I may as well get it over."

"Mother, must you? Why not say that you're not seeing anyone?"

"My dear," said Joanna dryly, "I've already answered two telegrams and three letters and several telephone messages in which she offered to come to me, and I think that nothing but word of mouth will have any effect upon her. But I'll talk to you this evening, if there's anything you want to know. John is dining here to tell us the result of his Medical Board."

Joanna left the room, with her decisive, unhurried step, and Char, ignoring Grace, said to Miss Bruce: "I have a lot of letters, sent on from the office. Perhaps you'd be kind enough to give me a little help this afternoon?"

"Certainly, Charmian."

Miss Bruce was gratified; but when Char had walked away without so much as glancing at Grace, she could not help saying to her, with a sort of flustered kindness: "I hope you'll find some way of amusing yourself, Miss Jones."

She had loyally adopted Char's prejudice, but was too kind-hearted not to try furtively to make up for it.

Miss Jones, however, was not destined to spend a solitary afternoon. Mrs. Willoughby was driven to Plessing by Captain Trevellyan in his car; and although Miss Bruce, casting sidelong glances from the > window of Char's boudoir, where she was busily taking notes from her dictation, distinctly saw him enter the house, she felt certain that he proceeded no further than the hall, where Grace sat reading by the fire.

Mrs. Willoughby went at once to the library, where she enfolded the resigned Joanna in a prolonged embrace.

"My poor, poor dear! Words, can never tell you how I've felt for you how much I've longed to be with you!"

But despite the inadequacy of words, Mrs. Willoughby had a shrill torrent of them at her command, with which she deluged Lady Vivian for some time.

"Poor Lesbia!" Lady Vivian remarked afterwards to Grace; "she enjoyed herself so much that I really couldn't grudge it to her!"

"He was so much, much older than you, dear, that it must almost feel like losing a father, and I know that that unfortunate girl of yours isn't very much comfort. She must be racked with remorse. Now, do tell me, Joanna, would you like me to take her off your hands for six months? Let her come back to London with me next week, and get her married off before it's too late."

"Too late?"

"Well, Joanna, she must be thirty, and, mark my words, whatever people may say about there being no men left, things are happening every day. Half the mothers in London are getting their girls off now, what with officers back on leave and officers in hospitals, and those dear Colonials. Girls who never had a look in before the war can do anything they like in the way of nursing, or leading the blind about, or working in some of those departments where the over-age men are. Char is just the sort of creature to prefer a man old enough to be her grandfa

Mrs. Willoughby's jaw dropped, and she made a repentant snatch at Joanna's hand.

"Forgive me, darling! How idiotic to say such a thing to you, of all people! But if you'll give me your girl, I'll undertake to find chances for her. She'll be very good-looking when she doesn't look so sulky and take such airs, and one could make capital of all the patriotic work she's been doing down here. And I always think it's rather an asset than otherwise to be in mourning, especially in these days. Black suits her, too, with that sandy colouring. Does she choose her own clothes, Joanna?"

"She does, Lesbia, and has chosen them ever since she was out of long clothes, as far as I remember. But--"

"Joanna, you've been culpably weak, and of course that poor, dear old man had simply no idea of discipline. But I can put the whole tlu'ng right for you in six weeks, when the dear girl comes to me."

"It's no use, Lesbia," said Joanna, half laughing.

"It's very kind of you, but Char wouldn't hear of it, and really at thirty I can't coerce her besides, there's her work here."

"My dear, you don't mean to say that you're going to allow that to go on?"

"To begin with, I couldn't prevent it. To go on with, I think it perfectly right that Char should do what she can in the way of war-work. There wouldn't be the slightest object in her giving it up now."

"But Sir Piers 'the memory of his wishes his memory!" almost shrieked Mrs. Willoughby.

"His memory will survive it, Lesbia. Besides, as long as he was himself, you know, he didn't mind her doing war-work. He quite understood the necessity, and was proud of her."

"But, my dear, wrong-headed creature, when she so deliberately and heartlessly went against his wishes at the last?"

"Well," said Joanna placidly, "she won't be doing that now, so she can go on working with a clear conscience."

"Joanna," said Mrs. Willoughby, with an air of discovery, "upon my word, I don't understand you."

Nevertheless, she devoted the major half of the afternoon to the object of her perplexity.

"One word, dearest, I must say," she declared at the end of an hour that, to Joanna's thinking, held already more than a sufficiency of words. "Have you considered what is happening to that delightful lad--"

"Never," said Joanna unhesitatingly. "And who on earth are you talking about, Lesbia?"

"That precious creature, Johnnie. Too guileless for words, my dear; but if there's one thing I do understand, inside out and upside down, it's men. I should have made a perfect mother young things adore me. Look at my sweet Puffles! But I'm miserable about John, who really has a perfect passion for me, dear lad. Lewis always says that all the boys of his regiment go through it, just like measles."

Joanna, who had heard this quotation before, ruthlessly disregarded it.

"What is happening to John?"

"My dear, do you mean to tell me you haven't seen it? But of course you havon't, at such a time. What a brute I am! Forgive me, Joanna, but you seem so utterly unlike a widow. I can hardly realize it. But, of course, that little secretary creature she's had her eye on him all along."

"I suppose, Lesbia, that you don't mean my poor old Bruce, who's been with me almost ever since John was born?"

Lesbia uttered a screech between laughter and reproach.

"What an absurdity! Of course I mean the little Canteen girl Jones, or whatever her name is. My dear, will you believe me when I tell you that when that poor innocent boy drove us up here just now and followed me into the hall, there she was, actually waiting to pounce upon him, sitting over the fire?"

"I can believe you quite easily," said Joanna, "all but the pouncing. We none of us knew that John was going to drive you over, so she couldn't have been waiting."

"Blind, reckless one!" cried Lesbia excitedly. "I can only tell you that ever since those evenings at the Canteen I've seen what was coming. Do you suppose that a young man wipes up dripping wet mugs for nothing? Besides, Joanna, look at the air-raid! Of course, my poor dear, I know that just at that time you were thinking of something altogether different, but *I* was there, if you remember."

"I remember hearing about it," Joanna admitted, with a vivid recollection of Mrs. Willoughby's spirited behaviour on the occasion in question having been described in unflattering terms by Captain Trevellyan. "My dear, after we'd all dispersed and the whole thing was over, that wretched girl lured him back into the basement, under pretext of fainting or something, and pretended to have hysterics on account of the fright she'd had. And I assure you that she hadn't seen anything at all of the raid, because she was the very first person to make a bolt for downstairs. In fact," said Mrs. Willoughby modestly, "really, for one moment there might have been a panic, if I hadn't dashed into the middle of the hall and called out that we were all Englishwomen and not afraid of anything. And after all that, the miserable girl goes and faints away in his hands!"

"I did hear something about it in fact, she told me herself, but it wasn't nearly as dramatic as that, Lesbia. And his coming back and finding her was pure chance. I think it was the last thing she wanted." Mrs. Willoughby opened her eyes to their widest extent, flung back her head, and exclaimed emphatically: "You will have no one in this world, Joanna, no one but yourself, to blame if the very worst happens. Mark my words, that uninteresting little creature, without a feature to bless herself with, is going to make poor guileless Johnnie ask her to marry him."

Joanna had some opinion of Mrs. Willoughby's shrewdness, if none of her discretion, and this prognostication gave her a sense of comfort which she had had no slightest expectation of deriving from the visit of condolence. It even enabled her to thank Lesbia with sufficient cordiality for coming, as she at last escorted her into the hall.

"When we shall meet again, dearest, I am utterly unable to declare," was a valediction which added considerably to her relief at parting. "My Lewis won't let me stay down here any longer, now that I'm fairly fit again. He's too sweet and self-sacrificing for words, poor lamb! ' Go back to London where there are a thousand jobs and undertakings crying out for you,' he says. I really can't bear to leave him, and the dear regiment, and my beloved Canteen, let alone you, whom I've always looked upon as the oldest, dearest of links with my girlhood. But, of course, my poor committees must be getting into the most ghastly muddles, and I know that all my officer proteges are in despair. They write me the most heartrending letters."

Lesbia shrouded herself in sables, wound a motorveil round and round her head, and cast a piercing glance round the hall.

"What did I tell you, Joanna?"

"You told me that John was here with Miss Jones, but I don't see either of them. Is he going to drive you back?"

"So he pretended, my dear, but I can't answer for what she--"

Trevellyan came into the hall and greeted Lady Vivian.

"I've not kept you waiting, Mrs. Willoughby, I hope? I went to bring the car

round." "Where is Grace?" asked Lady Vivian, not without malice.

"Just come in and gone upstairs. We've been looking at your turnips," said John seriously. "A very fine crop, Cousin Joanna."

"We shall all be living on turnips quite soon," Lesbia declared with acerbity. "Good-bye, my poor dear Joanna, and do think over all I've been saying to you.
Remember that a telegram would bring me at any hour, for as long as you please, and I'll take your girl off your hands whenever you like. I could make her quite useful in some of my war-work."

Joanna turned away from the door, thankful to reflect that neither her daughter nor Miss Bruce had been present to hear this monstrous assertion.

As she crossed the hall, Grace came downstairs. Lady Vivian smiled at her.

"You've a knack of appearing just when I want you. I've just seen Lesbia Willoughby off, since she mercifully refused to stay to tea. Has the second post come?"

"Yes. I've got a letter that I rather wanted to talk to you about, from Miss Marsh at the Hostel."

Joanna sat down, her hands lying idly folded in her lap, while Grace read aloud:

"DEAR GRACIE,

"You'll think it extraordinary, me writing to you like this, but we really do miss you here, especially in our room, and the whole place has been upside down since you went away. This is because poor Mrs. Bullivant has actually got the sack, if you can believe such a thing, for no reason on earth that anyone can discover. She had a slip from Miss V. dated two days before Christmas but it only reached her on Christmas Day tolh'ng her that other arrangements would be made at the New Year. Of course, we're all fearfully sick, as you'll guess, and Mrs. Bulh'-vant has been simply howling about it ever since, though she's as quiet as ever and never lets on. But she looks rotten, and Tony can hear her crying in her own room at nights. You can imagine what a jolly Christmas we've all had! The point of bothering you with all this, however, is that perhaps you can find out what she's expected to do. It's all very well to say, ' Clear out at the New Year,' but Miss Vivian's being away, and in such trouble and all, makes it all jolly awkward. We sent a petition signed by all of us to ask if Mrs. Bullivant could be kept on; but of course there's been no answer, and she simply doesn't in the least know what to do. Do you think it would be all right if she just hung on till Miss V. gets back?
Perhaps then she'll have read the petition and made up her mind to let her stay on as Superintendent. Of course, that's what we all hope, and, in fact, some of the girls are so sick about it that I shouldn't be surprised if some resignations were sent in. We've been hearing something that's made us all sit up re Miss V. and--"

"That's all about Mrs. Bullivant," said Grace hastily.

"Nonsense!" cried Joanna vigorously; "you've stopped at the most amusing bit. Unless it's marked private, for goodness' sake go on, and tell me what this scandal can be. I'm quite relieved to hear that Char's past holds anything exciting."

Grace began to laugh.

"It isn't marked private, and there really isn't much to read.

"and there'll be a good deal less said in future about how wonderful she is. Did you know that her father and mother, after he first got ill, simply begged her to stay at home, for his sake, and she absolutely wouldn't? Work is all very well, but I must say that seems jolly callous, and one can't help wondering whether it really was the work she was after, or just the excitement and the honour and glory of her position. I know you never--"

Grace stopped again, and Lady Vivian said: "She knows you never liked her well, go on."

"and most of the rest of us are feeling rather off the ' personal influence ' stunt just at the moment. Delmege, of course, takes a high line and goes in for loyalty, etc., etc. in fact, won't speak to any of us at present. But, as I say, that's her loss and not ours.

"Now, dear old thing, I'm going to leave off, as you're probably sick of my scrawl by this time, and it's high time I was off to my bed. Try and find out if there's any chance of Mrs. B.'s being allowed to carry on for the present, and send me a line if you've time.

"Everyone sends all sorts of love, and we shall all be most awfully glad to see you turn up again. This place is more putrid than ever without you, and with all this fuss going on about Miss Vivian; but I dare say it'll all turn out for the best if it makes us a bit keener about the work for it's own sake, and not for hers. After all, there is a war on!

"Yours with best love,

"DORA MARSH."

"Dora Marsh seems to me to be an uncommonly sensible girl," observed Lady Vivian thoughtfully.

She gazed into the fire in silence for a few moments before adding: "I wonder who's been talking to them about Char? The only person I can think of is Dr. Prince. I know he felt very strongly about it, and I don't altogether wonder, though it may seem rather hard on her to have her reputation for infallibility destroyed at last."

"I think," said Grace, "that there would have been some feeling at the Hostel, in any case, at Mrs. Bullivant's dismissal. She's been so kind and nice to us all, and worked so hard always, and, of course, everyone knows that the loss of the position is serious for her. She's very poor, and she has no home of her own to go to."

"Of course, it's unthinkable. Char must have some reason for dismissing her. I shall insist upon being told what it is!" cried Joanna.

There was more animation in her manner than Grace had seen there for some time, and she was quite ready to follow her upstairs in immediate search of Char.

The Director of the Midland Supply Depot was at her writing-table, leaning back in the familiar attitude that invariably recalled to Grace old-fashioned engravings of an Eastern potentate, her eyes half closed, her slim fingers tapping upon the table in front of her, and her slow, deep voice drawling in fluent dictation. Miss Bruce, far from possessing the skill of Mrs. Baker-Bridges, sat agitatedly scribbling on various odd half-sheets of paper. Further notes lay strewn all over the table and on the floor beside her chair.

She looked up with shamefaced but unmistakable relief at the interruption.

"Have you been victimized all the afternoon?" inquired Joanna kindly, but with her usual unfortunate choice of expression.

"Oh, no, no!" said Miss Bruce, almost with horror. "But Charmian must be tired. She's been working without a moment's rest, and it really does give one some sort of idea of all that she must do at the office every day."

Char rewarded her with a melancholy smile. "At the office there are the telegrams, and the telephone messages, and endless interviews to deal with as well. I don't think I ever get a consecutive hour's time there to deal with the correspondence without interruption. Now, all these letters which you see here could--"

Joanna interrupted the Director of the Midland Supply Depot without ceremony.

"I want you to tell me, Char, why you want that nice little Superintendent of yours to leave the Hostel. The staff there is in despair."

Char suddenly sat upright.

"That is a purely official matter, and it's disgraceful that there should have been gossip about it already."

"But why have you dismissed her?"

"Because she is quite inadequate to fill the post of Hostel Superintendent. I was there myself, and I never was in a worse-managed or more uncomfortable establishment in my life."

"I can quite believe it, my dear, but I'm inclined to think and Grace, who knows more about it than I do, agrees with me that she's never had a fair chance of running it properly."

"I don't propose to discuss the matter with my secretary, mother."

"But why not talk it over like ordinary human beings, Char?" said Lady Vivian, reverting to all her old half-impatient, half-humorous outspokenness. "I've no patience with you. What in the name of fortune is the sense of vexing and distressing everybody, when by a little decent management the whole thing could be put on to a proper basis? Grace, you've lived in that Hostel. If the Superintendent had a freer hand, couldn't it be made more comfortable?"

"Yes, especially with anyone as hard-working and anxious to make things nice as Mrs. Bullivant. She may not be a very good manager, but, indeed," said Grace pleadingly, "things have been very much against her. If she could engage the sort of servants that she needs, and if there were fewer people in the Hostel, so as to give more room, and better arrangements made about the hot water and the food, it could be very nice."

"You are all in that Hostel for the purpose of war-work, Miss Jones, and I should have thought that with that end in view a few minor discomforts could have been overlooked. When one thinks of our men in the trenches--"

"However much you may have thought of them, Char, it didn't prevent your going into rooms before you'd been at the Hostel a fortnight," Joanna interrupted briskly. "Those girls are just as much flesh and blood as you are yourself, whether you own to it or not. But I can tell you one thing, and that is that they're beginning to find it out for themselves."

"To find out what?" said the Director of the Midland Supply Depot, vexed to the extent of for once speaking shortly and in monosyllables.

Joanna shrugged her shoulders, and Grace said emphatically:

"Mrs. Bullivant is very popular, you know, and the staff can't understand her getting such a summary dismissal. After all, it's very serious for her, apart from everything else, because she's got to live."

"To which, I suppose, Char would like to reply, 'Je n'en vois pas la necessite,'" quoted Lady Vivian, with her irrepressible laugh. "But it really won't do, Char. You're dealing with human beings, and you'll have to make up your mind to it."

"I am dealing," said Char magnificently, "with an organization."

"Even so, my dear, it's made up of human beings. But as it's tea-time and I'm extremely hungry," said Lady Vivian, with a side-glance at Miss Bruce, "we'd better postpone discussion until this evening. I don't know whether you feel human enough to leave your papers and eat bread and jam with the rest of us, but I dare say that Grace and Miss Bruce won't give you away to the staff if you do."

The outraged Miss Vivian left the last word to the ribald spirit apparently animating her parent.

CHAPTER XVIII

CAPTAEST TREVELLYAN'S Medical Board had passed him fit for active service again, and he made matter-of-fact announcement of his approaching return to France in the course of that evening.

"Do you know when, Johnnie?"

"Next draft that goes, I suppose. I rejoin the battalion the day after to-morrow, and it might be any day after that."

Exclamations were left to Miss Bruce. Grace and Joanna received the news almost in silence, and Char remained monosyllabic.

"Will you smoke in the library, John?" said Joanna as she rose from the dining-table. "We'll have coffee there. We can also talk business, Char, if you want to."

"Then, shall I?" said Miss Bruce, looking at

Grace and feeling strongly inclined to say "Shall we?"

Joanna laid her hand on the little secretary's shoulder. "Of course not, Miss Bruce. You know we count you as one of the family."

In the library a certain tenseness of atmosphere prevailed, until Joanna had finally dismissed the coffee equipage, and leant back in a great leather arm-chair under the lamp.

John, next her, had taken up his favourite position on the hearthrug, and was smoking in meditative silence, his eyes now and then seeking Grace, whose head was bent over a piece of needlework.

Char, presumably from force of habit, had seated herself at the writing table, and Miss Bruce took a low chair beside her, gazing dumbly from her to Lady Vivian and back again, as though a divided loyalty harassed her thoughts.

Char broke the silence.

"Mother, you spoke about letting this place this afternoon. Is that what you mean to do?"

"No. I only said that it was in my power to let it, but as a matter of fact, since your Uncle Charles has no wish to make any change until the war is over, he and I have agreed that it had better be made use of. He is quite willing that I should do whatever seems best and most necessary."

Miss Bruce uttered an exclamation.

"Red Cross work, do you mean?"

Char made a movement to check her, as though unwilling to let any display of surprise greet Joanna's announcement.

"Of course," she said slowly, "I could find a hundred uses for a place like Plessing, from turning it into a hospital onwards. The idea had naturally occurred to me before, but as, I must say, mother, you've always discouraged any form of patriotic sacrifice by every means in your power, and done everything possible to ignore the very fact of there being a war, it never struck me that you would consent to such a plan."

John looked up.

"It isn't a question of consent, Char. The scheme is Cousin Joanna's, not anyone else's."

"As I am as I have been placed in the position of Director of the Midland Supply Depot, John," Char said quietly, "the voluntary organizations here, of whatever kind, come under my jurisdiction, and I must say--"

"Char," interrupted her mother, "you may say anything you please, but you'll never persuade any of us that you and I could work together comfortably, and I haven't any intention of trying the experiment. I shall offer this place as a convalescent home to be attached to the Military Hospital at Staffield. That will put it altogether outside the jurisdiction of your office."

"It's too far from the station."

"Not with a couple of cars and Government petrol," said John. "The doctors here are

overworked as it is."

"A convalescent home does not need the same amount of medical attendance as a hospital, and Dr. Prince is perfectly willing to undertake whatever is necessary."

"But you'll want a staff, and at least two trained nurses in the house."

"I have no doubt that they can be obtained. Char, I don't want to vex you and make you feel that I'm acting in opposition to all your own schemes," spoke Joanna impetuously, "but really and truly it wouldn't answer if I tried to run things on your lines. I must do something, and it seems a shame not to use Plessing. But I had thought of another plan, though I know Johnnie doesn't approve of it."

"No, I don't," said John stoutly.

Char had coloured deeply and her mouth was set. She spoke as though with difficulty.

"What is it?"

"Tell her, Grace. You thought of it," said Lady Vivian.

"To make Plessing the Hostel for your staff. Lady Vivian would give them their board and lodging, and superintend herself. You see, it would make an enormous difference if the present Hostel, which is much too small, were free. You could make it into an extension of the office, which is badly needed. The chief drawback, of course, is the distance, but we should have to come in by the 9 o'clock train every morning, and either bicycle back or come out by the 6.30 train.

They're putting it on again next month. You see, the days will be getting longer very soon, and we've all the spring and summer in front of us."

"I don't think it's practicable," Trevellyan said.

"Nor I," echoed Miss Bruce, watching the thundercloud on Char's forehead.

"I thought Char might prefer it," said Joanna simply. "You would keep your own rooms, my dear, of course, and it would be very much more comfortable for all of you than the present arrangement. As to the difficulty of getting in and out, there's no reason why we shouldn't see what could be done about driving one way. I don't know if the petrol ought to be used, but there are plenty of farm-horses, and we could hire a wagonette, or something of that sort."

"And what about the nights when we're all kept late, or a troop-train comes in, and the Canteen work, which is never over before eleven or halfpast?"

"You must give it up," Lady Vivian informed her placidly. "People can't work half the night as well as all day, and I've always thought that you had no business to ask it of your staff. That Canteen work is very heavy, and utterly unfit for girls who've been all day in an office. It isn't as if there weren't others to undertake it. Lesbia Willoughby says that the ladies of the regiment are quite ready to divide it amongst themselves in fact, they've rather resented having it so completety taken out of their hands."

"Mother, you had better understand me once and for all. Nothing will induce me to give up any single item of all that I've undertaken."

"But, Char, why?" inquired Captain Trevellyan mildly. "Is it the work you care about, or just the fact of doing it yourself?"

Dead silence followed the inquiry.

At last Char said, without attempting to answer it: "The Hostel suggestion is quite impossible, mother. Even if it were not for the practical objections, such as the distance from the work, I could not accept. My staff has been put into perfectly suitable quarters, and I should not dream of moving them. But as it has become more and more evident that Miss Jones is dissatisfied there "She paused, and looked at Grace.

Trevellyan made a sudden brusque gesture, but Grace said quickly: "I am afraid that I had better ask you to accept my resignation, Miss Vivian."

Char made no pretence at surprise, and simply bent her head in acquiescence.

Grace folded up her work and stood up. Trevellyan opened the door for her, and, with one look at Joanna, passed out of the room after her.

Miss Bruce gasped, as at a sudden illumination. But it was Joanna who exclaimed roundly: "Well, Char, you've put your foot into it with a vengeance! Unless I'm very much mistaken, John will be in no hurry to forgive you."

"Mother! why will you always obscure every issue of what is, after all, national work, by some wretched personal question?"

"Because, Char, I'm dealing with human beings, and not with machines."

"Oh, Lady Vivian!" cried Miss Bruce irrepressibly. "Forgive me, but you speak as though she she wasn't adored by her staff. Look how they all admire her!"

"Yes, and she takes advantage of it to work them very much too hard, and also to use her personal influence to obtain a sort of blind loyalty and perfectly unreasoning admiration that is bad for the work, and bad for the staff, and bad for her! However, Char, I don't mind telling you that I think a good deal of that nonsense is coming to an end. Your staff has not been at all impressed by your abominable treatment of that poor little Superintendent, and they've also found out that you insisted on going off to Questerham against your father's express wishes, and then posed as a martyr to patriotism."

"Oh, Lady Vivian!" groaned the secretary.

"Yes, I know I'm losing my temper, but I always did and always shall think that Char behaved in the most heartless and disgraceful fashion. It wasn't I who told her staff about it, or Grace Jones either, but I'm heartily grateful to whoever did. The work that we hear so much about may get a chance of being attended to on its own merits now, in a reasonable manner, instead of being overdone to a senseless degree, simply because ' Miss Vivian is so wonderful!'"

Joanna went to the door.

"Think it over, Char, and if you like to behave like a reasonable being, we'll talk over the Hostel scheme. Otherwise, John thinks there's no doubt of this place being accepted as a convalescent home. But you'll have to make up your mind, in that case, to see it being mismanaged by mere military authorities."

Joanna did not bang the door behind her, but she shut it with considerable briskness, and left the appalled Miss Bruce to assist Char's decision.

The Director of the Midland Supply Depot sat in an attitude of the most unwonted dejection, her elbows on the writing-table and her head in her hands. Miss Bruce hardly ventured to breathe in the heavy stillness that pervaded the room.

At last Char raised her head and looked at her. "Oh, Brucey," she said piteously, "they're all very difficult to deal with!"

The note of appeal, which Miss Bruce had not heard from Char since her earliest childhood, moved the little secretary to great emotion.

"Charmian, my poor dear child, it's very hard on you, after all you've been through already. I know that dear Lady Vivian has never altogether understood; and then her feelings about the war so different only, of course, now she needn't consider circumstances altered reaction

Miss Bruce floundered into a tangle of words, and ventured to put out her hand timidly, although aware of how much Char disliked demonstrations of affection.

It affected her with a profound sense of how far Miss Vivian must be reduced when she found her tentative hand received with a long, nervous pressure.

"Oh, what can I do? what can I say? Couldn't you make up your mind to this Hostel scheme, which would at least keep you at home?"

"I'm not thinking of myself 'though, of course, it's quite true that if Plessing becomes a convalescent home, under military ruling, I can't go on living here. Nothing would induce me to remain in a place where I had no official standing. My mother doesn't seem to consider that she's practically forcing me to go on living, under most uncomfortable conditions, in Questerham. Not," added Char hastily, recollecting herself, ' ' that I should dream of putting any personal consideration before the work, or of letting my own comfort interfere with it in any way."

"I know. I know! It's wonderful, the way you've never thought of yourself for a moment," cried Miss Bruce in all sincerity. "Even to your meals, for I know too well that half the time you never have any proper lunch at all, and your dinner at all hours. But I'm so dreadfully afraid of your breaking down."

"Not while there's work to be done, Brucey. But this winter has been appalling, with one thing and another father, and then all the difficulties here, and half the staff getting laid up with influenza before Christmas. They're few enough, as it is, for all they have to do, and now I suppose half of them will resign."

"Impossible!"

"Not at all impossible, with Miss Jones making mischief and talking all over the place about my private affairs, and then resigning in that absurd way. No doubt that will be made into a grievance, too."

"I thought," began Miss Bruce, and then hesitated, but Char looked so impatient that she went on rather desperately "I thought that you meant to send her away in any case?"

"Certainly I did. You must see, Brucey, how utterly out of the question it would be to have one member of the staff a sort of privileged person, who'd been out here to stay, when none of the others have so much as set foot in the place, and talking about my relations as though they were intimate friends of hers. It would be quite impossible."

If Miss Bruce saw the impossibility in question less clearly than did Char, she said nothing.

"No, Brucey, it's no good. I've set my hand to the plough, and there must be no looking back. I shall have to make up my mind to Questerham."

"But the discomfort!" wailed Miss Bruce.

"It may convince my mother that there is more than mere self-will and love of notoriety in my work. To me, Brucey, it seems almost laughable that anyone should attribute my work to that sort of motive, but, you see, she has never understood me."

"Never!" said Miss Bruce with entire conviction.

"The wrench will be leaving you, dear old Brucey," Char said affectionately.

"Charmian," said the little secretary solemnly, "I can't do it. I can't face letting you go alone to those horrible lodgings, and only Preston to see to your comfort. I don't wish to say a word against Preston, and I know how devoted she is to you, but there are things that she can't be expected to think of. If you leave Plessing, you must take me with you."

An emotion such as had never shaken Miss Vivian out of her self-possession before, moved her suddenly now.

"Do you really mean that, Brucey? Would you leave my mother, and the work which she would certainly find for you here, and come and look after me in Questerham? I do know that I'm difficult sometimes, and and I can't promise you always to come in punctually to dinner, but it would make all the difference in the world to have you there."

Miss Bruce's allegiance to Char dated from many years back, and needed no strengthening was, indeed, beyond it; but henceforward, come what might, she would never forget that Miss Vivian had said that it made all the difference in the world to have her there.

"I will come whenever you like, and wherever you go, and I will look after you as much as you'll let me," she said tearfully.

There was a silence before Char remarked practically: "You'll have to arrange it with my mother, Brucey. I don't want her to think that you're deserting her for me."

It was difficult to see how Lady Vivian could possibly think anything else, but the uplifted Miss Bruce knew no qualms of spirit.

"I'll tell her myself, my dear, and I know she'll understand. She'll be only too glad that you should have somebody with you. Indeed, she does care, very, very much, if you'll let me say so; but all that's passed has

"I know, I know! It all makes it the more impossible for me to stay here with her and at the same time try to carry on the work."

"Then you won't consider the idea of making this place into a

hostel?" "I've already said that it's out of the question."

Quite evidently, the Director of the Midland Supply Depot was herself again.

She rose, and was meekly followed by Miss Bruce into the hall, where sat Lady Vivian and Captain Trevellyan.

"Mother, I'm going to bed," said Char calmly. "With regard to your scheme of making this place into a hostel, by the way, I'm afraid it wouldn't answer. I'm most grateful to you, but as Director of the Midland Supply Depot, I must refuse the offer."

Joanna shrugged her shoulders.

"Then, my dear, as Director of the Midland Supply Depot, I'm afraid you must go on living uncomfortably in rooms, since I suppose you won't want to stay here when the place is full of convalescent soldiers."

"Not in the circumstances," said Char gravely. Miss Bruce advanced valiantly.

"I have told Miss Vivian that I'm quite sure that you you will see your way to letting me go and be of what use I can to her in Questerham, Lady Vivian."

"Leave Plessing?"

Lady Vivian's voice held surprise only, but the unfortunate Miss Bruce was again obliged to struggle with divided feelings. She gazed miserably round, but Captain Trevellyan returned her look with one of unmistakable reproach, and Char was fixing her eyes persistently upon the fire. And then reassurance came to her from Joanna's voice, unusually gentle.

"I'm very glad, dear Miss Bruce. I shall like to feel that someone is looking after Char who has known her all her life, and cared for her as you have. And you won't be far away, so that I shan't feel I've lost sight of you. You must come out and see me struggling with my convalescents."

She stretched out her left hand, and Miss Bruce, answering her smile only with a convulsive pressure and a sort of sob compounded of mingled relief, gratitude, and compunction, hurried upstairs with her handkerchief undisguisedly held to her eyes.

"Poor Miss Bruce! We shall make an exchange, Char," said her mother, "for I'm hoping that Grace will stay here and help me."

"In what capacity?"

"Any capacity she likes."

"I hope," said Char, in tones which held more of doubt than of hopefulness, "that you will find her more accurate than I have. Good-night."

She went upstairs in her turn, feeling oddly tired and with a disquieting sense of finality. Her way and her mother's had parted, and although Char knew little regret for a separation which had long held them apart in all but physical nearness, she felt to the full the disturbing element introduced by a definitely spoken renunciation.

She would return to her work on the morrow, and make the move from Plessing as speedily as might be. But even in thinking of her work Char felt, that evening, no solace, for the recollection of her mother's words as to the frame of mind in which the staff might receive her left her strangely bereft of her usual armour of self-confidence.

In the hall, Trevellyan asked Joanna rather wistfully: "Do you mind very much?" "Exchanging Miss Bruce for Grace? Do you think I shall lose by it?"

They both laughed a little, and then Trevellyan, looking into the fire, observed; "I'm glad you're going to have her. I shall like thinking that she's working with you here."

"I'm glad, Johnnie."

There was the ghost of a flicker in Joanna's voice. "She'll be a comfort to you."

"Yes, indeed she will. The difference of age hasn't prevented our being friends." "And and you'll look after her?"

"I hope so. At all events, I shan't allow her to do any nursing of wounded, since we know the unfortunate effect that the sight of blood has upon her."

Joanna was laughing outright now.

"Oh, did she tell you?"

"Yes."

"I think that was the first time she and I ever had any realconversation."

"Was it? It was rather talented of you, in the circumstances."

"Cousin Joanna." "Yes, John."

Captain Trevellyan bent a yet more ardent scrutiny upon the fire.

"It seems the wrong time to say anything about it, but you always understand, and she and I could neither of us bear that you shouldn't know it at once. I couldn't go away without telling you. Not," said Johnnie, suddenly turning round and facing her, "that anything is settled, you know."

"Except the only thing that matters," said Joanna softly.

"One thing that makes us both care so much," he said diffidently, "is that we both care so much for you."

She gave him both hands, regally, and he stooped and kissed them as he might have a queen's.

Presently she said: "I'm so glad, dear Johnnie. Nothing in the world could make me happier."

It was past eleven o'clock before John left her, and his final inquiry, standing at the hall door, made her laugh outright.

"You don't think anyone will guess, do you? She doesn't want anything said till her father knows, and unluckily I can't get down to Wales and see him now. There won't be time. But you didn't guess till I told you, did you?"

"My dear Johnnie," said Joanna, with a singular absence of any emotion but her habitual kindly satire in her voice, "you really remind me very much sometimes of an ostrich!"

CHAPTER XIX

GRACE JONES went back to the Hostel soon after the New Year in order to pack up and to make her farewells before going for a month's holiday to her home in Wales.

"And then Plessing!" said Miss Marsh in an awed voice.

"And then Plessing," Grace assented. "Lady Vivian hopes that it will be properly started by that time as a convalescent home."

She looked across the sitting-room to where Mrs. Bullivant was sitting, with a smile that held inquiry and congratulation.

"Fancy!" ejaculated Mrs. Bullivant, with a sort of timorous pleasure, "Lady Vivian actually thought of me, and suggested my taking over the work of quarter-mistress there. You know, looking after the stores and all that sort of thing. I must say, it's very good of her, and I shall like working there and Gracie as secretary and all, too. It'll be quite like old times."

"I hate changes," observed Miss Henderson gloomily.

"This place will be extraordinary, with you gone, Mrs. Bullivant, and Gracie, and probably Tony and Plumtree as well."

"Tony isn't leaving, is she?" cried Grace.

"Yes, she is. Sent in her resignation two days ago. The fact is, she was altogether upset by that fuss we had about Miss Vivian the other day, and so she's decided that she wants a change. And Greengage says she won't stay without her. They always did hang together, you know."

"I don't altogether wonder at poor old Plumtree," Mrs. Potter observed thoughtfully. "Miss Vivian has always had a down on her, hasn't she? But she and Tony will be a loss to the Hostel, and so will you, dear."

"I don't like leaving a bit," Grace declared; "you've all been so nice to me, and I've been very happy here."

It was undeniable, however, that happiness was not destined to be the prevailing characteristic of Miss Jones's last day in the office.

Miss Vivian, seated at her paper-strewn table with all the old arrogance, if not actually with an additional touch of it to counteract the humanizing effect of the crepe mourning band on her left arm, ignored her junior secretary as far as possible, but inspected her work with a closeness of attention that almost argued a desire to find it defective.

"You can hand over your work to Miss Delmege, Miss--er--Jones. She will take it over on Monday next."

"Yes, Miss Vivian."

"And bring me your files."

Char ran over the papers in the old way, with the murmured running commentary that denoted her utter unconsciousness of all but the task in hand, and at the same time made the extensive area covered by her official correspondence fully evident to the perceptions of whoever might be in the room with her.

"Papers relating to that man Farmer's pension those must go up to-day. That contract for the milk send it up to the Commissariat Department, and I should like to know why they haven't sent me down the balance-sheets for the month. Nothing is ever properly checked, it seems to me, unless I do it myself, though Heaven only knows when I'm to find time for it. I've got to go through the accounts to-day, some time or other.... What's this? One of the nurses from the Town Hospital wants to see me, and calmly writes to say so! I never heard such unofficial nonsense in my life, as though I had time to give personal interviews to every wretched little V.A.D. who chooses to ask for them! Miss Delmege!"

"Yes, Miss Vivian?"

"Take this letter and answer it in the third person. Make it quite clear that any application of that sort is entirely out of order. If she wants to speak to anyone, she can go to Matron; and if it's necessary, Matron can write to me about it."

Miss Delmege took the letter, and mentally framed to herself the sentences in which she would later on make it clear to Gracie Jones that Miss Vivian's manner never really meant anything, and that her summary dismissal of any such appeal was only the necessary concomitant to official authority. It had become increasingly clear to Miss Delmege that Gracie was somehow, by the very reticence of her unspoken judgments, at the bottom of the extraordinary prejudice with which so many members of the staff now viewed the arbitrary ways of Miss Vivian.

The clear, rapid undertones continued:

"Boiler at the Hospital burst; they should have reported it sooner, but I'll send an order to the shop people. Another list for transfer! Dr. Prince transfers his men without rhyme or reason all cases of myalgia and trench feet, too. I shall have to write and tell him to reconsider half of them, before I should dream of letting them leave.

"What's all that? case for massage, case for Shepherd's Bush, five transfers for convalescent homes. ... Send me up the Transport Officer. Miss Delmege, what are my appointments for to-day?"

"The new Superintendent for the Hostel is coming for an interview at two o'clock, and Dr. Prince rang up to say that he would come in for a moment at three."

Char raised her eyebrows.

"If I happen to be engaged or busy, he will have to wait. Is that all?" "Yes, Miss

Vivian."

"Thank Heaven!" piously ejaculated Char, entirely pour la forme, since the interviews which cut into her day's work afforded her the only relief she obtained from its monotonous strain.

"Then I'll get through these letters at once. Send those to Mrs. Potter; and. Miss Delmege, you can take these the rest are for the Clothing Department. Miss Jones, kindly deal with these files.... Send for Miss Coll Mrs. Baker-Bridges, to take down some letters at once."

Miss Delmege looked rather disturbed, and remained standing at Char's elbow without speaking.

Miss Vivian, as was customary with her when wishing to display absorption in her work, continued to turn over the papers on the table without raising her eyes.

At last she looked up and said sharply:

"What is it, Miss Delmege? You fidget me very much by standing there in that unmeaning way. Do you want anything?"

Miss Delmege cleared her throat nervously. Too well did she know the peculiar note of crisp asperity now sounding in her chief's voice.

"I'm afraid the stenographer isn't here to-day."

"And why on earth not?"

"She isn't well."

"I've had no application for sick leave."

"She only telephoned this morning to say that she didn't feel able to come to-day."

Char, with the calculated show of temper with which she greeted any departures from discipline, struck the table with her hand, and made the unfortunate Miss Delmege jump.

"I think you've all lost your heads completely while I've been away. Is this office under military discipline or is it not?"

The question being purely rhetorical, Miss Delmege attempted no reply to it, and merely drooped the more dejectedly over her sheaf of letters.

"You can tell Miss Collins that unless she can apply for sick leave in the proper manner, and with a medical certificate to say that she is unfit for duty, she may consider herself dismissed."

Miss Delmege, only too thankful to feel that the Director's wrath was not aimed at herself, hastened to the telephone to deliver the ultimatum. She returned scarlet, and with an air of outraged modesty that made Grace look at her in mild astonishment. Miss Jones's curiosity, however, only received satisfaction that afternoon, at the close of Dr. Prince's interview with Miss Vivian, when he casually remarked: "By the way, that pretty little red-haired typist of yours, the one who got married the other day, paid me a call yesterday."

"Then, perhaps, you can inform me why she thought proper to remain away from duty without leave to-day."

"Oh, you'll have her back to-morrow for a time, anyway."

Grace saw Miss Delmege make a hurried plunge into a small stationery cupboard, where she appeared to be searching for something elaborately concealed.

"I can't have that sort of playing fast and loose with the work," Char said icily. "If Miss Collins--"

"Mrs. Baker-Bridges," the doctor corrected her cheerfully.

"If my stenographer can't attend to her work regularly, she is of very little use to me."

"jShe's probably going to be of more use to the nation, let me tell you, than all the rest of you put together," said Dr. Prince.

Miss Delmege's agony of mind reached its culmination, and she let drop an armful of heavy ledgers with a clatter which effectually covered any further indelicate precision of utterance of which the doctor might have been guilty.

By the time that Grace had extinguished her own laughter in the cupboard, and had assisted Miss Delmege to pick up her books, the Doctor had slammed the door behind him, with a disregard for Miss Vivian's presence which might perhaps be accounted for by the searching cross-examination to which she had just subjected his proposed Medical Board cases.

"A doctor's profession, I suppose," Miss Delmege said to Grace in tones of outraged delicacy as they left the office together, "destroys the finer feelings altogether. I'm not prudish, so far as I know, but really, after what passed in the office to-day--"

"I wish you'd tell me what Mrs. Baker-Bridges said to you over the

telephone." Miss Delmege coloured and tossed her head.

"Some people don't seem to mind what they say. I never did like her, but I certainly didn't think she had a coarse mind."

"And has she?"

"Well, I wouldn't say it to anyone but you, dear, and I know you won't repeat any of it, but she was actually so pleased and proud at the mere idea that she said she couldn't keep it to herself, though she isn't even in the least certain."

The virtuous horror expressed in Miss Delmege's whole person at such deplorable outspokenness was so excessive that Grace dared not make any reply for fear of producing an anti-climax.

That evening, Grace's last at Questerham Hostel, her room-mate became disconsolate.

"I don't know what I shall do without you, Oracle, and this room will be simply awful. You've always been such a dear about my being so untidy and everything, and put up with all of it, and done such heaps of little things. I shall never forget how you washed up the cups and tea-things after our morning tea, dear, never."

"But I was only too pleased," protested Grace. "You've done a lot for me, if it comes to that. Look how often you've boiled your kettle for me, and had everything ready on nights when I came back late. I shall miss you very much, but don't forget that if ever you're in Wales you're coming to stay with us."

"I say, do you really mean that?"

"Of course I do."

"You are a brick, Gracie. The thing I like about you," said Miss Marsh instructively, "is that you don't put on any frills."

"Well, why should I?"

"Oh, I don't know staying at Plessing, and knowing Miss Vivian's people, and so on. There are others I could name," Miss Marsh said viciously, "who take airs for a good deal less in fact, for nothing at all, that anyone but themselves can see."

Miss Jones knew from much previous experience the subject denoted by that particular edge in her room-mate's voice.

"Are you worried?" she asked sympathetically, selecting a euphemism at random.

"My dear, I've got an awful fear that Delmege means to move into this room when you're gone. You'll see if she doesn't get round the new Superintendent. She's always resented being put in with twoothers, and that room of theirs will always be a threebedded one." v ' But Tony and Miss Plumtree are both leaving."

"Not yet, and, anyway, two others will be put in instead. Mark my words," said Miss Marsh tragically, "that'll be the next thing. Delmege and me stuck in here tete-a-tete, as they say."

"I do hope not."

"I shall resign, that's all. Simply resign. And give my reasons. I shall say to Miss Vivian right out, when she asks me why I want to leave--"

"But she never does ask why anyone wants to leave. Besides, you know you wouldn't leave for such a ridiculous reason as that."

"Well, perhaps I wouldn't! After all, I should be sorry to think I couldn't get the better of Delmege, when all's said and done. I've a very good mind to tell her quite plainly that if she's got her eye on that corner bed she'll have to come to an understanding with me first, both as to the use of the screen and who's to make tea in the morning and turn the gas out at night. I've heard tales about Delmege's trick of getting into bed in a hurry and leaving everybody else to do the work. And she and I have had words before now."

"I know you have," said Grace. "Perhaps that may prevent her from wanting to come here."

Miss Marsh looked gloomy, and then bounded up as a tap sounded on the door.

"What did I tell you? I'll take any bet you like that's Delmege nosing round now. I know the way she swishes her petticoat such swank, wearing a silk one under uniform! Well, I'm not going to interfere with her."

Miss Marsh bounced behind her screen.

"Come in," Grace called.

"Say I'm undressing," Miss Marsh issued a whispered command.

Miss Delmege stepped elegantly into the room, her favourite "fawn "peignoir chastely gathered round her.

"You alone, dear?"

"No, she isn't. I'm undressing," said a sharp voice behind the screen.

Miss Delmege ignored the voice, and laid a patronizingly affectionate hand upon Grace's shoulder.

"What thick hair you have, dear! Quite a work brushing it, I should think. Now, mine is so long that it's never had time to get really thick, though I know you wouldn't guess it to look at it, but that's the way it grows. As a child I used to have a perfect mass. Mother always used to say about me, ' That child Vera's strength has all gone into her hair, every bit of it.' It used to make her quite anxious, to see me without a bit of colour in my face and this great mass of hair."

"What made it all fall out, Delmege?" came incisively from behind the screen.

Miss Delmege tossed the long, attenuated plait of straight fair hair which hung artlessly over one shoulder, and simulated deafness.

"I just looked in as it's your last night here," she told Grace. "We shall miss you, I'm sure. Tell me, dear, have you any idea who is coming into this room in your place?"

"Not any," hastily said Grace, as Miss Marsh's boot was dropped on the floor with a clatter that argued a certain degree of energy in removing it. "I suppose it will be arranged by the new Superintendent."

"It might be kinder," said Miss Delmege thoughtfully, "to have all that sort of thing in order before she arrives. She'll have plenty to do without changes of bedroom. But of course this is a room for two, there's no doubt about it. I've sometimes thought of a move myself, and this might be a good opportunity--"

The second boot was violently sent to rejoin its fellow.

"Strange, the noise that goes on in here, isn't it with only the pair of you, too. I wonder it doesn't disturb you; but perhaps you're used to it?"

"If you don't like noise, Delmege, don't come in here," exclaimed the still invisible Miss Marsh. "I never could bear creeping about without a sound, like a cat, myself."

"I dare say not," Miss Delmege returned, with a certain spurious assumption of extreme gentleness in her little refined enunciation. "But I hope we all know what give and take is in sharing a room especially in war-time."

"There's more take than give about some of us, by all accounts, especially in the matter of kettles and early tea," was the retort of Miss Marsh, spoken with asperity.

Miss Delmege turned to Grace.

"Well, dear, as I don't propose to have words either now or at any other hour, I shall say good-night. Do you mean to say you manage with only one screen?"

"Quite well. Besides, there are two round the other bed."

"I dare say that's very necessary," said Miss Delmege pointedly, as she moved to the door. "Goodnight, dear."

"Good-night," said Grace, not without thankfulness.

"Good-night," repeated Miss Delmege to the screen. "When I'm in here, I shall certainly insist upon having an extra screen. I can't imagine how anybody can manage with one only. And each will keep to her own side of the room, too, instead of leaving her things all over the other's. What I call untidy, some of these arrangements are. But, of course, it's all what one's been used to, isn't it?"

Leaving no time for a reply to this favourite inquiry, Miss Delmege shut the door gently behind her.

Grace, proceeding to bed under the flow of eloquence directed at her from behind Miss Marsh's screen, conjectured that the bedroom would know no lack of spirited conversation between its inmates in the future.

The next morning Miss Marsh asked her at breakfast: "Shall you go and say good-bye to Miss Vivian?"

"I don't think it's necessary, is it?"" Grace said hesitatingly.

"I can easily find out for you, dear, if she can see you for a moment," Miss Delmege kindly volunteered.

The opinion of the Hostel instantly veered round to an irrevocable certainty that a farewell to Miss Vivian was not necessary.

"After all, she'd only say she was too busy to see you."

"Or say she couldn't conscientiously recommend you for clerical work, as she did to poor Plumtree when she gave in her resignation the other day."

"After Plumtree has toiled over those beastly averages for the best part of two years!"

It was evident that the temper of the staff, for one reason or another, was undergoing a very thorough reaction indeed.

Only Miss Delmege remarked firmly: "I know nothing about Plumtree's work, I'm sure, but if there's one thing Miss Vivian is, it's just. Quite impartially speaking, one can't help seeing that, and especially being, as I am, in the position of her secretary. As I always say, I get at the human side of her."

"Parthuman, I call it," muttered Tony, Miss Plumtree's chief ally.

"Wherever a recommendation is possible, Miss Vivian always gives it," inflexibly replied Miss Delmege. "I can answer for that."

Few things received less consideration in the Hostel than Miss Delmege in process of answering for the Director of the Midland Supply Depot, and Miss Marsh, Tony, and Miss Henderson dashed simultaneously into discussion of a project for seeing Grace off at the station.

"We can get off at lunch-time, and your train goes at 1.30, doesn't it,

Gracie?" "Yes, and I'd love you to come; only what about your lunch?"

But everyone said that didn't matter at aD, and that, of course, dear old Gracie must have a proper send-off.

"How nice they all are to me!" thought Grace, and recklessly purchased a supply of cigarettes, which she left with Mrs. Bullivant, for the consolation of the Hostel during many Sunday afternoons to come.

"We shall meet at Plessing," the little Superintendent said, kissing her affectionately, "and it will be a great pleasure to work with you, Miss Jones dear, and you must tell me all Lady Vivian likes, you know, and how we can help her most."

"You'll like working for her very much," Grace prophesied confidently. "Good-bye, dear Mrs. Bullivant, and thank you for all your kindness to me."

She ran down the steps and would not look back, conscious of emotion.

At the station the members of the staff were to appear when possible. But as Grace crossed Pollard Street, glancing involuntarily at the familiar office door, Miss Delmege, with a most unusual disregard for propriety, emerged hastily, hatless and with her neat coils of hair ruffled in the wind.

"Good-bye, dear. It's sad to lose you, but I'm sure I hope you'll like your new job. I must say. it's been a pleasure to work with you."

"Oh, I'm so glad! How kind of you!"

"It's not everyone I could say it to," Miss Delmege observed, with great truth. "But there's never been the least little difficulty, has there? We shall all miss you, and I must say I could wish that some others I could name were leaving in your place."

Grace knew too well the nameless being alluded to, however feebly disguised by the use of the plural. "Couldn't you get away to the station?" she asked hastily.

"Well, dear, I would, but really, with so many others there to tell you the truth, that Miss Marsh is beginning to get on my nerves a bit. Besides, you see, if I went off early, Miss Vivian might think it rather strange."

On this unanswerable reason, Grace took a cordial farewell of Miss Vivian's unalterably loyal remaining secretary.

At the station Tony and Mrs. Potter hailed her eagerly. "We got down early, but the others are coming. There's an awful crowd, dear; better hurry."

Grace, in obedience to their urgings, purchased her ticket, while Mrs. Potter looked after the luggage and Tony took possession for her of a corner seat facing the engine.

"Here you are, and remember," said Mrs. Potter earnestly, "that you can get a cup of nice hot tea at the Junction. There'll be plenty of time; I found out on purpose."

"Thank you very much," said Grace gratefully. She stood at the window, and presently Tony and Mrs. Potter were joined by several other members of the staff, all hurried, but eager to take an affectionate farewell of Gracie.

"Marsh ought to be here can't think why she isn't. She was tearing about like mad so as to get off in time," said Miss Plumtree.

"That girl will come into heaven late," Miss Henderson prophesied, and looked gratified when her neighbour emitted a faint, shocked exclamation.

"Give her my love if she's too late, and say I'm so very sorry," said

Grace. "You'll be off in a minute now."

"Mind you come back next month all right. We'll come down and meet you." "I should like that so much. I shall look out on this very platform for you all."

"Oh, Gracie! shall we any of us ever see this awful platform without thinking of those troop-trains and the ghastly weight of the trays?"

"Never!" said Grace with entire conviction.

"There's the whistle you're off now."

"And here's Marsh she'll just do it. Look at her!"

Grace hung out of the window, and saw the ever tardy Miss Marsh hastening up the crowded platform, making free use of her elbows.

"I started too late--that wretched Delmege pretended I was wanted--so sorry, Gracie dear. Mind you write."

"Yes, yes. And please do all write to me when you have time, and tell me all your news. And we'll meet again next month, as soon as I get back."

The train was moving now, and only the panting and energetic Miss Marsh hastened along beside it, her hand on the carriage window.

"Good-bye, good-luck. I shall miss you dreadfully in our room. Don't be surprised if you hear that Delmege and I have had words together; that girl simply gets on my nerves."

"Stand back there, please." "Good-bye, Gracie!"

"Good-bye."

Grace stood at the window and waved to the little group until the blue uniforms were lost to sight and only the nutter of Tony's handkerchief was still visible.

The Hostel days were over, but she would remember them always with a smile for the small hardships that had been tempered by so much kindness and merriment, and with a faithful recollection of the good companionship that work and the comradeship of workers had brought her.

To John Trevellyan in the trenches, Grace wrote something of her thoughts two days later, amid much else.

"I'm so glad I went to Questerham, apart from everything else, for the experience. The Hostel life was sometimes uncomfortable, but it was always amusing; and when all was said and done, everybody was ready to do anything or everything for anyone else. I can't believe I was only there such a little while, for more happened to me there, and I got into realer touch with more people, than ever before.

"And now the New Year is only just beginning, and there have been so many changes and happenings already. I wonder so much what else it is going to bring to all of us who were together in Questerham."

CHAPTER XX

To Grace Jones herself the New Year, speeding on its way until it was new no longer, brought much work in the convalescent home at Plessing, the glad realization of Joanna Vivian's need of her, and innumerable unstamped letters bearing the field postmark. The quality of Miss Jones's peculiar philosophy was much tested as the months went by, but it was characteristic of her to be much heartened and rejoiced by an announcement confided to her soon after her return by Miss Marsh.

"The boy I was such pals with has been sent back on sick leave, and they're not sending him out again. And if you'll believe me, dear, I've been persuaded into saying yes. He wants it to be quite soon, and really I don't mind if it is; the Hostel is quite changed nowadays, and not nearly as jolly as it was, now the new Superintendent makes us all so comfortable. Besides, I don't mind telling you between ourselves, Gracie, that I can't help fancying me going off like that and coming back with a wedding-ring and all, will be rather a knock in the eye for our old friend Delmege."

If this kindly prognostication was verified, Miss Delmege gave no sign of it, beyond introducing several additional shades of superiority into the manner of her congratulations.

"Strange, isn't it?" she observed with a small and tight smile, "to see the way some people put all sorts of personal considerations first and the work afterwards! Personally, I agree with Miss Vivian on the subject."

In agreement with Miss Vivian, on that as on all else, Miss Delmege continued to find solace. The promotion of Miss Bruce to Grace Jones's vacant place in Miss Vivian's office was a source of disquiet to her for some time, but the bond of a common admiration at last asserted itself, and found expression in their united efforts to persuade Miss Vivian to her lunch every day. There was also infinite consolation to Miss Delmege in her assertions, frequently heard at the Hostel, that nowhere was the human side of the Director of the Midland Supply Depot so touchingly and unmistakably shown as in the occasional unofficial lapses which led her to address her secretary as "Brucey."

The Hostel saw rapid changes when Tony and Miss Plumtree had both become munition-workers, and Mrs. Bullivant had gone to Plessing. The war-workers became the victims of a series of new superintendents, each of whom found insuperable difficulty in accommodating herself to the arbitrary ruling of Miss Vivian, and either departed summarily or received a curt dismissal. Finally, an energetic Scotswoman established herself at the Hostel and, as Miss Vivian had become exceedingly weary of the quest, remained there unchallenged. She was a better manager than little Mrs. Bullivant. and made drastic reformations in many directions, several of which were ungratefully received by the older members of the community.

"For I must say," Mrs. Potter told Miss Henderson, "it was a good deal more sociable in the old days, when we made toast for tea over the sitting-room fire on Sunday afternoons, and Dr. Prince dropped in and told us all the news."

It was Tony and Miss Plumtree who dropped in now, and did their best to bridge the gulf that had yawned so long between the munition-workers' Hostel and that sacred to Miss Vivian's clerical staff.

"It's all very well," Miss Plumtree instructively remarked as she lounged in holland overalls and a pair of baggy but entirely unmistakable garments from which Miss Delmege kept her eyes studiously averted. "It's all very well, but working at munitions gives one a bit of an idea as to what one's working for. You people may think it's all Miss Vivian's personality, etc., etc., but I can tell you that's a jolly small part of the whole show."

The independence of Miss Plumtree's manner, as well as a new and strange slanginess developed both by her and by little Miss Anthony, was noted by their old companions without enthusiasm.

"After all," Tony chimed in patronizingly, "you really have the best of it.
Troop-trains simply aren't in it with our work. Standing all day long, and shifts of twelve hours at a time and if you turn green, that little reptile of a Welfare Superintendent pouring water all over you and telling you that there's nothing the matter."

A shade of reminiscence, almost of regret, passed over her face.

"At all events, Miss Vivian never did that and she was pretty to look at. Everyone is hideous at the works--especially Jawbones."

"And who," Mrs. Potter distantly inquired, "is Jawbones?"

Her tone implied that there were nick-names and nick-names, and that those in use amongst the habituees of the munitions-factory would meet with little or no admiration from the refined inhabitants of the Hostel.

"That's what we call the Superintendent," Tony said airily.

Miss Delmege, her lips drawn into an extremely thin line, uttered her solitary contribution to the conversation, before retiring with marked aloofness to the bedroom where she hoped to defeat her old antagonist, Miss Marsh, by annexing all three screens and the largest kettle of hot water.

"I must say, it does seem to me that a happy medium might be found between doing your war work entirely for the sake of whoever's at the head of it, and calling your superintendent 'Jawbones'."

The conclusion was so irrefutable, that even the new-born independence acquired by the munitionmakers could produce no adequate reply.

It might even be inferred from the unusual thoughtfulness with which the holland-clad enthusiasts took their departure, that neither was devoid of an occasional pang at the memory of the old days of blind obedience and enthusiastic loyalty to the ideal which Char Vivian, with all her autocratic charm arid occasional flashes of kindness, still represented.

As Dr. Prince had said, "the Vivians of Plessing stood for the highest in the land."

The doctor seldom came to the Hostel now, for time had brought him more work than ever, and he spared himself none of it. Only at Plessing could he sometimes be persuaded to spend half an hour in talking to Grace or Lady Vivian after his medical inspection was over.

"A wonderful work you're doing here," he told Joanna with satisfaction. "I wish all our great houses could be turned to such good use--and all our lady-workers too," added the doctor with some significance. "When all's said and done, nursing is women's work and no one else's, and the ruling of hospital discipline and the disposal of cases for Medical Boards, or anything else, ought to be left to the Medical Officer. That's my opinion, right or wrong, and will be till my dying day."

To Joanna Vivian, presiding over the altered establishment at Plessing, time brought many outlets for the unquenchable spirit of energy that would always possess her. She brought gaiety to her work, and laughter that was as unofficial as her inveterate habit of referring all questions of discipline to Dr. Prince, and the management of each individual branch to the helper in charge of it. Joanna's staff was not a large one, and each member of it had her own special and peculiar interest in the work given into her hands.

It was in vain that Lesbia Willoughby, from London, wrote impassioned accounts to her poor dear Joanna of the many activities in which her days and nights appeared to fly past. "Wounded Colonials, blinded officers, Flag-days, hospitals, canteens, Red Cross entertainments I have my finger in every single war-pie that's going, and I can't tell you how too utterly twee some of the dear fellows are with whom I get into touch. If you'll only trust that sulky girl of yours to me for six months, I could do wonders for her, and probably get her off your hands altogether. After all, dear, we can never forget that you and I were girls together, can we?"

"Lesbia never means to forget it, that's clear enough," was the sole comment of Lady Vivian.

She did not go through the form of transferring Mrs. Willoughby's invitation to her daughter. It gradually became evident that the Director of the Midland Supply Depot would accord but little of her fully occupied time to a convalescent home not supplied from her own depot, and as Joanna said to Grace, with her habitual slight shrug: "It may be just as well, my dear. I'm not Miss Bruce, and Char and I haven't the same way of looking at things. She vexed and disappointed her father, and no amount of eloquence about her high and mighty motives will ever make me altogether forget it. I shall never be able to hear her talk about her position as Director of the Midland Supply Depot without thinking what a fool I was not to smack her well when she was a child."

Thus Joanna, half laughing, but with the eternal loneliness that all John's steadfast loyalty and Grace's loving companionship would never altogether assuage still underlying the dauntless youthfulness in her blue eyes.

For Trevellyan the months succeeded one another, strangely monotonous. In company with a hundred thousand others "somewhere in France," he moved between the mud and noise and blood in the trenches, and the eternal dreary billets where letters from home and the need of sleep were the only considerations. But to his Grace in England Johnnie wrote cheerily, of hope and good courage, and peace dawning on a far horizon, and of the prospect of ten days' leave.

To Char Vivian, Director of the Midland Supply Dep6t, the advancing year, imperceptibly enough, brought certain solutions and enlightenments.

The personal fascination that she could exert when she willed would always secure for her a following of blindly devoted adherents, but her influence was not always strong enough to retain their admiration. Insensibly, Char modified a little of her arbitrariness.

"They put so much else before the work," she said helplessly to Miss Bruce.

But Char's perceptions were never lacking in acumen, and she became more and more aware of the truth of Joanna's prognostication that the work of the Supply Depot would be done for its own sake, and for that of the cause in whose name it existed. And it was perhaps that awareness which brought to her a gradual realization of motives in her own self-devotion hitherto unacknowledged to herself.

The Director of the Midland Supply Depot might sit day after day and hour after hour at her paperstrewn table, issuing orders and receiving the official interviews and communications that so clearly indicated the high responsibility of her position, but Char Vivian grew to exercise a certain discretion in the matter of her return to the meals and rest so anxiously watched over by Miss Bruce, whose adoring loyalty was hers beyond any possibility of shaking.

In those occasional, unofficial concessions to her imploring solicitude might, after all, be numbered the most creditable achievements of Miss Vivian.

LONDON, 1917.

Made in United States
North Haven, CT
04 April 2022